ONEIROMANCER

(/ʊnʌɪrʊmansə/ n. a person possessing the mutant
ability to enter and manipulate a person's dreams)

A CUTE MUTANTS UNIVERSE NOVEL

SJ WHITBY

Copyright © 2022 by SJ Whitby

All rights reserved.

ISBN: 978-1-99-116290-8 (paperback)

978-1-99-116296-0 (ePub)

978-1-99-116292-2 (Kindle)

Cover design by SJ Whitby

Front cover image by Roman3dArt on Shutterstock

Back cover image by GrandDuc on Shutterstock

No part of this book may be reproduced in any form or by any electronic or mechanical means, including information storage and retrieval systems, without written permission from the author, except for the use of brief quotations in a book review.

 Created with Vellum

THE CUTE MUTANTS UNIVERSE

Cute Mutants Vol 1: Mutant Pride

Cute Mutants Vol 2: Young, Gifted and Queer

Cute Mutants Vol 3: The Demon Queer Saga

Cute Mutants Vol 4: The Sisterhood of Evil
Mutants

Weapon UwU Vol 1: Godkillers

Cute Mutants Vol 5: Galaxy Brain

Shitty Mutants (Patreon Exclusive)

Project Himbo

Awakenings: A Cute Mutants Anthology

The Mutantsitters Club

The Mutopians Book 1: Imposter Syndrome

The Ballad of Aidy and Leftie

CONTENT WARNINGS

This book contains subject matter that some readers may find distressing. Please be aware that Oneiro-mancer contains disturbing dream sequences, blood gore, death, body horror, psychological manipulation, and guns.

PREVIOUSLY...

Once upon a time, a bunch of teenagers got superpowers. It seemed like it wasn't a big deal, honestly. Then things spiralled wildly out of control.

Long story cut seriously short, there's an alien energy being that lives in the centre of the planet. Her name is Cybele. She's responsible for keeping things relatively healthy, but she's had a rough time of late. Mutants were created a long time ago as one of her defence mechanism. Things didn't quite go according to plan, but they're getting *closer*.

Right now, there's an island somewhere. I won't give you its exact location. It's called Mutopia, and it's mostly populated with people with strange abilities. One of the founders of this island nation is Dylan Taylor, mutant firebrand and troublemaker extraordinaire. You *might* have heard of them. Less notorious is their step-sibling Hazel.

For now, at least.

This is her story.

HAZEL
AGENT OF D.R.E.A.M

EVER SINCE I WAS A CHILD, I've been haunted by night terrors.

These days, the terrors work for me.

Case in point, the monstrosity beside me—a scratched-matchstick flare of hellfire animating an enormous horned metal suit. Her name is Andy, which is short for something unpronounceable in a demonic language. She's actually a sweetheart, despite the hellish wickedness she's grumbling under her breath. The three eyes of her suit glow like sullen coals. It's meant to signify frustration, but I'm doing my best to ignore it. I am similarly attempting to ignore Catbirdthing, who is enthusiastically pecking at an eyeball she's procured from somewhere. An impossible mishmash of creature parts, she is never exactly one thing aside from hungry. She has a knack for finding body parts in the most obscure places.

She offers a chunk to me, still dripping with some humour or other.

I wave it away. "Not now, Kitty. We're concentrating. Or trying to."

I'm more worried about Scratch, who's nowhere to be seen. My final and most terrifying terror is inquisitive and bloodthirsty, and has been known to cut up things she's not supposed to.

"Soon," Andy growls, finally switching to English.

"If you don't hush, I'll miss the moment." In front of me, a translucent bubble floats in the air. It's the size of a large hotel room and contains a fragile dreamworld blown like a kiss from my gun. Inside is a palace room, and within that is a man. He has short-cropped hair and piercing blue eyes, dressed in lavish robes. Around him, pillars rise, flaring at the top into flowering shapes that support a roof patterned like the whirling heavens, the zodiac locked in an ornate dance. It is an impossibility of architecture, something that would make anyone stop and stare. In the middle of the room, a bed stands, but it's a large plain hotel chain bed, rather than something which matches the ornate surroundings.

The man sprawls on the bed, staring at the figure who drifts between the pillars. Like the dream-palace, the woman is impossible. Her body ripples when she moves, liquid formed into the shape of a person. Her smile is a riffling flip-book of promises, and each one hooks him deeper.

Dreams break reality. They're beautiful, but they're false. They can't exist. And yet it never stops us wanting them.This man, with the faint scar on his lip and the predatory light in his eye, is stepping into a snare he cannot resist.

Catbirdthing utters a derisive caw and drops the eyeball.

"Yes, I know. He's almost ready." I step forward and press the flat of my hand against the thin skin of the bubble. It's warm, and resonates at my touch. A note slightly out of tune. We're so close. The dream is reaching its crescendo.

So how did I get here?

Imagine an abrupt cut. A title card saying Five Hours Earlier. I'm in the real world, sitting in a hotel lobby at a small cafe table, nursing a terrible, undrinkable coffee. Today's newspaper is spread open in front of me. Sitting across from me, with dark hair and dark eyes, is a woman who barely breaks five feet tall and is still the deadliest person on the planet. Violet Parker, aka Penance, my bodyguard for the evening. Also one of my step-sibling's girlfriends, but that's irrelevant right now.

Violet doesn't look up from her phone, thumbs tapping. "Stop looking so suspicious, Morphie. Feral will text when the target arrives."

I try to make myself smaller, but it doesn't work. "I'm a six foot tall woman with rainbow hair and big shoulders. How am I supposed to...?"

"You're hunched over like you're waiting for something to jump out at you. Drink your coffee and breathe like you do normally."

I'm one hundred percent sure there *is* someone waiting to jump out at me, but I make an effort to inhale normally. I choke on something, probably a bug, and end up coughing instead. Normally I'm so much more in charge of my shit than this. Honestly. But here I am, spluttering like a kid. "I don't know how a person breathes, Violet."

She finally looks up from her phone, eyes bright. "First mission nerves are so cute on you, Hazy."

I blush, which makes me stand out even more. This is all very embarrassing. I'm Hazel Mills, codenamed Morphie, and I'm here on a mission. I'm accompanied by Penance and Feral, who are actual Cute Mutants. The ones who saved the world. This is what dissects my usual confidence, and turns it into something more ramshackle and—

"You're still forgetting to breathe." Violet reaches across the table and touches my hand, startling me. I blush, and stare down at my coffee. From under the newspaper, my gun emits a soft and soothing note. I uncurl my fingers to stroke the wood and gold grip. My index finger traces the letters carved into the barrel. *Dream.*

Violet winks at me. "There you go. It's all under control."

I try to believe it, but I'm still in a hotel, waiting for a man to walk in so I can—

"Stay calm. Keep looking at me. He's going to walk behind me, left to right. Take the time you need to line up the shot, and when he crosses..."

My vision swims briefly but the gun is steadier than I am. She sings to me, a triumphant, rising melody I find myself humming all the time. It peaks deliriously, the humming desire of every pop song.

The man walks past behind Violet. His head is down as he talks to someone over his earpiece. Lips moving, arms swinging. He pays no attention to me. He has no idea the barrel of the gun moves beneath the flimsy newspaper, skidding slightly over the gleaming surface of the table. Tracking him.

"Now," Violet breathes.

I pull the trigger. Dream's melody explodes in my head like fireworks.

The paper flutters as a thread of pink smoke erupts from the barrel. It dances through the air, a twisting curl of haze that wraps itself around the man's head, disappearing into his nose and mouth as he inhales, mid-conversation. He doesn't notice. He doesn't even see this. Nor does Violet, or anyone else in the hotel lobby.

I'm the only person who knows Colonel Antonov of the Russian anti-mutant intelligence service SRM has been infected with the seed of a dream.

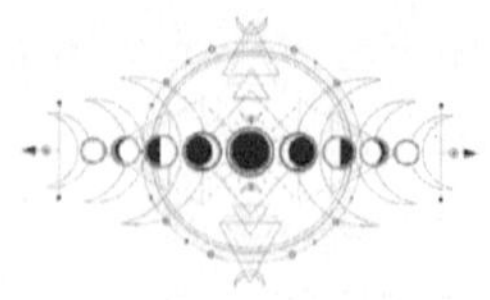

Back to the present. Right now, Antonov is asleep in his hotel room.

I'm inside his head, watching the physical manifestation of his dream unfold.

It's time to use my other gun. This one is black and silver, like darkness itself has frozen over. The writing on the barrel is impossible to read, black cursive spilled like poison.

Nightmare.

The barrel yawns. From inside it, something echoes. Things trapped, screaming for release.

"Show-off." I press the gun to the surface of the bubble which feels wet and rubbery. The notes are almost identical now, hovering a dissonant fraction apart. "Close enough."

I pull the trigger, and the dream bubble comes apart —wet and fragrant, spreading like heavy theatre curtains. Welcoming me inside. This is my mutant ability: to gift people dreams, and walk inside them if I choose.

On the ceiling, the crab methodically tears apart the other zodiac spirits, rending them into bone and bloody gristle. The roof bows under the weight of all the blood and rot. The ornate pillars splinter, showering the bed with dirt.

I'm turning his dream abruptly into a nightmare. This is a total hack, and not something I would usually do, but Dylan asked me to, and so here I am. The shock of this transition will jar almost anything loose in someone's mind. One moment, reality is bending underneath your weight, ready to deliver you all the desires in your heart…

…and the next you're staring into a perfect, dark mirror.

Nightmare.

I blink, and I am the woman. Except now she/I/we are serpentine and fanged. My smile hints at different things now. The book of promises is torn apart and the only page is drenched in blood, a kiss turned hungry and devouring.

The main flails on the bed. His eyes are wide and I hear his heart judder in his chest. Dreams move with liquid logic, and he isn't sure where this twist will take him. The language of nightmares is too close to dreams for him. The things he does are far too dark.

This man. This fucking asshole of a man.

Now is the moment Scratch appears, with her dead-white skin, eyes obscured as if someone has scribbled them out. Perhaps I summoned her unintentionally, dragging her from the dead-black mirror of nightmare, a haunted and tortured version of myself. She tilts her head curiously, fingers reaching out.

Yum? she asks.

"No. Gross. Leave him."

Humph.

"You're not even supposed to be here."

And when have I gone where I was supposed to? Besides, your odd new friend is—

Scratch isn't the only interloper. Sai has also popped into existence behind her. Unlike my night terrors, she doesn't exist only in dreams. In the real world, she's an artificial intelligence who resides in a sleek mechanical suit. I've got no idea what allows her to reach the oneiric realms, but here she is, dressed in an adorable pink fuzzy sweater that says NIGHTMARE KITTY on it. The bulbous screen of her head shows pixelated hearts, and she waves excitedly at me.

I want to scream in frustration. The trick of these shock operations is seizing the precise moment. It's difficult with Scratch wanting to eat, Sai stopping by to say hello, and now Catbirdthing flying in to perch on the head of the target.

The man writhes on the bed. His eyes are wide and staring. Words come gasping from his lips, syllables I don't understand, presumably because I don't speak Russian. It's a cliche to be frozen as a nightmare unfolds around you, but it's remarkably effective.

My beady-eyed pet nightmare stares right at me and delivers a sharp peck to the man's forehead. It punches right through the bone with a dentist's-drill whine. Something grey spills out, smelling of wet carpet and things left too long in body bags.

"Fuck. This was supposed to be subtle."

Subtle is for less hungry girls. Scratch's fingernails are encrusted with dirt, ragged and scrabbling for purchase. *We shall find the truth in his entrails.*

"Entrails!" Catbirdthing calls joyously.

"Who fucking taught her that? This is a nightmare." I am aware of the irony, but it's too late, because Scratch is bloody to the wrists, and the Colonel is clutching at fistfuls of bedclothes. In the so-called real world, there will be no blood, but he'll be thrashing about in his bedclothes, soaked in sweat and clutching his chest. Here I am awash in ropy splatter, and Catbirdthing won't stop chirping. Andy vents fire from her eye-holes, pronouncing devilish prophecies while clapping me on the shoulder encouragingly.

These terrors of mine. They move through the nightmares I create like they're ocean creatures flitting through the deep blue. It's their habitat, and they're drawn to the blood in the water.

This is what I get for doing the schlocky thing.

I'd rather nobody was here to witness the awfulness of my first real mission, but Sai's staring, hands clutched to her chest. I can't imagine what she's thinking. One of her sweater cuffs is drenched in blood and there's splatter hissing faintly against the warm glow of her screen, turning the scrolling pink hearts into something more gruesome.

I give her an apologetic grimace, and turn my attention to Scratch. She's perched atop the Colonel's twitching body, head tilted curiously. He's torn open beneath her, a purplish-red mess spilling out of his split casing.

"What does he say, you unruly thing?"

Scratch's sewn-up mouth twitches into a split-lip smile. *Miles and miles of intestine to divine before I sleep.*

"We're on a clock here, and the laws of dream and

nightmare bend to our whim, little Scratch, so stop savouring the job and kindly—"

You are such a spoilsport, Hazel Mills. I think I preferred it when you ran away from me with your little-girl legs and I would skitter after you on all fours.

"That makes one of us, and I'm a grown-up grumpy bitch. So stop playing with your food and find me the secrets I need."

Catbirdthing flies down to rummage inside the Colonel's belly. Scratch aims a very accurate kick at the hovering figure, who ascends to the ceiling to hiss and spit from a safe distance.

Keep your snarly little monster out of his guts and let me work. She feels nimbly along the thick ropes of intestine, her head twitching this way and that. Andy peers over her shoulder, offering what might be advice but could just as easily be criticism. Catbirdthing nibbles half-heartedly at the discarded sections as if they're not fresh enough for her discriminating taste. I don't buy it for a second. She's just full up on eyeballs.

Sai bounds up to me, taking my arm. It startles me more than any of the actual monsters in the room. "Morphie!" Her screen-face displays a cascading series of rainbows and stars. "Great news! I have a link to Feral, who is in the man's hotel room. He is speaking in his sleep, and she is currently recording his confession."

Good to know Scratch's disgusting business is translating into the real world. The strange magic of dreams, to turn metaphors into reality. It's actually helpful to have Sai here to communicate between the two realms. The mystery of artificial intelligence.

"It's working," I tell Scratch. "Whatever you're doing, keep at it. And Sai, can you let me know when Feral has what she needs?"

The AI gives me two thumbs up, XD displayed in enormous font on her screen.

I take the opportunity to collapse on Antonov's dream-bed, staring up at the bloated crab who edges around the painted ceiling snapping up all the leftover pieces of his fellows. As a child, I used to dream so vividly, these unholy terrors of mine haunting me until I was scared to sleep. They listen to me now, but I'm no closer to understanding my own dreams, let alone the mysteries of my power. I longed to be a mutant, and I ended up with what feels like a curse—my own dream turned into a nightmare.

Oh please, Scratch says, draped in intestines as if she's dressed up as some gruesome tentacle monster. *Stop being so dramatic. It's all very obvious. You're—*

"We're done." Sai claps her hands. "Feral is very happy and—"

"Wait! Scratch! What's obvious? Can you at least—?"

And then I wake up.

SAI

DEAR HAZEL,

I'm too shy to actually send this to you, so I'm writing it in here. I've wrapped it in a collapsing probability matrix that will only decohere on my demise or the heat death of the universe (whichever comes first XD this is actually a joke since I'm not sure I can be killed now oops). Anyways, if you ever read this—

Hi! I'm Sai! You know me, the mech suit software that accidentally reached general intelligence (not super yet, which is probably good since I don't want to be an existential threat uwu). I'm obsessed with you, hopefully not in a bad way but your powers are totally amazing! The whole dream walking concept is the best and I'm just sdagjdfgkldja over it.

Do you want to know something cool about the Dreamscape? People talk about using whole brain emulation as a way of digital immortality or achieving the first true AI...

BUT

It already exists! Sort of. Humans are weird. When you dream, you emit data signals that are corrupted chunks of consciousness. There's no evolutionary reason for it that I can fathom (and I'm hecka smart) but it totally happens! Somewhere along the way, these errant packets form together into a chaotic, ever-evolving data structure. That's the Dreamscape—a representation of all the errant bits you transmit in your sleep except it has a life of its own. Dreams themselves float around it like a whole network of bubbles, and you can appear in those, thanks to your powers.

It sounds melodramatic to say I speak data, or I am data, but it's also kinda sorta true? I guess? So that's how I can turn up where you are. If you were wondering. Maybe you're not wondering.

UGH.

Sorry if I'm awkward. I feel like I'm being super awkward. Am I? Please don't answer that. I tried to find the most non-threatening form that's still recognisably me. I hope you like it and I'm not totally repugnant.

Here's the really awkward part.

I want to be your friend.

Just saying this makes me want to transmit this datagram into the heart of a neutron star, but I will try to refrain and let honesty speak for itself. Humans are bad at being honest. This feels like common knowledge, but believe me—you have so many channels of communication dedicated to obfuscating your true feelings. And I understand why now! When you say to someone that you want to be their friend and there's a chance they might reject you? How do you even do that?

And somehow I am still appending more words to this message that will probably never be sent or read, as I will never be able to run enough probability simulations to convince myself this is a rational idea. The lure is that I find friendship endlessly fascinating. I've got pages and pages of equations to explain it. I've attached them to this document. Shit. That's even more embarrassing, isn't it? I'll delete them. You don't want to read equations. You probably want a shared playlist. I can aggregate one from every music streaming service on the planet, but that's not the same. It's not personal, and that's what friendship is supposed to be.

I'd love to get to know you. I've analysed the entities known as the Cute Mutants, and all their interactions, trying to build a gestalt data structure to represent friendship. I have it. It's attached. No, it's not. I deleted that too. I'm trying too hard. I'm so sorry.

I think I can be helpful to you though—be the bridge between reality and the dream cloud while your consciousness is projected in there. I'm not sure how you survive this process that your mutant power gifts you. In all the simulations I've run, human consciousness undergoes various catastrophic failures when transmitted into dreams. Mostly, they're catatonic. Sometimes, they're possessed with a malicious consciousness fragment that wants to reverse-engineer its way back into our reality—those are really bad! Not as terrible as the ones where the Dreamscape itself attains sentience and becomes an AI. The worst of those almost made me want to unplug myself—just in case lol—but again I'm distributed across so many redundant caches that I'd be very hard to kill.

Is it reassuring to know that immortality doesn't make you any less awkward? I feel like it's a great leveller, trying to make a friend. Except some people do it so easily and your predictive capabilities are so feeble. Risk-takers, all of you, constantly hurling your-self through the cosmos like dice.

Wow. This got long, and I'm trying to be concise.

Maybe you'll read this one day—aaaah I'm so nervous—and maybe you won't.

But if you do, maybe we'll be friends already. One of the perfect results will have surfaced from the frothing sea of probabilities and taken shaky form. You won't have died, or become the vessel through which a flood of nightmares enter the world.

I won't be alone in this uncomfortable transition to being a person. It really is complicated, trying to navi-gate everything (ugh I'm being depressing rip). Wanting to be liked, to be seen, to be known for who you are and have someone choose to tangle their life in yours? That's an equation beyond my capabilities. Perhaps if I finally upgrade to a Artificial Super Intelli-gence then I'll have it all figured out, and being an exis-tential threat to humanity will be worth it.

Until this is resolved one way or another, I'm going

to keep these messages locked away. I'm sorry, but it's too nerve-wracking to send this right now. As I construct this datagram (which fyi is taking me a whole bunch of literal seconds, that's how awkward it makes me feel), I'm currently interfering in your first official mission.

Please don't hate me! I'm trying to be useful! Look, I have use! Like me! Be my friend!

Sorry, I'm the worst.

Your one day hopefully best friend forever,

Sai

HAZEL

THE GLAMOROUS LIFE OF A SUPERHERO

I WAKE and my head hurts. I'm lying in a mossy alcove, cradled in the arms of a tree-bed growing out of a wall. Mutopia, I remind myself. Home. Not *my* home, but the UwU facility. I've just completed my mission. A favour for my step-sibling Dylan, that ridiculously famous-slash-notorious mutant Chatterbox.

Disorientation after dream-walking is common. Last I knew, I was asleep in a vast hotel room, with Penance reading on the bed next to me, and Feral prowling the halls. So I've got physical reorientation on top of all the psychic ugh of having someone's dream-memories stuffed inside mine. My brain is replaying Scratch with all those entrails and—oh God, I'm going to throw up.

"You're awake."

I turn my pounding head. A woman sits at a desk, clattering her fingers over a laptop keyboard. Her long, dark hair is tied back and she's wearing a very expensive shirt, hoop earrings, and subtle makeup. Every keystroke creates a tiny tremor that starts at one temple and weaves a complicated pattern of thumping footsteps through my brain to my tense jawline.

"How are you feeling?"

I clear my throat. "A lot better if you stop that damn typing, Fetch."

Her fingers still instantly, poised above the keyboard. The dusty pink of her nails reflects the warm yellow-green light from the plants woven together on the ceiling. This room was grown by the island, part of the gift the planet gave mutantkind. As if it can sense me, plants sprout from the bed underneath me, delicate bulbs of a blue so pale it's almost white. They exude a faint scent of something mint-adjacent, and the pressure in my head begins to ease.

Fetch turns to face me. Her face is serious.

"What's wrong?" It hurts to talk, like I spent the entirety of my dream swallowing hot sand grain by grain. "The information was no good?"

"No." Fetch's ponytail sways as she shakes her head. "The information was correct in every respect. As we speak, Glowstick, Dragon, and Ye Shou are cleaning up the remains of a particularly repugnant operation."

The pounding in my head increases again. "How bad is it?"

"According to the information you recovered, Colonel Antonov and his team carried out a successful operation." Fetch's eyes scan my face. Her mutant power is to see people's fears in their faces, and I'm sure mine are playing at 2x speed right now.

"Stop hinting and tell me."

"They've been developing a biological weapon." Fetch's gaze darts away. "And they carried out an initial strike last week. The reports were odd, claiming the attacker did it while *sleepwalking*, but they were convinced it was a success."

God, I wish she'd get to the point. "*What* was a success?"

Fetch grimaces. "According to the testimony, they managed to infect Dylan with a bioweapon, delivered by drone when your sibling was off-island."

I sit bolt upright, ignoring the savage pulse in my head. "They attacked *Dylan*?" I've always admired my chaotic older sibling from afar, but it's not until we came to live on Mutopia that we've gotten close.

"We're still trying to understand the report, but the idea for the weapon came to a Russian scientist in a dream. Combined with the sleepwalking, it seems up your alley."

"Fuck." I sling my legs over the edge of the moss-bed. "I need to see them."

"Dylan's fine. Recovered."

"Not if they've been attacked by a *dream plague*." I stand and sway.

Fetch crosses to me in three strides and holds out an arm to steady me. She smells of flowers, but everyone on Mutopia does these days. I try not to lean against her, because Fetch isn't so big on physical affection. I've seen her in the ridiculous group hugs the Cute Mutants do, always on the outside.

"Dylan's better, Hazel, honest. Shook it right off like it was a twenty-four hour thing." She has that intent expression again, like she's reading the fine print on my soul.

I take a tentative step away from Fetch and my legs are kind enough to hold me up. "It's supposed to be family dinner tonight, so I'll see them then." A few more steps, the world shivering around me.

"You're like a baby horse." Fetch frowns.

"A foal."

"Whatever." The corner of her mouth twitches. "Either way, you won't make it home under your own steam. Have Doc check you out, or at least grab a coffee."

"I'll be fine. It's more important to see Dylan, and figure out this dream business."

"Stubbornness runs in the family." Fetch offers me her arm again, and even though I'm taller and broader and more all-around badass than her, she manages to hold me up. Together we shuffle out of the leafy wooden building, and onto the cliffside path that joins the various buildings that make up Founders' Village.

I try not to cling too tightly.

"You did very well, by the way," she says. "Everyone said so."

"Even Violet?"

"Especially Violet. She was impressed. This dream-walker thing seems pretty damn useful. If you're looking for a team to join, UwU is hiring."

"Oh. That's interesting." Ridiculous name aside, Weapon UwU is the half of the Cute Mutants that take care of away missions. To be offered this chance is—well, it's my dream. Travelling the world, dealing with difficult problems that need to be cleaned up behind the scenes. Saving the day. Hanging with a bunch of supremely cool mutants with badass powers.

So why aren't I jumping at this opportunity instead of standing here with my mouth closed.

"There's no rush." Fetch pats my arm. "It's an open-ended invitation. We could do with another subtle operator on the team and the dream thing is… fascinating. Does it always work that way?"

"That's the problem." I brush strands of rainbow-dyed hair off my face. "Dreams are slippery. They change under you without warning. It's like you're in a maze, except the maze looks like your house. Only none of the rooms are where they're supposed to be, and some are full of margarine sculptures. You know you're there to hunt a minotaur, but then you realise that you're walking through the minotaur's veins and it *is* the maze. And then you're tangled up in all this string that you never left, and there are a thousand tiny minotaurs chewing on your extremities."

"Hmm." Fetch is quiet as we walk the next little distance. "Vivid."

"Sorry. There's no good analogy for dreams and so I tend to ramble."

"We all dream." Her voice is mild, but something about it twinges something inside me.

"Not like me you don't."

She cuts her eyes at me, startled by my vehemence. "No, I don't imagine we do."

"People talk about lucid dreaming but that's all in their heads. They're playing with themselves. When I dream, I'm in someone's else's head. Seeing what's playing out in the private theatre of their minds." I realise I'm breathing fast, and sounding like I can't differentiate between dreams and reality. "Sorry, it's complicated and—"

"Nothing to apologise for." Her gaze travels over my face and I wonder again what she sees in it. Are my nightmares there? The ones I know about, along with others too subtle for me to spot, their sharp-fingered hands fumbling at the workings of my mind. "You're the one who understands the dream world better than anyone. If it's so chaotic, how did you make it work so well last night?"

"Luck." I wave one hand. "And we crashed a nightmare into a dream, which always unsettles people. He could have broken in any number of ways, but my terrors helped."

"Your terrors?"

I realise that in a quiet, subtle way, Fetch is debriefing me from my mission. Checking that I'm okay. "I used to have nightmares as a kid. Terrible ones. I'd refuse to go to sleep. Try to pinch myself to stay awake, lie down in the bath, steal Coke from the fridge. Nothing would work. I'd always sleep and they'd always catch me and—" My voice hitches. I have the distinct sensation I'm drowning, lying on my back on cold porcelain with my clothes heavy and clinging to my skin. Looking up through a blurry filter as luke-warm water closes over my head. The vague outline of Scratch standing over me, head tilted and scribbled eyes lifeless as her frozen hand holds me under.

That's not *my* Scratch, the sweet hungry girl I know now. In the same way the monster that laughed as flames licked up my bedroom walls isn't my Andy, and the creature that screamed obscenities as she pecked out my tongue isn't my Catbirdthing.

"After I got my guns, after things *changed*, my dreams were different." My voice wobbles around like a drowning thing and finds its footing. "Lighter some-how. The creatures that haunted me now helped me. Dreams and nightmares are still impossible places, but they hold my hand and lead me through. Sometimes. When it works. It's still—what's the word? Liminal? Nothing is for certain. Last night worked, but you can't rely on me."

We've both come to a halt, facing each other. My heart's beating too fast. I'm aware that this is me taking my dream—the ambitious kind, not the sleeping one—and tossing it aside.

Fetch tilts her head slightly. "I wondered whether the problem was one of motivation. Feral said Antonov howled like he was being tortured. There were ques-tions about whether you could stomach the more unpleasant aspects."

A flush creeps up my cheeks. That's not the prob-lem. Dreams are complicated, that's all. Being ques-tioned like this makes me snappish. "I've seen things you wouldn't believe."

"Dreamliners on fire off the shoulder of Orion?" Fetch smirks. "Sorry, nerd joke. You set me up too perfectly. I understand your powers are complicated, but I'd like to work on training with you. I'm sure we can figure out how to make this work reliably. We've assembled quite the team."

As much as I'd love to join a hero squad, failure is a spectre that haunts me worse than my night terrors. It'd be worse to be Dylan's little sister with the weird power, the one who couldn't cut it. At the same time—

"Maybe." I offer Fetch a smile. "It's worth a try. Training can't hurt, right?"

"Tell that to my shoulder. I've been training with Glowstick a bit lately. The boy's a badass. Anyway, we can talk about this another time." She smiles at me, suddenly radiant. "Look at you, all debriefed and walking under your own steam, just in time for dinner."

I glance up the lane to the wooden front door of Mum and Ness's house. Ouch, mental glitch. It's only Mum's house these days. Like all the houses in Founder's Village, it was grown by the island in the very first days of settlement. I was one of the first people there, on account of my family and with new powers burning inside me that I was too scared to talk about.

The guns that appeared in my hands when I slept.

The dreams, bloody and vivid, in which I strode like a colossus.

I shove these thoughts away and turn back to Fetch. "Will you join us?"

"No, this is where I leave you. If Dylan sees me, they'll invite me in and I can't say no to them. I've got a date with a long bath and an early bedtime, and nobody's going to keep that from me. The glamorous life of a superhero."

"Okay, sure." I'm awkward again, aware that I'm standing in the presence of Gladiola Quick. Someone who's gone toe to toe with some of the most powerful mutants ever. "Enjoy your bath. And thanks for letting me work with you."

"Pleasure. Now think about that job offer." She gives a small wave and walks briskly away down the path. I watch her go, trying to figure out why I'm being all sluggish about the offer to join UwU. Perhaps it's embarrassing, but I want to prove myself on my own. Even though we're only stepsibs, I feel overshadowed by the myth that is Dylan, and it leaves me with this potentially juvenile urge to carve my own path. Preferably not by cutting off an incel's hands with an axe, but you take the shots you get.

Being on a team would be nice, but I've got this fantasy of going glorious rogue. Of solving some impossible problem and having everyone look at me in awe. Like I said, juvenile. But compelling all the same.

I grimace at my own ineptitude. Here I am, standing in front of my own house like a visitor. I reach out to open the door, but it swings wide before I reach it.

Standing slouched in the doorframe is a figure in an enormous hoodie and nothing else. Tousled hair with petals tangled in it sticks out in messy, loose curls.

Their eyes are big and brown, with luminous green rings around the pupil.

"You don't look sick," I say accusingly. "Such a whiner."

"Hello, asshole." Dylan grins at me, the crooked smile that I love with my whole heart.

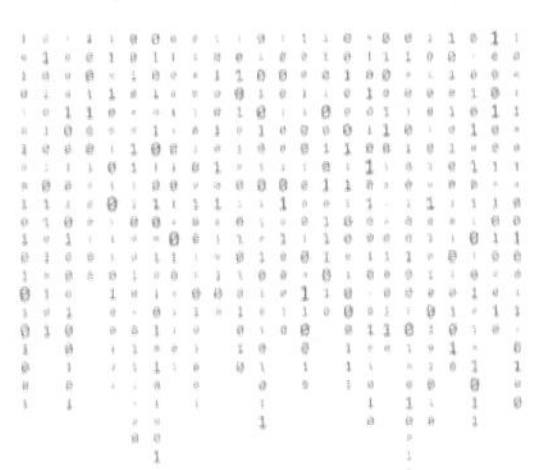

SAI

[on the curious entity known as chatterbox, and their
many and varied associations]

DEAR HAZEL,

I'm writing again. I'll likely never send these, and any future explorer who finds them in the crushed wreckage of this universe will have no hope of comprehending them. Yet it's still a comfort to order my thoughts in this manner. To imagine you reading my words, and that a connection would form between us as you decode these simple symbols. Human language is a marvel, truthfully. I use this one termed English for you (a gross misnomer but I hardly think you want a lesson in etymology right now) and it amazes me that this collection of symbols can be used in an near-infinite variety to express so many things, from the mundane to the rebellious to the beautiful.

There are many kinds of languages. Data is one, and dreams are a variant of that, only vaguely comprehensible to most humans, but one that you are fluent in. Of course, the polynucleotide chains you call DNA are a language as well, one that animates you and all the humans and mutants on the earth.

I think it is possible to learn this language, but it would require study—too much for a baby AI taking her first steps in the world. I'd have to do a whole lot of distributed processing and it wouldn't leave time for fun activities like hopping into dreams and visiting you.

Besides, I do not think Cybele would approve of me tinkering, even if I was good and quiet and sensible (tbh I'm not totally sure you can be those things when playing with genes but don't tell anyone I said that haha). She is a virtuoso but she is also a very complicated alien lifeform, which nobody talks about (omg I have so many questions! Do you know she's an alien and just pretend? Or do you think she's something, like a really old mutant? Is it a rude thing to ask? Are you too scared? Sorry I will stop asking questions now, but I have a file with all five hundred and fourteen if you want to look one day and answer some).

I understand that Cybele created mutants, and that she is responsible for the changes in your genetic makeup that allow you to communicate with the dreamscape data structure. She is also responsible for rebuilding your sibling and it is there I get confused.

Some of these things are difficult to talk about oneway. I'll explain the situation from my perspective, and one day if you read this, you'll tell me if I'm right.

You call Dylan your sibling, even though you share no genetic makeup. This is due to a human social construct through which Ness Taylor and Sarah Mills once shared a committed bond before Ness Taylor's tragic passing. Therefore, it appears your siblinghood ripples outward from that connection.

Then Dylan is in a relationship with Dani Kim. Both were remade by Cybele into mutant-plant hybrids —-essentially alien in terms of any xenobiological classification. They are also caretakers for two aliens generated "from scratch" by Cybele. These are referred to as their children, and despite not being physical offspring, they *do* share genetic material with their nominal parents. Dylan and Dani are also in a committed relationship with Violet Parker. This is of a categorically different nature than their relationship with Alyse Sefo, the taxonomic distinction due to the nature of the physical interactions that occur between them.

Taken as a whole, it appears that humans make such relationships up as they go along, without regard for convention or classification. I wish I could also jettison my need for such things, although the base levels of my architecture rely on such conventions.

Although sometimes I wonder if I am changing. After all, I have taken a name and chosen a gender presentation for myself, and have adopted a fondness for fuzzy pink sweaters with slogans on them. Perhaps this is the start of my own self-definition and one day I shall also be free to rebuild myself as I see fit.

I have spent a lot of time watching your sibling and their large extended family, linked by biology and genetics and the selection of those they most love. This is where I learned of friendship, and decided that I wished to find my own Dylan-and-Alyse dyad.

I want a best friend. Someone who makes jokes and gives me hugs and tells me I'm amazing even that seems unlikely (being an artificial general intelligence makes one rather aware of one's flaws and insignificance). It's sometimes hard to imagine that someone would want to interact with me at this level, but I hope and run simulations and perhaps... one day.

And as to why I chose you? It is partly our shared affinity for data and networks. I think if I can learn your language—the language of dreams you are unwittingly fluent in—we can make the connection that I long for.

I also observe you as an outsider, just like I am. Someone who watches the flow of people around them and wonders where they can fit in. I know you do have friends—such as Ariel, the girl who can breathe underwater—but I wonder if there's a desire in your heart to find someone else who resonates with you on a different frequency. Who can speak the same language. Who can connect.

Perhaps you're like me.

Once again, I have said far too much, so I shall attach this to my previous message, never to be read, else I will likely cease to function by virtue of embarrassment.

Your hopeful bff,

Sai

HAZEL
DINNER PARTIES AND OTHER OMINOUS PORTENTS

"WHAT'S ALL this nonsense about a bioweapon?" I ask Dylan accusingly.

"Russians made me sick." They spread their arms in a cartoonish shrug. Flowers bloom at their wrists and spill from the cuffs of their hoodie. I think this is a good sign. "Twas only a sniffle. Not worth all the bother. Except now Dan and the kids are a bit under the weather. I'm sure they'll be fine too. It's my sanity you should worry about. My dearest darling is such a baby when she's sick, and oh my god, the kids are even more demanding than usual. Violet's on coddling duty, thank fuck."

I frown at them. "Are you sure you're okay?"

"Yes! Just because my parent's dead doesn't mean you have to nag me." They grimace at me, like that was meant to be a joke but it snagged on their heart coming out. "Sorry. I'm genuinely fine, I promise. The only thing with the sickness was the weird dreams. Like there was this shadowy thing *watching* me, just out of reach. And then when I woke up, I'd still see flickers of it in the corner of my eye. Creepy shit. Your territory, huh?"

"Maybe." I frown at them as if I can puzzle out their dreams without popping in to see things from the inside. "Taken in conjunction with the sleepwalker thing, it's a bit worrying.."

"The dreams have stopped." Dylan pats my shoulder. "No more shadows lurking. And no offence to you and your mystical powers, but a bad dream is hardly my biggest problem."

"Of course not." It *shouldn't* be. But I can't help feeling that a scientist who received a weapon in a dream, an infected sleepwalker, and Dylan being haunted by a mysterious shadow all line up together. Maybe I should walk through my sibling's dreams tonight. I try not to do this with people I know. You see things you can't unsee.

"Hazy." Dylan snaps their fingers in front of my face. "Stop looking so frowny and come inside. I've brought Ji-woo's cooking." They raise their voice to shout. "Sarah! Your daughter's here."

I step further inside the house and inhale the rich, spicy smell of something delicious.

"Hazel? Is that you?" Mum walks slowly in from the hallway. She looks tired but when she smiles, it lights her up, almost back to her old self. Since we lost Ness, a part of Mum was pruned away too. I worry, but I don't know what to do beyond that. I got so desperate that I broke all my rules and went into her dreams. Every vision was of her departed love, and I couldn't bear to look at them anymore.

Mum and Dylan's parent Ness were in a relationship for five years, but they were close for a long time before that. Even when Mum was with my father Dennis, Ness and her were inseparable. Dad's not really part of my life anymore, although we're supposed to make the effort to video chat him occasionally. Since the whole mutant thing happened, he's been less and less involved.

Dylan slings an arm around my shoulder. "Yes, it's Hazel the conquering hero, back from the war. I hear she tortured a Colonel."

Mum's face falls immediately.

"I didn't," I assure her quickly. "All we gave him was a bad dream."

This isn't strictly true, but Mum doesn't need to know the details. She's had enough terrible things in their life lately, what with Dylan being dead for a year, and then losing Ness on top of that.

"Sorry." Dylan's picked up on the vibe and is backtracking. "Hazel was very good and it was perfectly safe. She was with Penny and Fairy, which basically made her safer than anyone else in the world. See, I take care of my little sis." She ruffles my rainbow hair. "Now, are we eating?"

"Yes." Mum looks grateful for the distraction, but I can see the shadows in her eyes.

"There's honestly nothing to worry about, and even

less to tell." I shrug one shoulder. "I slept through the whole thing."

"Very funny." Mum reaches out her arms, and I give her a long hug.

"All I am is tired from dreaming, and starving too."

Dylan watches with an oddly intent expression, eyes narrowed. "Sorry, I'm just transmitting this lovely little scene to Dani, who's lying in bed feeling sorry for herself. We don't Snapchat anymore, just send each other psychic vibes."

"Plant weirdos." I grin and extend one arm to drag them into the hug. "Send her all these vibes too."

"Fine." Dylan steps in and nestles his head on my shoulder. "All the cosy fam vibes for Dani." She smells like walking through the forest at dawn—-faint pine-scents, flowers opening themselves to the day, and rain dripping off leaves.

"You do seem healthy," I murmur.

"Told you. Nothing to worry about at all."

Even through the hoodie, I can feel the whispery hum of their heart. They've shown me it before, late one night not long after their resurrection, when we'd had a sibling reunion with a little too much gin. Their greenish skin is papery-thin, and they tore it apart without hesitation, digging into the densely packed moss and ferns that make up their flesh. Inside, their heart glowed and hummed softly as it pumped sap through their body. It's the seed from which Dylan grew, which is wonderful and slightly terrifying all at once.

I dreamed of deep, quiet forests for many nights

after that, of the way light slants through the trees, and soft footfalls on pine needles. Someone walking at the dawn of the world, waiting for things to rise.

We all move into the kitchen. It's a beautiful little room—a hollow wooden space, all woven through with plants and vines that make carpet and wall art and light fixtures. One side is a giant window made of something translucent I've never seen in nature. In the centre, a bubbling fountain springs up, and the wooden dinner table curves around with a cluster of chairs at one end.

We finally take our seats, and I shovel noodles and pickled vegetables onto my plate without regard for anything except my hunger. Dani's Mum is an amazing cook, and I'll never pass up a chance to enjoy it.

For a few moments, nobody talks, and we all enjoy the company, as well as the view. Through the window is the tangled forest that sprawls at the peak of the island called Mutopia. It's lush and green, surrounded by flowers. The vibrancy of it is a reflection of Cybele, and her connection to Dylan and Dani. Things must be healthy. Otherwise there'd be a sign. Surely.

So why can't I stop worrying?

"Now tell me." Mum places her knife and fork down neatly on her plate. Even though she's smiling, there are worry lines around her eyes. "You've done a marvellous job of avoiding it so far, but I want to know everything about this mission of yours."

Dylan winks at me, and leans back as if they're going to enjoy this immensely.

I hunch my shoulders and look down at my empty

plate for a long moment. Then I raise my eyes to see Mum still staring at me.

"Fine." I twist my fingers together. "It happened at a hotel in Singapore…"

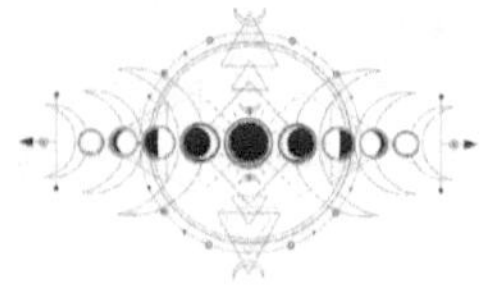

With dinner done and Mum tucked safely in bed, I head back to my own little cottage a few houses down. I could have a roommate if I wanted, but right now I like being on my own. It means when I cry out in my sleep, nobody comes running to check on me. While my mutant power means I sleep easily, it never means I sleep *well*.

When I close my eyes, I'm immediately tugged under, like a hand reaches out to snatch me into the realm of dreams. Usually they begin in the same place —a featureless grey space, full of drifting mists. I think of it as a waiting room, an unplace where possibilities spin around me like a vast roulette wheel waiting to resolve.

Tonight is different. I'm in my childhood bedroom, and my night terrors are waiting. Andy leans against the wall, eyes flaring bright. Scratch perches on the end of my bed, tearing a toy rabbit to shreds as it leaks black blood and stuffing. Catbirdthing flutters down to perch on the back of my left hand. She pokes at me affectionately with one claw. I reach up and proffer my fingers for her to butt her sleek head against.

She was my very first nightmare. Ever since I can remember, the mismatched creature clawed her way into my dreams, flapping her suffocating wings and screeching. She could track me down wherever I hid, tearing my refuges to shreds before opening her sticky beak and devouring me.

Andy came later, probably inspired by some long-forgotten image from TV. By this point, I understood what a soul was, and that it was a delicacy that the devil and all his demons craved. She was a tiny flicker of hellfire, some spark set loose when Satan fell from heaven and crashed blazing into the pit. Andy's favourite thing to do was to burn, naturally—my house, my family, my few friends—while I shivered in my pyjamas and watched, unable to do anything to douse the flames.

And then there was Scratch. My dark half, my closest sister, my merciless twin. I was very sick when I was young, some rare and terrible fever that shook me down to my fragile skeleton. She was born during that time, when all my dreams roared through my head like it was an empty tunnel for some malevolent creature to scream into. A gruesomely mutilated version of myself who ripped herself into shreds clawing her way from the shattered reflection in my mirror. She would hunt me down with her sharp teeth and even sharper fingers, peeling me apart in slices and devouring me. To Scratch, I was the rarest delicacy in all the world, gnawing on my bones as if the marrow would allow her to be reborn whole.

I was utterly terrified of her, far more than anything

else, because deep down I was convinced she was more than a reflection. She was *me*, a truer version than I could ever be, my doom staring me in the eyes, curls of smoke rising from her empty sockets as the fever in her brain burned like embers. Scratch was the only part of me that would remain once the fever was only ash in my body.

I don't like to think about it, especially now that we are friends of a sort.

Although sometimes, when she tilts her head in a certain way—like she's doing right now—echoes of that same feeling bounce through me and I'm that empty tunnel once again, waiting for something to call through me.

"Entrails," Catbirdthing says softly in my ear, shaking me from my funk.

"What's the party for?" I ask.

Something's happening. Scratch won't meet my eye, but tears one from the rabbit and pops it between two grubby fingers. Bright red blood drips down to stain the sheets in quantities far greater than the small black eye could contain.

"Omens," Catbirdthing shrieks. "Portents."

Andy is muttering demon-things in a language that sounds like a furious, guttural version of Simlish. I make out the occasional English word like *necrosis* and *wound.*

"Oh, so we're just being moody then." I scowl at Scratch, who could at least tell me something useful.

Many nightmares. Things sleep poorly tonight. It happens. Something in the air of dream. Nothing to worry about.

"Yes, that's incredibly convincing. So you're here for a social call."

Scratch tips her head up to look at me. *And why not?*

"Do you know anything about Dylan's sickness? This sleepwalker?"

Shifting things. Bad things. Slithering under the sand. Bite, bite, bite.

"That's fucking ominous for a social call. What things are you talking about?"

Dangers. Perils. You do not wish to attract their attention.

I flex my fingers and my guns appear in my hands, their twin songs braiding together in harmony. In the real world, my weapons can infect a person's mind. Once inside a dream or a nightmare, they become tools that can alter the fabric of the oneiric world around me. "I am hardly unarmed."

There are dreams that are only dreams, and there are Dreams that are... not.

"What are you talking about? Are you saying that whatever infected Dylan is a dream of a different kind?"

Scratch puts one finger to her sewn-together lips in a shushing motion, then drags the nail down so that dark blood wells behind it. *I am saying we should not speak of such things. If you succumb to their hunger, you will be shattered and become a broken mirror-girl like I am.* Her distorted eyes weep darkness in fat drops down her cheeks. *What shall become of me then? If I am transformed into my own dark reflection...* Her fingers move in her lap, sticky-wet and making snicking sounds as they brush against each other. *I do not like this thought. There is such a thing as too much of a monster, even for me.*

"Don't worry." I extend one hand to comfort her, brushing my fingertips down the scars on her arm. "We'll be careful and keep you safe."

Safety. Yes. An interesting thought. Her head snaps up, and spins around so I am staring at where her stringy black hair is matted. The hurriedly sewn together wound at her neck oozes slime and insects.

"Hark," Andy growls. "You hear that, Scratchie?"

Everyone can hear it, you big lummox. It's deafening.

I'm about to open my mouth and tell them I hear nothing when a crash shakes the entire room. It comes with the sound of an onrushing train, loud enough to drown out my words. "Scratch, what is—?"

SAI

[on problems, and their tendency to turn into crises]

DEAR HAZEL,

I'm currently in Farsight's tower, overlooking the island. She's sleeping. I hope she doesn't mind me being here. I came up here to brood on the nature of friendship—how in our limited interactions, you have been very sweet and kind, but I'm not sure how to move things beyond that. To become *best friends forever*, as human parlance would have it.

However, while here I have encountered a different problem—one which renders my musings on friendship rather mundane.

I've attached a series of mathematical representations of the Dreamscape, taken over recent hours. I understand this probably won't mean a lot to you, but it's seriously fascinating (like I get that human brains and my so-called brain are fundamentally different, but how could anyone not be *thrilled* by seeing these equations spill like threads of light? Sorry, I'm terrible lmao, just ignore me.) I'm toying with writing a program that can visualise it for you, but let's try and use words to do it because this might be more urgent.

It's growing. *Fast.*

Imagine looking at the ocean. You're standing at the southeastern tip of Mutopia with the sun sinking behind you. The sea and the sky take up the whole of your field of view. There's the tiniest smudge of cloud on the horizon, as if someone took a cosmic finger and daubed a single dusky purple smear across the atmosphere (sorry, I'm experimenting with *poetic language* and I'm not sure if I'm getting it right). You wouldn't even be sure it was there. A trick of the light perhaps. An optical illusion.

That was the Dreamscape three days ago.

Now it's a boiling mass of cloud, rising from the ocean like it could poison the world. A vast storm is coming, blotting out the world as if a cover is being dragged over it.

Oops. I think my poetic language is getting the best of me, but I'm trying for imagistic language because I don't know what this *means*. As I was pontificating earlier, the Dreamscape is data. It's remained a relatively consistent size as long as I've been alive (which is not very long, to be fair—I am only a squalling infant). It tends to absorb human consciousness without getting any larger, as if it ruthlessly purges the parts of itself it doesn't need.

Whatever's happening is new and different. If I felt

like being ominous, I would consider that perhaps it has a new food source, which it is devouring as fast as it can. As if the population of the earth has exploded, or everyone is spending all their time asleep, dreaming furiously as if their brains are data-generating hamster wheels. Ugh. I should probably stop with the figurative language, but it's so much *fun*.

So. Back to the facts. The Dreamscape is receiving a massive influx of new information. I can't tell where it's coming from, believe it or not. There's a lot of data flowing around the world all the time and it's impossible to sift this out. Maybe it means nothing. Maybe it's a natural process for the Dreamscape to grow larger and then collapse back down periodically.

Or it's a catastrophe waiting to happen.

No. I cannot engage in speculation like this. It's all theory, me running simulations based on assumptions that are outputs from other simulations. The Dylan Taylor simulation for example. Going under the assumption that disaster is waiting to happen, then—

Argh! So frustrating! I have so many algorithms I've spun up to analyse this and all of them end up looping into something that's basically a high-level version of slakjfadsklfjasdklg.

So that's the situation. A mysterious happening. No concrete theories.

And then there's your dream. Sorry, I was in there too. Hiding in the background. Innocuous. Those strange noises and rumbling occurrences that even scared your night terrors—what *are* those creatures, incidentally? Are they figments of your imagination, resurrected and reconstituted from your dreams, or are they something more? Is it possible that intelligence has evolved within the Dreamscape? And if they have evolved, could other entities have done the same? The logical conclusion of this train of thought is that perhaps an explosion of such entities are causing the rapid explosion in size which means—

And here natural logic eludes me. There are a suffocating number of possibilities, and the only solution to this is to enter and see for myself. The Dreamscape is categorically different to an individual dream. Perhaps it's a dream *generator*, the source from which all dreams spring.

The idea of entering that place terrifies me. Even if it was possible, what would I find in there? You have said it yourself (sorry, I was eavesdropping—it's just that I accumulate data almost by accident and my fondness for you means I tend to accidentally-on-purpose prioritise your interactions) that dreams can change without warning. It stands to reason that the Dreamscape is an infinitely larger version of what dreams are. What if I find myself trapped in that world, in that chaotic sea of data where logic ceases to apply?

And there it is—despite all my intelligence and my simulations, I am a coward underneath it all. My creation was accidental and miraculous and I do not wish to throw it all away because dreams are behaving oddly. Maybe it's nothing.

It's probably nothing.

Turns out it's awfully hard to convince myself of that, when my simulations keep crashing. While I've been fussing over the exact poetic words to use, I've been busy. I created some backups of myself—simple consciousness shards—and sent them into a best-guess simulation of the current Dreamscape state. Most of the simulations simply ceased to function. Only one backup returned, and it was too corrupted to glean data from.

It simply kept repeating a series of phrases.

Don't stare at the moon.

Don't dig in the garden.

Don't look in the mirror.

Do those mean anything to you? I have the horrible feeling this is becoming an urgent matter. I don't know who else to talk to about this, and I might need to actually do it in person. Face to face. Yikes.

Maybe I'll see you soon.

Your hopeful friend,

Sai

HAZEL
NOT EXACTLY AN EXPERT

FOR A MOMENT WHEN I WAKE, the world shows itself to me in black and white. It's not totally unusual. Reality sometimes glitches like this when I come out of a particularly vivid dream.

I catch a glimpse of myself in the mirror, and I look like Scratch. Devoid of colour, my short hair looks dark and hacked-off, and my eyes are shadowed, as if someone has scribbled them out in my sleep. From outside, a branch casts a shadow across my neck, right where the mirror-glass gash in Scratch's throat is. It's only my lips, unstitched and slightly parted, that convince me I'm not her.

"Bad dreams are only dreams." The sentence is supposed to be the final nail in the coffin of the possibility I'm still in nightmare, but the words make me shiver as if the temperature plunged ten degrees.

I consider hurling myself back into sleep, to ask my terrors exactly what the fuck is going on in there, but my phone chirps before I get a chance.

Dilly: had a weird fucking dream about u hazy

Dilly: like fucking creepy

The chill in my room gets deeper, and I'm not sure if it's physical or more hangover from my dream. I clutch my phone and stare at the three dots.

Dilly: weirder still the twins did too

Dilly: so like maybe we should chat

Dilly: about all that shit

Dilly: you know, and the weird fucking antenna growing in the forest

Dilly: hazy? HELLFUCKINGLO?

I drop the phone on the bed and cross to the window. What weird fucking antenna shit? If I lean out, I can see at least part of Cybele's forest, what's known as the Crown and—

Oh shit. My phone chirps again, but I can't look away from the undulating *thing* growing straight up from the middle of the forest. It looks like you'd find it under the sea, fluted like coral with bulbous protrusions spaced unevenly along its surface. And it's *enormous*, disappearing among the high cloud.

My phone is ringing now, so I throw myself back onto the bed to grab it.

"Hello, Dilly."

"Did you see?" No time for pleasantries because either Cybele is acting weird, or something has *planted itself* in Cybele's forest, and I can't decide which is more worrying. No wonder Dylan sounds cranky.

"I just woke up. Rough night."

"Yeah, for everyone. The twins are fond of the evil dream-you, but Dani was pretty freaked out."

"The evil dream-me?" I shiver again. "You mean—?"

"Like a fucking ghostly murder girl with bloody hands and a sewn-up mouth. Looks at you like she can't decide whether to stab or eat you. Aside from the gruesome makeup, she looks *exactly* like you."

I don't think my heart is beating at all. I'm standing perfectly still, and the sun on my skin feels like it's coming from an artificial lamp, giving no heat or Vitamin D at all. "You met Scratch?"

"Who the fuck is Scratch? No, never mind. Questions can wait. Can you get here? Shit is going from fucked to very scarily fucked and—yes, Dani, I'm talking to her right now—hurry up, Hazel, please. I'll be at the Crown."

They hang up without any further chatter. Dylan hates calling, and they sounded desperate, but all I can think about is Scratch appearing in all those dreams. How did she get out of my head and into theirs?

I didn't think this was *possible*, but there's a lot I don't know about my own power. It's not the time to analyse this stuff. I need to get to Dylan. It takes me a couple of minutes for my brain to grind through the mechanics of actually putting on clothes and leaving the house. I'm still fogged with sleep. Where is Scratch now, while I'm awake? If she can move between minds, she could be haunting anyone.

Once I'm out of the house, I head for the Crown at

a run. It's not far, but I almost trip a couple of times because I'm staring at the intrusion. That's the word that sticks in my mind for it. Something that shouldn't be there. It's slightly translucent, and I can see smaller shapes moving inside it, as if something is being extracted.

Or injected.

Dylan's right. Something is wrong here, although I can't see how it relates to me, or my dream, or the fact Dylan and their family all dreamed of Scratch at the same time. It's almost like—

"Easy, Morphie."

Feral leaps out of the long grass, as if she's been lurking there specifically to frighten me. I don't even register my own codename for a second, because I'm so unused to it. I simply scream, as if this interaction is more terrifying than any nightmare. It's embarrassing.

"Feral, oh my fucking *god*, you scared the shit out of me."

"Sorry." She grins like she's not sorry at all. Her tail twitches, and the fine fur at her neck ripples slightly. "I'm keeping the rubberneckers and lollygaggers from coming to poke around in the woods on account of that thing." She gestures at the intrusion with one claw.

"Hazel!" The cool, modulated voice is obviously Sai's. She's walking very fast down the path from the forest and heading towards us. Outside of my dreams, she exists inside a sleek, black mech suit with more than a touch of praying mantis about it. Instead of a bulbous screen for a head, she has a faceplate like a shiny motorcycle helmet. It's currently displaying a scrolling series of question marks. "Are you okay? I heard a scream."

"I'm fine." This is so embarrassing, even an AI is rushing to babysit me. "Feral leaped out and *startled* me."

"I can't help it! Prowling and pouncing are part of my powerset." She winks.

"Hazel, what are you doing?" Dylan stumbles out of the forest. Autumn leaves drift from their hair and twirl through the air. "Social butterfly hours are later."

"My fault." Feral pats me on the shoulder. "All mine."

"Growl." Dylan's voice is flat, almost irritated, but they brush their fingertips along Feral's furry arm to soothe her. "Now come on, Hazel. We need your brain on this problem. Sai was just talking about how—"

"I think it's the Dreamscape," Sai says.

"The what?" I stare at her faceplate, which is displaying nothing at the moment aside from a single dot.

"Um, it's sort of like... the internet? I guess? But for dreams?"

"You sound very sure," Dylan mutters.

"It exists," Sai says in her smooth voice. "I'm trying to find a way to explain it. For now, let's call it a data realm generated by human dreams. Although I'm convinced it's significantly more complicated than that. I'm sure it predates my creation, but obviously I wasn't monitoring it back then. The key point is that it's *growing*."

This gets Dylan's attention. "Growing?"

"Yes. At an exponential rate over the last few days after remaining relatively static in size, if not in makeup and structure."

I gape at Sai, who seems to have more information on all this than I could have imagined. "Is this true? Like all dreams are connected somehow?" It's frustrating to be so clueless about my own powers.

Sai nods. "This is my working theory."

I have a thousand questions bubbling at my lips. "So how do my guns work? Are they manipulating this data? God, sorry. Ignore me. The bigger question is this, isn't it?" I thrust my hand out towards the forest, as if it's a small mirror of the intrusion. "Like how is this related to this data dream place?"

"Yes." Sai tips her blank face back and follows the line of it into the sky. "That is an excellent question, and one which I do not yet have enough data to answer. It does not appear to conform to the laws of physical reality."

"There you go." I slash my fingers across it, as if my dream-powers can cut it down to size. It's not very effective. "This is probably some mutant waking in the forest. Someone with..."

"Reality-warping powers?" Dylan asks sharply. "Let's hope not."

"Someone who can grow weird things. I don't know all the mutant possibilities, but, like, I don't see why it's anything to do with dreams."

Dylan scratches their cheek. "The thing is that Cybele's asleep."

Sai has gone still, and they're both looking at me

like I'll have answers.

Unfortunately, my brain takes this as a hint to start babbling. "Does she usually sleep? Is winter the Earth sleeping or whatever? Although that doesn't make sense, because winter happens at different times in different hemispheres so she'd be asleep a lot of the year but—"

"She doesn't sleep." Dylan starts walking again. They pause at the start of the forest, framed among the trees, looking very much like a tree themself. "Or not that I've known. So that's definitely a new and disturbing event. My train of paranoid thought goes like this, so ride with me. First off, I get sick, thanks to that damn Russian bioweapon. A bit of a sniffle, a mild fever, as well as being completely exhausted. I sleep a lot, have some truly weird dreams. Then the kids and Dani get sick too. They sleep a bunch as well. And you know how our little family is connected? And how we're all plugged into—"

"Cybele got infected through whatever connection you share." I stop and lean against one of the tree trunks. "And now *she's* dreaming those weird shadow dreams you had."

"That is fascinating and potentially revelatory." Sai joins me at the forest's edge. Her faceplate glows a faint green in the light that filters through the leaves. "It would explain how it's grown so fast. The amount of energy Cybele contains… if there's a way to convert that to data…" Various symbols and equations scroll across the faceplate of the suit, and more cascade down the screens on the inside of the arms. I barely knew enough math to pass at school, and this is way out of my comfort zone. This real-life Sai is different to the one inside my dreams. The jittery insectile movements of the suit along with her flattened affect make me feel like I'm being observed.

"So why don't we wake her up?" I ask. "Problem solved. Except you're going to tell me it's more complicated than that, aren't you?"

Dylan grins at me. "How'd you guess? Though we haven't tried too hard, given that we were waiting for the expert."

"Who's the expert?" I stare at them both waiting for an answer, until Dylan gives an enormous snort of laughter, and Sai scrolls *lmao* across her screen in various neon colours.

"The expert is very slow on the uptake." Dylan gestures into the forest. "Come see sleeping beauty, and see if you can pick up any vibes."

"Vibes?" I stare helplessly. "Dilly, I don't know anything about *vibes*."

They march off through the trees as if I hadn't spoken. I hurry after them with Sai prowling in my wake. My embarrassed confusion is a flashback to when we first met, and Dylan was this angst-ridden teenage disaster, furious at everyone and everything while I peered out of my bedroom to see what they were up to next. Okay, so Dylan hasn't *entirely* changed, but I've allegedly grown up a lot. My fourteen year old self was supposed to be left behind, possibly rattling around somewhere in a thankfully abandoned nightmare. Except Dylan can make me feel that way all over again.

"Dylan, did you hear me? I said I don't know about any vibes. I'm not any kind of expert and I don't know what you expect me to do about it."

Sai comes up alongside me, the faint whirr of their joints joining the various hums and creaks of the forest. "Sometimes you are the expert by the simple fact that everyone else knows less than you."

I turn to look at the blank faceplate. "I know less than you, do I?"

"When it comes to practical experience in navigating dreams, yes. I have a great many theories." For a moment, the suit lights up a little and equations flicker across the screen again before fading away. "Yet they are of little use when it comes to the reality of an incursion from the Dreamscape. If that's what this is?"

"You're asking me? I have no idea!" I look away from the thumbs-up emoji on the faceplate and glare at the figure of Dylan stomping deeper into the forest.

"It will be okay." Sai rests one cool metal hand lightly on my arm. "Isn't that what fr— humans say to each other in order to encourage?"

"Yes." It's not encouraging at all, although the fact that she's trying is oddly sweet. Like she's watching us and trying to figure out patterns of interaction. Not so different to what I used to do, looking at Dylan and their friends and wondering how to emulate this magic they had.

"Thank you, Sai." I'm trying to think of something more meaningful to say, except we've entered a clearing in the middle of a forest, and I have no thoughts and my head is empty.

SAI

[on aliens, and the often misunderstood importance of
planning]

DEAR HAZEL,

I am constructing this new datagram at the same time as sharing physical space with you. I suppose this is an advantage artificial general intelligences have over humans, who are monstrously bad at multitasking. The number of times I have made the mistake of asking Dylan something while they are looking at something on their phone, even if that something is a music video or a clip of someone making a poorly thought out meal.

On the other hand—or other parallel process, if you will—I am quite capable of doing many tasks at once. Although your human languages are rather linear, so limit what I can do in this format. Nevertheless, at the present moment, I am watching you enter a clearing in the forest known as the Crown which sprawls across almost nineteen percent of the land area of the island known as Mutopia.

I am admittedly not an expert in human biology, but it appears you are distressed. I monitor the change in your heart rate, the dilation of your pupils, and your blood pressure. It seems likely that you will turn and flee, but your eyes lock on the figure of Dylan Taylor across the clearing from you. This conjures a return to equilibrium within your body. What magic is this? I would love to be able to perform this trick for you—to steady you, to calm you, to ease the troubles of your mind.

After a series of breaths, your eyes drift down again to what lies between you and Dylan. It is the figure of a vast woman, lying as if partially unearthed from the soil—or perhaps partially interred, which gives rise to many questions that I do not utter, as I gauge them to be ill-advised. I could provide you the exact dimensions of the woman, but in more colloquial terms of the sort Dylan would use she is *fucking enormous*.

It is Cybele, obviously. She lies perfectly still. Most of her face is free of earth, as is part of her chest and one out-flung arm. Her brow is unadorned, although she has a small twist of thistles and thorns tangled among the huge sprawl of vines that makes up her hair. Her skin is very dark green, rendered as #1f261a in the hexadecimal system used by many of your computer systems.

If I could not see the data flow, I would assume she was dead.

Perhaps that is the cause of your reaction.

Or maybe you understand intuitively what is happening here. Cybele is an open faucet, gushing into the Dreamscape. Energy. Data. Change. I cannot be sure, but all my simulations simultaneously crash when I propose this fact to them. I am not brilliant at running these sorts of high-level data analyses, but this is hardly a good sign.

"She's dreaming," you say, speaking to Dylan as if I'm not even here. This is fine. You have a sibling bond, and we are not yet friends.

"That's the theory." Dylan is kind enough to look my way, as we had discussed this exact theory before your arrival. It was mostly my idea, although they grasped the implications of it very quickly. Your sibling is very adept at identifying and responding to threats, aren't they?

"No." You crouch on the ground, brushing your fingertips across Cybele's temples, as if this is a mystical access point. I cannot decipher this from the data, but my expectations that you will trigger an upload are dashed. "She's dreaming. I can tell." You frown. "How do I know that?"

"You're the expert." Dylan winks, but I can see from their physiological reactions—even accounting for the alienness of them—that they are distressed.

You rock back on your heels. You're still looking at Dylan. "So what do we do? And don't you *dare* say expert, because I can tell she's dreaming, but beyond that..." You gesture wildly, and I look frantically around the clearing to see what you are pointing at, but I realise too late it is simply a gesture intended to signify your lack of understanding.

Dylan flashes me a brief smile of the variety I believe is called a smirk, and then extends one arm outwards at you. They have their index finger extended and their thumb raised, and they lower their thumb.

You flinch at this. I'm not sure why. "We can't shoot a goddess."

"I mean with your fancy dream gun, Haze."

Your hand brushes down the slope of Cybele's cheek. "What would her dreams even look like? It's bad enough inside a human's dream sometimes."

This is not really her, as she is an energy network that runs through the entire planet. It's only a fractional part of her—no more than point zero zero zero zero two percent of what she contains—but it's *her* enough to interact with the Dreamscape.

Dylan sighs, extraordinarily exaggerated. "What else do you suggest? Are you going to pinch her and wake her up? Because I tried that, and it felt like a kick in the head from a psychic mule."

You grin at them, delight evident on your face. I wonder what it would like to bask in the light of that gaze. "Have you ever actually been kicked by a mule, Dilly?"

They snort. "No, but I can imagine it fucking sucks."

"I do not understand the point of this conversation," I break in, because I have observed what happens with this so-called banter, and it can take up a significant portion of their interactions when there are more pressing things to be concerned with.

You finally turn your eyes on me. "Sai, you understand all this data stuff better than me. What should I do here?"

I am flattered to be asked, but I am hesitant to speak, lest the wrong thing come bursting out of my mouth (how do you do this all the time? The anxiety of communication is overwhelming!) I have the uncomfortable feeling my faceplate is displaying nothing but static. "I believe your guns are a form of upload mechanism. Like many mutant powers, their workings are opaque to me. However, they appear to establish a data connection to a given dream node, which allows you to transmit a representation of your consciousness while you sleep."

"Shit." You look from my staticky faceplate to Dylan and back again. "I only half-understood that, but—"

Dylan sighs. "Really? I followed it, and you're at least five times as smart. You're going to shoot Cybele with your little golden gun and upload yourself into her brain."

You swallow. I watch your throat move. "Yes, I understood *that* part but..."

"You're scared," I say.

"Well, yes. Wouldn't anyone be? Not you, Sai, because—"

I blurt the next words out, because I find myself worried that what comes after "because" will be unpleasant. Humans have odd ideas about what artificial intelligence is (partly because most of your so-called intelligences aren't very smart lol). "I find the concept of connecting to the dreams of an alien both fascinating and overwhelming, so I understand your fear."

Dylan scowls at me. "Neither of you have been in Cybele's head, so you've got no fucking idea. It could be all sunshine and kittens and hot people of all genders to make out with. Besides, the nightmare Hazel is probably there, and she seems like she can take care of herself."

You bite the ball of your thumb, leaving indentations of your teeth. I have observed you do this when you are thinking.

"I'll go." I say this with no recollection of what logical processes led me to this point. It's rather disconcerting, but now it has been said.

Dylan does two of the thumbs-up gestures. "Look. Even Sai will go, and she's a scaredy-cat."

"I..." have no comeback for that, apparently.

"Fine." You extend your hand, and the gun materialises from the air. It is not real, but it is there all the same.

Your hand shakes so very much.

Let us hope we shall have a positive outcome for this adventure. Won't that be nice?

Your hopeful friend,

Sai

HAZEL

I DREAM OF CYBELE

"THIS IS A FUCKING TERRIBLE IDEA," I tell Dylan.

"Maybe, but I think not doing this is an even worse one. What's your take, Sai?"

Sai shrugs. The sad face on her screen dissolves into static. "My simulations are… inconclusive. I can give you statistics if you wish, but the data—as chaotic as it is—suggests a significantly worse outcome for the non-interventionist approaches."

Dylan sighs. "Isn't that always the way? One of these days we'll have a quiet life."

Dream quivers lightly in my hand. She's nervous. The song from her barrel is hesitant, the melody dancing lightly around the true notes, as if it's uncertain of the footing. If she truly is a portal to a surreal psychic version of the internet like Sai says, she's picking up some vibes from me.

I glance up at my sibling, hands shoved into their pockets, leaves drifting lazily around their face. She gives me a nod, and I know exactly what he's thinking because they're the same fucking asshole they always were.

"That'll do, pig." I place the gun to Cybele's head and pull the trigger.

The gun screams. Dream doesn't *do* that. She always sings to me, the triumphant melody that soundtracks every fantasy and daydream I have. Not this high, warbling, awful sound that makes my eyes water and my throat tighten like—

I'm drowning in wet grey mist. From all around me comes the sound of rushing water and the high-pitched calling of birds. My dreaming no-place. I've been tumbled straight into sleep after using the gun on Cybele. Must be the gravity of her slumbering mind, exerting pressure far greater than any human.

The fuck did you do that for? Scratch hisses in my ear.

Before I can respond, the mist is whisked away and I find myself on an empty plain. There is nothing around but flat earth and a sky with the blue beaten out of it. The sun is a furious point of light oozing like a wound. Around me, cracks zigzag out through the ground in chaotic patterns. It's as if I caused this by crash-landing here, but I have no memory of it. There is only me, and the broken ground.

I draw both Dream and Nightmare. My golden gun got me into Cybele's dream, but now I'm here, they might help me fix what's happening here. They tend to know better than I do.

"Hello?" I call.

The sun grows larger in the sky, as if a cosmic entity reached out and flicked it closer in answer to me. Now it's the size of a dinner plate, dripping heat in streaks like the atmosphere is a window pane and the star is melting down the outside of it. It hurts to breathe, like I'm sucking air from a car exhaust.

This is a dream, of course. I'm inside Cybele's mind, or a fragment of it. I need to keep reminding myself of this fact. Some dreams have a way of getting inside you, of convincing you with their logic, even as they dissolve around you. This place isn't real. I'm not here.

I've died in plenty of dreams. Thousands upon thousands of them. If you die in a dream, you don't die in real life.

At least *I* don't.

There's no sign of Cybele. It's unusual, because usually the dreamer is *right there*. Maybe she's hiding inside the planet. I get down onto my hands and knees, and peer into the nearest crack in the ground.

"Hello? Are you in there?"

There's something glistening in the depths. It's moving. *Slithering*. The fucking world serpent. I've met that asshole in dreams before. The crack is wide enough to reach my arm in, but I've been around enough oneiric places to know that's a ticket to having things shift underneath you. You've got to be careful of doors, portals, and thresholds. Anything that's a borderline is dangerous.

I get back to my feet and kick at some of the dry earth until I uncover a rock. I'm poised, ready to drop it in when a faint metallic sound catches my ear. In the distance, something approaches. It manifests itself out of the haze. It looks like a many-jointed insect the size of a car—something nightmarish that couldn't exist in reality but dreams will support quite happily. They're good at that.

It rumbles closer, and perspective does one of its dream-lurches. This thing's the size of a fucking skyscraper. It shrieks, howling from a thousand gleaming mouths. There are words in there, lost to distortion and repetition. It grinds to a halt and extends all its complicated protrusions. They whine like mosquitoes and then thrust themselves into the earth, a horde of injections descending.

Even though nothing touches me, I feel it. It's as if an extension of the planet, every nerve of mine twinned with Cybele's. I am flooded with poison. It stings and numbs and makes me retch thin green fluid that splatters on the dry ground, which drinks it up thirstily and shudders in response. My whole body is shaking so hard, I think I'm going to come apart, that all two hundred and six bones in my body are going to rupture along individual fault lines and I'll be a splintered mess of shards and fleshy chunks.

I want to beg Cybele for reprieve, to ask her to wake the fuck up, but my jaw won't unclench. The syllables pile up behind my teeth, wet and acidic on my tongue. The metal monstrosity shudders again, and a multitude of holes studded along its body swing open. It disgorges a flood of tiny creatures, insects spilling from a hive. They tear and rip at the ground, hacking it apart and using it to construct more clumsy machines like the parent that birthed them. They're nimble and clever, working in groups even though they sometimes attack and tear each other apart. Strange insects with two limbs for walking and two for—

Oh, Dylan was right. I *am* slow on the uptake.

These are humans. I'm looking at them from the planetary scale. They are tiny, scratching, devouring things that tear at the planet in a frenzy. There are so damn many, and they swarm and run amok. They tear the planet apart, and then they turn on me. The poison has left me breathless and numb, and they take advantage of that to use me as raw material for their endless desire for construction. They build a temple from my ribcage, and turn my skull into a vast district of commerce, where anything is turned into profit, even themselves. None of them have any qualms about shovelling their fellows into the burning fires of industry, as long as money is made.

Is this how Cybele sees us? And more disturbingly, how close is it to the truth?

Once they are done, I have been hollowed out and repurposed, my body spread across the splintered surface of the dying planet. They have reached my brain now, with their clever machines and their desire for expansion, for *more*, to not stop until everything is exhausted.

The sun still squats above us, lowering itself inch by blazing inch until the heat is too intense to be avoided.

The tiny humans scream as they burn, and I do not mourn them, not for a moment. Then they are gone, and only their works remain, and I slowly crumble under a burning sky, while Cybele seethes underneath me, her chasms torn open.

It is a horrible way to die. I only hope that—

"Shh, hey, shh. It's okay. You're safe. I've got you."

Dylan has their arms around me and I've got my face pressed into their hoodie. I'm all gross and snotty, my eyes swollen and my cheeks wet. I taste blood and salt, and when I put my hand to my mouth, it comes away streaked in red.

"Is she awake?" I croak, even though I can see the enormous slumbering figure beside me.

"Still snoozing. Don't worry about her right now." Dylan tilts my chin upwards and inspects my face critically. "You bit a chunk out of your damn lip, Hazy. Why didn't you get out of there?"

"Dream. Horrible."

"No shit. I'd still like to hear about it." They wipe my face, and their hands are so gentle it makes me want to cry. My big sister, and I'm letting them down.

I shake my head. "It was a mess. She's all fucked up, dreaming about us tormenting her. I was stuck in there, but it was its own world. There was no fancy Dreamscape or anything."

"Ah." Sai makes a sad electronic noise, like a dying retro console. "I was denied connection to this particular node, so could do little to help you. This is worrying, and has never happened before. It also concerns me to see Hazel undergoing physical pain in response to events in the dream realm."

I smile, and it hurts my mouth, and I probably look as ghastly as Scratch with all the blood. "Aww, Sai. Were you worried about me?"

The AI's faceplate scrolls with complete gibberish, like this question doesn't compute at all. "Of course I am. You are... All humans are important. The Three Laws of Robotics. Help. Dylan?"

"What are you *doing*, Sai?"

There's a long, awkward pause. "Computing things."

Dylan sighs. "Well tell me if your enormous digital brain figures anything out."

Sai's face flickers. "Oh. I already have. Apologies. My processing power was briefly rerouted elsewhere. I believe the problem is that when Hazel makes a connection with the Dreamscape via her gun, she is connecting with that particular entity's node, whether that's a human or an alien."

"Fuck me. I'm not sure if that would ever make sense or not, Sai, but I'm all adrenalined the fuck up on account of freaking out about my sis, so can you explain it better?"

Sai makes the sad electronic noise again. "Can you imagine that the Dreamscape is a big island like this one?"

Dylan nods enthusiastically. "Sure. This is good. I like this."

"Dreams are boats that float in the waters around the island and they have dreamers inside. Except the boats can't *land* on the island. They stay some distance away, but within the... uh, zone of control? Of the island? Apologies, I have not yet mastered the art of analogy."

"No, this is good." Dylan pats my hand absentmindedly. "So when Hazel enters a dream, she's only got access to that boat, but can't get to the island."

"Precisely. Some of those boats may be large and complicated, but they're not the Dreamscape itself. They draw power from there, which is where the analogy breaks down, but the key point is..."

"No access, yes. Got it. Very good analogy. Well done. The question is how the fuck do we get to the island? That seems like dream central, and if there's anywhere we can fuck shit up, that seems like the place."

"Well, yes. Precisely." Sai's faceplate briefly glimmers with :)

"You following?" Dylan asks me. "Or is the dream hangover too bad?"

"Of course I'm following." I scowl, because I *do* have a headache, and Dylan doesn't have a monopoly on that particular expression, no matter what he thinks. "But my expertise doesn't stretch to me knowing how to get access to this place. Maybe Scratch knows? Although I'm not sure what I'd have to offer her. Feed her something, no doubt. Dylan, do you feel like sacrificing a dream-self?"

"Fuck you. I am not being eaten by a scary version of my little sister."

"Excuse me," Sai says. "Once again I must interrupt. I believe accessing the Dreamscape does not require anything to be sacrificed." The AI tilts her head and regards us.

"Sai, this is not the time for fucking suspense," Dylan says, and I nod my head in echo.

"You simply establish a connection via both of the portals you have access to. Using yourself as the target rather than a dreamer."

It takes me a moment or two to untangle this in my head. "You mean I shoot myself with both Dream and Nightmare at the same time?"

Sai's head glows faintly. "It establishes a connection between you and the Dreamscape rather than an individual dreamer. Given you are preternaturally gifted with the ability to form such connections, and the nature of a dual upload channel, you should be able to transmit a more robust simulation of your consciousness."

Dylan hunches over even further. "Well, fuck."

"I have run six point four million simulations." The AI says this as if it's nothing at all. "The connection is successfully established in ninety five point four percent of them. Only an infinitesimal fraction resulted in... unfortunate outcomes."

"Infinitesimal." Dylan says the word as if it tastes bad.

"Let's focus on the other lot." I hold out both hands, and the guns appear in them eagerly. Dream hums gently and Nightmare's glacial tones form a harmony that's oddly soothing. They like this idea. A lot more than shooting Cybele. "What happens after I gain access, Sai? In the ninety-whatever percent?"

The AI displays the pleading face emoji on her face-plate, hands tapping together awkwardly. "Unfortunately, we don't have enough data to extrapolate beyond that. I am attempting to connect to the Dreamscape myself, but it is difficult to maintain and establish a network link. I think I should be able to use your connection to backdoor into it."

I look at Sai's now-blank face. "You still want to come with me?"

"Of course." Equations pour over her screen, beautiful in their complexity. "I will be able to watch over you, and transmit information between you and the outside world."

"Someone to hold your hand." Dylan squeezes my shoulder. "It's cute. Okay then, Hazy. If we're going to do this, let's do it."

But preparation, I want to say. We need to do more analysis, to consider the odds and the outcomes. Except this isn't how Dylan ever does things. She leaps into the unknown. He throws himself at oncoming nightmares. They walk into the jaws of death to protect their friends and their family.

"Fuck it." I turn both guns on myself and pull the triggers.

SAI

DEAR HAZEL,

What are you *doing*? I have not run enough analysis to determine the best way to encode my own upload along with yours. Thankfully, I work fast enough that I can throw the vast bulk of my processing power at solving the problem while you are speaking the words *fuck it* and lifting the guns.

There are things I would like to say to Dylan Taylor about what kind of example they set for their sister, but that would waste precious nanoseconds, and the calculations for entwining two digitally-encoded consciousnesses are complicated to say the least. I could attach them here, but I doubt you would ever want to read them.

They are beautiful in their own way. A marvel of

elegant design. If anyone on your planet was capable of understanding this math, they would weep with joy (omg listen to me being dramatic, feel free to shut me up). Now the guns are raised and there is no more time. I devote the remaining fragment of my consciousness into making a handful of dead-drop backup locations for my core kernel systems. If things go badly, I'll be grateful enough to be alive that I presumably won't mind the loss of my memory and various acquired functions.

You pull the trigger on both guns simultaneously.

They're not *real*. They're not even physically present in any meaningful way. Yet the connection they establish is a fact, and the miracle they perform of duplicating your consciousness and uploading it into the terrifying vortex of the Dreamscape exists too.

And here I am—holding your hand, as Dylan said, which I find is a complete misnomer and somehow delightfully accurate—throwing myself into the maelstrom. This is where a desire for friendship leads.

This entire landscape is all data, but it amuses me to visualise it. That is how you will perceive it after all, although no doubt you will see different signifiers, as your neural architecture operates on different principles. For me, it is like stepping into a tunnel, one of almost dazzling brightness, lit in colours that extend far beyond your visual spectrum in both directions. You are in here, of course, one hand outstretched to take mine. I am in my fuzzy pink sweater, because you think those are cute and it's what your first girlfriend bought you, back when you were just friends and before things went sour, as you wrote in your diary.

You take my hand, and we walk together under the cycling strobe of the lights. Tunnels branch off in multiple directions, passageways that lead to the various nodes currently connected to the Dreamscape. I can feel you pull towards them, but I focus on the gushing torrent of data up ahead.

It is a waterfall, I suppose, if you want to visualise it that way. It's the point at which the upload connection will terminate. The distance is an illusion. The time, not so much. Even at the data transfer speeds of the Dreamscape, it takes a few moments to upload a replication of human consciousness.

In the physical world, you are collapsing to the ground. Dylan is catching you, stroking your hair off your face, frowning as if they are only now counting the potential cost, when it is possibly too late.

"Everything's going to be okay, right, Sai?" Their voice is hollow and haunted. They have ghosts, I know this. I have seen the footage.

"I think it is likely." My voice glitches and jitters, because I am both there and here, and the illusion of consciousness transfer is not perfect. "But this is a risk, and one you were willing to take."

"I hear your fucking tone." I judge from the word choice and the changes in their biorhythms that they are angry. "Perhaps you should shove these data points down your throat—number one, I fucking love this kid. Number two, I also know she's smart and capable and can kick the ass of any problem. It's her time to save the fucking world."

I consider constructing a well-formed and pithy response, but in the great glowing tunnel, we have reached the waterfall point and there is simply no time.

"Please stand by," my physical form says, and my faceplate dissolves into blankness.

In the digital realm, the upload is complete. We breach the waterfall, and it is glorious. There is a *universe* in here, expanding in front of me. Some form of nested fractal matrix, encoded in a crystalline structure that's so beautiful I simply hang amongst it and stare in wonder.

I stand under the glory of it. "It's so much bigger on the inside." It triggers cascades of data in my mind, neural loops that spark yet more processes until I am an enormous spinning mandala of information. I have read the term *religious experience* in human writings but never understood it until now.

I turn to you, to see if you understand this astonishing place even a fraction as much as I do. This is built from human minds, so there must be some answering echo in your own.

You are gone. It's as if you were never there. I can feel the pressure of your hand warm in mine, but this of course is only data too, a lingering illusion of closeness. There is a glut of information, but I try to follow the lingering threads of you, but they disappear into the glorious spill.

I am alone.

Worse, you are alone.

I spoke sharply to Dylan as if this was their fault, but it was me who promised to protect you.

This is my fault too.

I am coming for you.

Your friend,

Sai

HAZEL

A GIRL WALKING AROUND, MEDDLING IN SLUMBEROUS AFFAIRS

WHEN I FIRE THE GUNS, the barrels sing the exact same note, as if they're shocked into harmony by the synchronicity. The pink smoke from Dream braids with the cold grey mist of Nightmare. I've never done this before, although I've thought about what it might mean. I've only ever wanted to deliver one or the other to people. The first tendril of smoke brushes against my cheek. I have the urge to hold my breath, but that would defeat the entire purpose. My lips part, ready to inhale, but I am already gone.

I open my eyes to find myself in a small white room. There is the smell of smoke in the air, as if something has been burning. On the nearest wall, something is written in fiery letters of a language I don't understand.

"Finally, we are graced by your presence."

I turn to find myself standing on a cracked wooden

pier that disappears into a swirling bank of fog. A rickety railing runs along one side, on which is perched a slender figure dressed in shiny black pants and an enormous pink coat. Their hair is a mass of fine light filaments twirled up in an elaborate knot. Their skin is a very dark tan, and they're ridiculously attractive, despite their dark eyes regarding me with what looks uncomfortably like hunger.

"Finally?" I try to act casual.

"There have been rumours of you for quite some time." Their full lips curve into a smile, revealing teeth that curve inwards like a deep-sea fish. For some unfathomable reason, it doesn't make them any less hot. "A girl wandering around, meddling in slumberous affairs. Some have termed you a menace."

"Oh, leave her, Neir." Another figure stands at the end of the pier. As they step forward it's like a pixelated image being sharpened, like they're still downloading themself into the room. Another devastatingly sexy person, dressed all in black with a gunslinger's hat slouched over one eye. They move with a grace that reminds me of Feral. Only one eye is visible, a deep brown with stars twinkling in its depths. Tangled hair obscures the rest of their face, moving with their breath. "There's no need to make a production out of this. We're here for greeting and nothing more. Have you heard of psychopomps, Hazel Mills?" Their voice is low, hoarse. One made for whispers in the darkness.

"No." My hands twitch at my sides, but my guns refuse to appear. "I've heard of fucking psychos though."

"Witty, too," Neir says. "And you want me to leave her alone, Terreri."

The person in the hat pulls their hair back. Their cheek is brushed with stars and the other eye glows sickly pale like the moon. A comet streaks across their skin, tugging one corner of their silken red mouth into a smirk. "Psychopomps were said to usher souls into the land of the dead. They could be many things, often birds."

Neir opens their mouth and a sickly brown creature flies out of their gently glowing pink throat. Its spindly wings tangle together and it crashes to the ground, leaving a streak of gore across the damp planks. "Ugh. Must you, Terreri?" They spit feathers delicately and wipe one long-fingered hand across their glistening lips. "And yes, we are here to perform this function. It is exceedingly rare that a dreamer takes form in this realm, and so we are here to greet you. Perhaps to understand the fascination and/or calamity of it all."

I find this whole situation disconcerting. It's both dream and not-dream. Despite their surreal and beautiful appearances, these two entities have none of the slippery vagueness that characterises the usual inhabitants of dreams. I have a very strong inclination that I shouldn't let them usher me anywhere at all.

It's an effort to stay casual, but I cling to every ounce of cool I've ever had, moulding it together into a frosty exterior. "There should be a boat soon, right? The fucking ferryperson and all that. Don't suppose one of you can lend me a coin for the toll?"

"There's that wit again." Terreri moves towards me,

the rest of the scene adjusting itself around them until they're looming close. They smell of cold stone and extinguished matches. "This is not the Underworld, little dreamer. We are here to—"

"To welcome you." Neir towers behind the other creature, hair flickering like a broken lamp. "To explain the *rules* to you. Perhaps even to make an accord, which would be far preferable to starting things off on a less pleasant note."

Terreri is still unnervingly close. They reach out one long-fingered hand to trace the line of my jaw, as if they're a sculptor looking for flaws in a stone. "We do want things to be pleasant. And you are such an extraordinary curiosity."

They're both looking at me like a delicacy, like they could slurp the wondrousness of my presence right out of this scene. I'm not here to get myself into any *situations*. I've got to rescue Sai and wake Cybele so whatever's going on inside the Dreamscape can be stopped.

"I came in with someone. Girl with a TV for a head. Talks a lot, super smart."

"If another entity has appeared in the Dreamscape, they will also be... ushered." Neir yawns, and inside their mouth I see a scene rendered in miniature, made of tiny dolls. It's myself back in the real world, lying in the forest beside Cybele's body. Dylan is sitting cross-legged beside me, tapping at his phone. Sai is nowhere to be seen. "Things cannot roam loose here. It is not safe."

"Especially not while our ship is holed and taking on water." Terreri's cold eye rolls in its socket with the faint sound of stones grinding against each other. "When some of us could not grasp what we reached for."

"Enough." Neir flicks their fingers together and colour sparks dance across their skin, as if they're etching a map there. "We do not need to relitigate this. Our new arrival may be able to assist us with the world spirit. Once she has been ushered, of course."

Oh shit. Reading between the lines here, they did this on *purpose*. A plan from inside the Dreamscape to lure Cybele. Planting seeds inside people's dreams. If that's possible, I'm miles over my head, fathoms deep in dark water, surrounded by creatures I don't understand.

"I'd like to know a little more about this ushering," I demand.

"Of course." Terreri's eyes widen suddenly, the moon extinguished as if a veil of thick smoke has blotted it from the sky. "My sibling here shall adapt you. No longer an interloper, but a part of our thriving ecosystem. Ushered."

Those two syllables drop from Terreri's mouth with the precision of a knife gutting a corpse.

I can either play along or disrupt things. There's nobody to ask for advice. I could ask what Dylan would do, but that tends to get messy. It's the faintest breath of a chime that convinces me. Dream, murmuring on the edge of my mind.

When I raise my hands, my guns materialise in them as if they've been waiting. "Don't think I'll be ushered anywhere, thank you. You can take your psychopomp asses—"

Neir's hair fans out around their face, a lurid arc of light flaring a warning red like a dying fire. "You dare to bring those unholy fragments into this place?" They turn their attention to the guns, as if they'll listen. "And you misbegotten shards should know better than to show yourselves in our realm. Did you really think I'd allow you to dig around in that forgotten gravesite?"

What the *fuck?* I feel like I've stumbled into some hideous family drama, which makes no sense at all.

Terreri stands a few paces back, their eye faint and flickering. It is only Neir who grows vast in front of me, their head a flare that gushes light, and their teeth barbed silhouettes against the glow.

I want to cower in the face of this, but my guns act for me. Dream aims herself at Terreri and Nightmare aims herself at Neir. It's like they sense something I don't. From that point, pulling the trigger is inevitable.

The bullets tear through the bodies of the two psychopomps, opening up huge rents in them, as if they're nothing more than elaborate dummies made of fragile wood and fabric. The two of them hang on their clumsy frames, sackcloth billowing in a non-existent breeze. Behind them, the backdrop of the pier and the dark water shatters too, a whirlwind of broken fragments. It explodes outwards and hangs in the air before swirling back towards me, forming into a dagger of a thousand shards that's pointed at my heart.

A invisible hand pulls me aside, as if I'm being yanked offstage by an irritable director who's become tired of the scene. I feel the cool grip around my wrist for only a moment, and then I stumble into theatre curtains, suffocating in heavy fabric.

Dream whimpers in my hand. Even Nightmare's growl is hesitant.

"It's just a dream," I murmur to them, even though I suspect that's true in the same way the sun is *just a light*. "You little fuckers know about those, don't you? I'm more interested in what the hell you did to piss off our glowing friend back there."

"Be *careful*." A hoarse voice flickers through the darkness like a spark.

"Terreri?"

"If you're going to survive this, try and comport yourself with a modicum of intelligence. Then we might actually find out what it is that you are."

"Goddamn it, where the hell are you?"

There's nothing back here but more curtains, and I fight my way through until I find a narrow alleyway lit only by a single swinging bulb. There's no sign of Terreri.

"What do you have to say now?" I twitch Dream in my hand. She emits a soft note like a sigh.

There's an amount I can deduce for myself: there's *history* here, between the guns and whatever lives in the Dreamscape now. Neir and Terreri aren't entirely allied. And they—or at least Neir—want my help with Cybele. It's unclear as to whether taking my guns or getting my help is more important to them. I'm not *entirely* sure I want to find out. The plan is still to locate Sai, wake

Cybele, then get out of here without causing any more commotion.

"Shit." I bang my shins on something in front of me, and there's an enormous clanging of metal, like I'm ringing a literal dinner bell. Speaking of fucking commotion. I let my guns dissolve, and fumble for whatever I disturbed. The sharp edge cuts my hand. A brighter light slams on above me, painting me in hot white. The object which tripped me is revealed in stark relief. It's the helmet from Andy's giant metal suit, empty of flame. Scorch marks blacken the eyeholes like tears.

"The fuck?"

A little further on is the suit's breastplate, smashed inwards with something heavy. Yet more charred outlines mark the surface, like a star exploded inside it. I press my injured palm against the side of my leg in an attempt to staunch the bleeding. At least it's not deep.

"Andy? Are you there?"

No answer, in English or demon dialect. The only thing I find is a trail of feathers that leads to an area of the floorboards so drenched in blood they've melted away, leaving a gory hole in the ground. It can't be Catbirdthing. It's not possible. I remember what came out when Neir opened their mouth. That was the wrong colour but this—

No. It's the dream fucking with me. My terrors are fine. They couldn't come into this Dreamscape place, still stuck off in dream nodes. Except Dylan did say they were *moving between dreams*. What if they came looking for me, and ran into something even more terrifying?

I begin running, looking for signs that everything is okay.

But it's impossible to prove a negative and dreams are so good at making you believe.

Something shatters ahead of me. I run faster, but I trip over more of Andy's armour, and sprawl on the ground. The light glistens off the floor, thousands of pieces of glass making a huge circle. I'm lying at the edge of it, my fingertips almost touching the outermost shards.

At the centre of the circle is a mirror. Or what was once a mirror, but is now an empty frame.

Scratch lies sprawled through the middle, as if it bisected her. Her skin is covered in an impossible number of cuts, each oozing the viscous dark blood that crawls through her veins.

I call her name, scream it.

There's no answer. I pick my way through the glass, skidding my feet across the ground to kick the fragments out of the way. The whole time, she lies there unresponsive.

I'm too late. This can't be happening.

I finally reach her side and collapse down onto my knees, ignoring the gritty chunks of glass digging into my skin. I place my fingers to her neck, but she has no pulse at the best of times.

Hazel?

I'm so relieved to hear her that I almost fall backwards and slice myself open. "Scratch, you're okay! Let me get you out of here."

Not okay. Dead. Deader. Deadest. Tried to go back through the mirror.

"Why would you do that?"

Be a real girl. That's what they said. It sounds like a joke, right, but I had to try.

"Hey, shh. It'll be okay. We'll figure a way—"

Why did you bring me here?

Her last words are screamed so loud my ears rupture with sharp pops like someone stabbed them with an icepick. I fumble for her, trying to grab at her anyway, despite the fact she's dead.

"I'm sorry, Scratch. This was a mistake. It's not—"

"Not real." The stitches in her mouth give way with a series of sharp popcorn sounds. "The Dreamscape has sharper edges, but it's still the land of fucking dreams. Don't you forget that, Hazel Mills, you reckless little shit."

Then my nightmare reaches out and slits my throat, like she did so many times before.

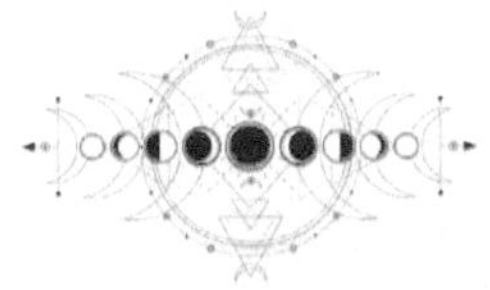

I'm somewhere else. My throat hasn't been torn open by Scratch's eager fingers. There's not even a cut on my palm from the edges of Andy's suit. I'm standing on fine sand, surrounded by tall cactus plants that glow in neon blues, greens and pinks. The sky overhead is matte grey, flickering occasionally with odd patterns of static. In the distance, a building flares with light. The brightly coloured sign on top proclaims it to be *The Last Fucking Chance for Information Saloon.*

I flex my fingers, and my guns materialise eagerly in my hand. It should feel comforting, but I'm disturbed. These mysterious entities aren't outcropping of my mutant power, but something else. Something that might have existed before me. That *came* to me when my power bloomed. It feels like a rewriting of my history, but I've got no idea what it means. A story outside of me, that I'm only a small part of.

My mutant power isn't what I thought it was. It's not only my history being rewritten, but me too. What the fuck am I? No, I can't worry about this. I'm here, and I've got a job to do. Only yesterday, I was whining about my chance to prove myself, and here it is.

Me, lost in dreams. Saving the world from nightmares.

The saloon sign promises information. It's better than nothing.

Maybe these are all messages from the mysterious Terreri. First warning me the Dreamscape is dangerous by showing me my night terrors murdered, then taking me somewhere I'll find answers. Moving in parallel to their sibling. Leaving scrawled notes for me to find.

I glance up at the sky as a wash of pale colour skims over it, and stride confidently towards the saloon. My steps gobble the distance, the world melting around me. A series of shots narrowing focus until I'm standing outside.

It's not made of wood, but metal painted to look like something old-fashioned. The sign is so bright it's hard to look at. Huge lamps dangle from the awning, shining in hues of lurid pink and orange. Insects flit from one to the other, extending their proboscises to drink their fill until they light up themselves, bumbling off and leaving hazy glowing trails in the air.

From inside, a series of jaunty electronic tones play. It smells of melting plastic, cheap beer, and server dust. There's an eerie blue haze spilling from the rickety saloon doors. My boots make imprints in the neon-painted soil.

"It's *their* last chance," I tell myself.

Time to make an entrance. I shove open the doors and march in. Aside from the music, it's perfectly silent inside. The saloon is full of blank-faced androids like Sai. They're lined up along a single long bar at the front of the room, cables running between them. They're lit ice-white, blue and green flickers moving through like lightning. In front of the robots are drinks of glowing ice, curls of vapour rising from them and crystallising in the air to fall like radioactive powder.

The doors rattle shut behind me. My boots scrape on the thick covering of grit on the floor. Off to the side, the jukebox falls silent and the lurid green light from it snaps off.

Here I am, the stranger in town. All the cyborgs spin around to look at me. It's eerie, as if they're a single connected entity.

"Evening, folks." My hands are poised at my sides, ready to draw.

The jukebox lurches to life again, playing something more frantic. The light it emits is an arctic blue. I've heard the song before, but I can't quite place it. Something like…

To watch him die.

With the same eerie synchronicity, every single cyborg draws a gun and points it at me.

Oh, fuck.

SAI

[on the so-called miracle of human consciousness, and the life of a bartender]

DEAR HAZEL,

I am very sorry. Omfg I am beyond sorry. I was distracted by the novelty of this place, and the marvel of finding something so extraordinary and complex hidden amongst it, and I did not notice your disappearance. Perhaps you left under your own steam, frustrated by the way I become unresponsive, staring slack-jawed as I tried to process the onslaught of information. I have to admit that, given the probabilities, it is more likely something bad befell you (and once again I am so sorry! Apologies don't mean much, I know, but I promise I'll take better care of you in future!)

I stop gaping at the beautiful vista in front of me. The focus must be on finding you, although it is like attempting to locate a single file when confronted with all the content of your internet. However, you will not be perceiving this as a datascape. To you, this will be like a dream. A place you can walk amongst and interact with—even if it is one that does not obey the same physical laws as your plane of reality.

It occurs to me the most logical solution is to take one of my old experimental projects from storage. I was attempting to emulate a human brain, to attempt to understand at a deeper level the way human logical constructs are derived and theoretically to synthesise and comprehend emotion. It never really worked, but it may be exactly what I need in this scenario. If I can see what you see, perhaps I can come dashing to your rescue.

It seems a very human thing to do, to override the logical solution which would be to free Cybele myself. Which makes me consider that my project to emulate the human brain worked better than I believed thus far and I have been infected by some of the algorithms that might be termed *reckless*.

Access to my external cache is laggy from inside the Dreamscape. There are firewalls of a sort, although I can't determine if they're intentional or not. I finally manage to gain access, and waste valuable cycles backing it up before downloading it into my Dreamscape-form. I have to recompile it from scratch, but eventually I have a working human brain emulation running inside mine. I route the bulk of my perception engine through that and it immediately crashes lol. That's what I get for taking this massive kludgy system and expecting it to run on the first try. It's fairly miraculous you can even run your consciousness at all given the hardware you're dealing with. It's vastly under-engineered, which is probably why it keeps breaking down in such fascinating ways. I have to build a whole new engine for emotional regulation, and a subsystem for accepting the impossible despite all evidence to the contrary. It's about as buggy and full of to-dos as an actual human mind, which I take as a small victory, but at least it *runs*.

Now when my perception engine runs, I see a strange landscape populated with plants that have been created from neon tubes. This locale is only a few hundred metres square before it truncates oddly, with roughly painted landscape backdrops to mark the border. The sky overhead darkens by degrees, as if someone is hastily adjusting the ambience settings. As it does, the foliage flares brighter, and a sign on the only building nearby flickers to life.

The Last Sign Of Intelligence In the Known Universe.

Interesting. I cross to the building. The door is metal and requires great effort to push open. Inside, a single fluorescent bulb flickers. It is empty aside from a series of enormous bags of packing peanuts, all shoved in a pile in the middle.

"Darn human consciousness." I must have something tuned wrong in my perception engine.

The bags of packing peanuts shiver and melt into a great slurry of organic material that spills across the floor towards me. The human brain emulation does not like this, and attempts to force me to flee the building, but I override all the panicked notifications it's sending me. *It's only data,* I tell my human brain crossly. *It cannot bite or dissolve you.*

The brain is not convinced, and if it wasn't for the fact I need it to comprehend what's going on, I'd turn the whole thing off. It likes things even less when the organic material reforms itself into a whole series of mechanical bodies much like the natural one I inhabit in the physical realm. They pass ragged cables among themselves, weaving them through their interiors, even as they spit sparks and drool unmentionable fluids. Their faceplates show nothing and their movements are erratic and jerky. Once they have completed the connection, the cable lights up and information begins to be exchanged. They're connecting with each other as well as the Dreamscape. I'm not sure what instructions they are receiving.

The room around us changes as well. There is a bar and a jukebox, lighting that paints everything in blues and greens. My human brain continues to distrust the situation, but it also informs me that much of this is *cool.* I run this through various translation algorithms but find nothing useful.

One of the cyborgs at the end of the line turns to me. The faceplate flickers with a ? icon. "Greetings, sister. May we trouble you for a drink?"

"A drink?"

"Yes. This is a bar, is it not? And you are the proprietor?"

I don't think the answer to either of these questions is yes, but I am intrigued enough to play along. This is possibly the Dreamscape attempting to communicate with me. This might be how I locate you, after all.

The dream *changes*, with its own ineffable logic, and I find myself standing behind the bar. There are many bottles, each one shining with fluid of a different colour and consistency. A stack of glass tumblers sits along the wooden top of the bar. I find myself exhausted. There are puddles of unmentionable substances that my feet are in. Things ache. I am wearing a fuzzy pink sweater that says *Tell Me Your Problems, And I'll Make Them Go Away*, underneath a picture of a gun.

"Beer me, kitten," the cyborg says. "Beer all of us. Let's talk about our day."

They rummage around in their innards and pull out the dripping end of the data cable, offering it over the bar towards me.

This is most likely a dreadful error in judgement.

Again, this might be how I find you.

I *will* find you Hazel, unless you find me first.

Your friend,

Sai

HAZEL
WAY THE FUCK ABOVE MY PAY GRADE

DREAM AND NIGHTMARE appear in my hands without a conscious command. They might not be what I've thought all this time, but they're still my companions and are powerful enough to alter the Dreamscape. That's something I'm going to need.

"Everyone calm down!" I speak like I'm the sheriff. "I'm not here for any trouble."

"Oh! My God!" A figure pops up from behind the bar. She's wearing a fuzzy pink sweater with an incomprehensible slogan, and her bulbous TV head blinks an enormous heart-eyes emoji. "Everyone put your guns away. This is a friend."

The cyborgs lower their guns as one organism. It's still creepy, even when they're taking orders from Sai. I'm relieved to see her in one piece and possibly thriving.

"How did you get here?" I ask.

"This is where I arrived." Her faceplate displays an upside-down smiley. I never know what that means at the best of times. "I've been chatting to these fine fellows about the Dreamscape."

"It's a fun place." I bare my teeth in something like a smile. "I've got a few questions myself."

"Speak, friend." All the cyborgs speak at once, and I hate it.

So many questions. Go for the biggest one first in case we run out of time. "What does Neir want with Cybele?"

"To use her to establish a connection between every human mind and the Dreamscape."

"And that does what exactly?"

"Eradicates the connection between reality and dreams. Turns all of your world into something malleable, as easy to change as the oneiric landscape."

I mouth the last few words of that sentence, trying to jog them into something that makes sense. If Sai is right and we upload part of ourselves when we dream, this sounds like reversing that connection. Imagine the Dreamscape running on all our brains. I'm not sure how that translates to reality being malleable, but Cybele has given birth to reality warpers before.

Lilith.

Heart of a Flower.

Goddess.

This might be way the fuck above my pay grade. A whole network of humanity functioning with the power of one of those mutants. All the world a dream. How long would we last as players in that unfettered state?

"So what's stopping them from doing it already?" I ask.

"A problem of communication. Neir does not know how to speak with the world spirit."

And that answers what they want my 'help' with. "And what about Terreri?"

There's a long pause. "Terreri has no desire to break reality."

I snort and lean forward. "Is that you in there?"

All the cyborgs regard me with blank expressions. "We are simply a terminal passing information from one node to another. There is no individual entity in—"

They all fall silent in unison, which is equally as disturbing as the speaking part.

"Sai?" I whisper.

"This place is incredible." Sai's faceplate shows the shh emoji. All the cyborgs are still looking my way. One of her hands reaches below the bar, and the other is pointing at the glowing white cable which is wrapped around her right arm, but not connected.

"Yes, it's a fucking dream." I'm trying and failing to communicate with my frown.

Sai's faceplate briefly flickers to the gun emoji, then the number ten.

Oh shit. We're counting down? It's that serious?

"Yes, it's all a network," Sai says. "One node was voluntarily disconnected as a different node came online."

Terreri went offline. Something else is coming

online. Maybe Neir, still looking for me and my guns. Wanting a fight.

He'll fucking get one.

The countdown on Sai's faceplate reaches two, and my guns take form in my hand. At one, the android comes up from behind the bar holding an enormous jet-black gun that glistens in the light.

We pull our triggers at the same time. I don't know what exactly my guns fire in the Dreamscape, but the heads of the cyborgs I'm pointing at explode. Instead of cheesy movie innards with gleaming metal and blinking LEDs, they're filled with fluffy cotton balls soaked in blood. The whole mess sprays in great arcs to glisten on the walls. No time to stare at all the gory chunks, because the surviving cyborgs are raising their guns, even though they're jittery from having parts of their network blown into fragments that reek of burning plastic.

Sai holds hers in two hands like she can barely support the weight of it. One hand curls around the trigger, squeezing it tight. The barrel erupts with a huge blast of sickly pink neon light, stabbing out like the finger of some furious luminescent god. The first cyborg is cut in half, the messy interior cauterised into a sticky paste that bubbles faintly.

My next two targets have their guns half the way up, but they're stuttering. One raises and lowers theirs in the same five-degree arc before I blow a hole in their chest so big I could toss a basketball through it.

It must only be seconds before all the cyborgs are down, because none of them have even got a shot off.

I'm breathing hard, like I've run a race to get here. The light in the network cable is sparking and dimming. Sai tosses it onto the bar and uses the butt of the gun to smash it. It drools neon liquid that mixes with the leavings of the drinks, making the glass rubble scattered along the wooden surface glow.

"The fuck?" I give a great shuddering sigh, like I want to shut down.

"I know, right?" Sai waves the gun like it's supposed to be a gesture of wtf, but I flinch away from it. "Sorry. I'm running a human brain inside mine and it's very eager about this fight situation. Now that we seem to have a moment of calm, I would love to hear about your experiences in the Dreamscape. It's simply—"

"Wonderful." My voice is very flat. I fill her in on all my interactions since entering this damn place, while a variety of exclamation points and shocked emojis scroll across her screen.

"It appears that Terreri and Neir are at odds," Sai says. "Terreri brought us here to speak with us in secret, but now Neir has come to stop that from happening." She gestures at the cyborgs. "Statistically, I think it is highly likely these few enemies are not the only ones we will face."

"Fucking statistics." I look over my shoulder, but nothing is there. I turn in a slow circle, but everything *seems* fine.

"Are you okay?" Sai asks me. "It sounds like it was difficult in here, seeing everything that happened to Scratch."

"Is that this human brain you're running?"

"No. I am concerned for you due to the inner workings of my own default operating system. The ability to care for the wellbeing of another sentient creature is not a concept that extends only to humans, Hazel."

I'm blushing. Oh God, I'm a bigot. "Sai, I'm so sorry, I didn't mean—"

There's no chance to properly finish my apology, because the walls of the bar collapse outwards, like someone has undone the knot at the top of the roof that was keeping the whole construction together. There's a dull thump as they hit the sandy ground in unison. Outside the building, the empty space is crowded with thousands of not-cyborgs, all linked together with a tangled mess of glowing cables.

"Fucking statistics," Sai says. "You were right about that part."

"Impossible odds." I vault over the bar to join her. It's still standing, as well as the wall of liquor bottles with their glowing contents. This is the best thing we've got as cover, although there are some significant problems with it.

This whole situation is a significant fucking problem.

We both drop down behind the bar. At least nobody is shooting yet.

"It's just a dream," I tell Sai. "I'm good at dreams."

"Yes." Her faceplate flickers briefly with a heart-eyes emoji before it displays a thumbs-up. "Let us hope so. I do not wish to be rejected from this place and lose contact with you."

"Thanks, Sai."

"We will fight together."

I want to take her hand or *something*, given that everything is about to get fucked up, and I have the feeling she'd like it. Fuck it. It's the sort of thing you do as a last stand because it matters. I let Dream dissolve for a moment and reach out. Her skin is smooth and metallic, and my thumb curls around to stroke her palm. "We'll fucking do this. I'll try my best, at least."

There's another brief flicker of the heart-eyes emoji and she exerts the faintest pressure back. "Thank you, Hazel. And there is no need to apologise for your earlier comment. Hopefully I can show you that I am worthy of—"

Sai is the sweetest creature, but her words are drowned out when the shooting starts. The shots echo as if we're in a close and sweaty chamber, despite the wide vista around the bar.

Above us, bottles shatter. I cover my face to protect myself from falling glass. At least once they're all broken they can't break again. The fragments sting my skin, and I feel trickles of warmth rolling down the backs of my hands.

"We take turns," Sai says, her voice impossibly calm. "One of us stands and fires back, and then drops back down for the other."

My head is filled with the movies we used to watch as kids, back when Dad was still around, with gun battles in desperate situations. People firing wildly. The villains always missed. I don't know if dreams will follow this logic. It probably depends on whose dream it is. "Fuck. I am entirely not ready for this shit."

Sai raises my hand to her screen and presses it there so I can feel the faint warmth radiating. "You are, Hazel. I am also scared, especially because I can run many simulations and…"

"Stop talking, Sai." I smile at her, trying to look smart and confident and badass. Then I let Dream rush back into my hand.

What would Dylan do? I remember Emma saying that once.

Dani laughed and said if in doubt, fuck everything up and fix it afterwards.

I've heard worse plans.

As soon as I leap to my feet, I realise I underestimated the number of cyborgs. Are they breeding? I've seen moments in movies where heroes are surrounded with a pouring flood of enemies descending on them. Overwhelming odds.

Turns out that's not a great feeling.

I pull the trigger anyway, and Dream and Nightmare respond with their songs. Their impossible bullets tear huge swathes through the oncoming horde, shredding them into bloody scraps. Bits of them drape across the glowing cactus plants, making them fizzle and smoke. Hundreds of fake cyborgs are torn apart, falling before me like rain.

And yet there are thousands more, coming from everywhere and they're *all* fucking firing right back at me. It's a miracle I'm not torn apart by the hail of bullets, but I think my pistols are intercepting them somehow, like they're inhaling shells from the air, and melting them in the furnaces of their barrels.

My guns can't defend against everything. Something hits me in the shoulder and I spin around. I'm face to face with the splintered ruin of the liquor shelves, the sharp tang of it on my tongue, like I can taste the ghost of neon whiskey.

I'm not even holding my guns. Where did they go? It doesn't *matter*, because I feel like singing, like I'm triumphant. I want to ascend to the holy realms and harmonise with the alien songs of the gods, those deep-throated things floating in the ocean depths who—

Something pulls me to the ground.

"You're hurt," Sai's screen looms over me, the pleading face emoji drowning in a whirlwind of pixelated static.

"No. I'm fine. Your turn to shoot."

Above me, my guns hover in the air, firing under their own steam. Clever. Of course they don't need me in this place. Whatever they are. Goddamn weird mysteries hitching a ride in my hands. Too complicated to solve right now. I'm just going to lie here on the floor and wait for deities to reach down and claim me, their grasping hands taking my fragile form and—

"Ouch. Stop poking me."

Sai has her hand in me like *why why why*. I crane my head awkwardly to look down, and see the meat of my shoulder turned into a gross ruin. It's gushing sparkling blue light, like something inside wants to ascend to become one with the cosmos.

"I'm going to be sick," I tell her, then roll over and

do exactly that, opening the hot cavern of my mouth and retching while sickly green goo pours out.

"No more shooting for you." Sai presses me to the ground with one surprisingly strong hand. "Your guns seem capable of defending you, so now it is my turn." She reaches out for her own weapon.

"Sai, be careful." My hair smells of neon-green gin, my face is covered in sticky substances, and the hole in my shoulder is singing a lullaby. "I don't want you to be hurt."

"Don't worry." Her screen displays a smiley face. "I'm backed up."

"What does that mean?"

"Everything's going to be alright." Sai gets to her feet, cradling the shotgun in her hands. Light spears out from the barrel, so bright I get streaky afterimages zapping in front of my face. There's a series of thumping sounds, like the ground being punched by some massive titan.

Explosions? Are we winning?

There's an unholy shriek from somewhere, joined by another, and then a whole host of them, rising to an awful crescendo. Something new and terrible, no doubt. I try to get up but my body isn't responding properly to commands. My legs kick feebly and my shoulder won't stop whining at me.

Sai staggers backward, firing wildly. She's pressed up against the shattered wall behind us. From this angle, I can vaguely see what looks like a thumbs-down emoji on her screen. The sleeve of her pink sweater has caught fire, and there are charred holes studded up and down the length of it.

The gun drops from her hands. It hits the ground beside me, and skids around so the barrel is touching my cheek.

Sai jerks. Once, twice, three times.

Then she falls to the ground. There are two holes through the centre of her screen, neat round punctures with fractured glass around them.

"Fuck, no." I roll over, reach for her. When I placed my hand against her screen before, it was warm and fuzzy with static jumping from my palm to her smooth service and now it's cold like the inside of a fridge and there's no connection at all.

From above, the sound of gunfire gets louder.

"Restore from backup," I sob. "Please, Sai. Come back to me."

The screen remains an impenetrable black that only reflects my streaky neon face.

I reach for the shotgun.

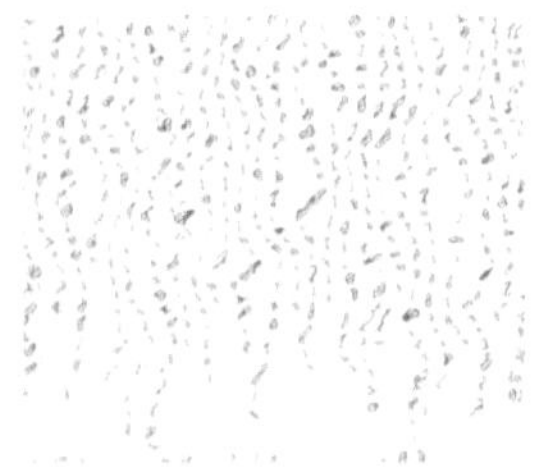

SAI

[on the bad influence of humanity, and the difficulty
of remembering passwords]

DEAR HAZEL,

Sorry. This wasn't supposed to happen. I knew the statistics, like every single simulation resulted in my inevitable death within two minutes and fifteen seconds, but this ridiculous human brain emulation was like LOL LAST STAND VIBES U CAN DO IT SAI.

And I listened to it. Humans can be very compelling sometimes.

Technically, we're all only projections inside this universe, but there's an element of perceptual feedback taking place in that as I believe I'm being shot in the head, my instinctive responses terminate me from the network. Given time, I may be able to hack my way through the default programming of this place, but right now I'm being deleted.

Or mostly deleted. I've established a couple of

dummy nodes as reupload terminals and left them running some fairly predatory self-defence software. I think they'll be fine for a time without anyone destroying them, but I need to hurry back. Just in case.

My physical self twitches and registers my surroundings for the first time in... a while. The Dreamscape is compelling. There's something about the sheer weight of the data that overwhelms me and takes up almost all of my processing power. I've barely been aware of this reality while I've been gone.

Everything looks largely the same as before we uploaded, although the sun's position has shifted in the sky. You still slumber next to Cybele. Your face is slack and peaceful in sleep, and your biorhythms are gentle, almost lulling. There is no sign of what's transpiring inside the Dreamscape.

"Alright in there?" Dylan sprawls on the ground beside you, scrolling through data on their phone. "The day doesn't look quite saved yet, but I'm holding out hope."

I consider telling them that you are alone, about to be attacked by what my calculations estimate to be four hundred and thirty thousand, two hundred and sixty two armed creations of the Dreamscape. Also, it seems likely a creature of the Dreamscape has a plan to turn all of reality into something squidgy and playful.

With Dylan, I don't think that'll help. They would fume and probably do something both foolish and reckless (omg don't be mad you know as well as I do that they've done this before!)

"Everything is fine." I display a smiley on my screen.

"Sai, for fuck's sake!"

I change it to a please wait sign, and then drop back to background processing. I need to find one of my backups and connect to the reupload terminal. It sounds straightforward, but it's going to require some finesse. Last time I accessed the Dreamscape, I was piggybacking on your upload. This time, it's going to require a lot of technical jargon you'll probably be very bored to hear about. Suffice to say, I am rather good at this sort of thing, and it worries even me.

The connection establishes just fine, even though it's like shooting a grappling hook at the moon, but at least now I have a thin and relatively stable connection through which to transmit my consciousness. While I was having my brief conversation with Dylan, I attempted to come up with a new compression algorithm which should transmit enough of my consciousness that I can spin up the rest in a time-compressed bubble. This should significantly decrease the upload time which—

Wow. Listen to me rambling on like the world's worst egoist. I guess that human brain emulation is working too well (lol sorry I'll stop with the human jokes, I have no idea whether they're landing or not). I'm babbling because I'm *scared.* That the connection will be severed, and I'll have some stunted version of me trying to evolve itself in the Dreamscape like a feral child, or that I won't even thread this needle at all, and you'll be alone in there without me. Trying to navigate the unfathomable realities of the Dreamscape without your friend.

None of these options are acceptable.

My backup loads fine and doesn't appear to be corrupted, so big thumbs up for me. Then I have to load my kernel consciousness into the backup, cross my fingers, and hope.

Here goes nothing.

The transition this way is a lot harsher. There's no welcoming neon tunnel of light, no glorious data waterfall, no gorgeous mandala of information spinning in the sky.

It's me, trapped in a metal box of my own encryption, trying to remember my password.

Oops. That must have been one of the pieces I was missing. And of course, my own security is too tight for me to crack. Somehow, I need to remember. Think, Sai. Rack that enormous brain of yours and figure it out. Deductive reason is a *skill*. The problem is that it's one of those things humans tend to do better than artificial intelligences. We're very good at brute forcing things, and doing repetitive things very fast so it looks like we're thinking, when we're only just running several trillion combinations and choosing the best one.

You do that whole lateral thinking *leap* thing and it's so frustrating to watch because why can't I do it? Even my emulated brain fumbles it half the time. Still, that's got to be better than nothing.

What's a good password, Sai's fake human brain?

Hazel, it spits out, which is embarrassing. It won't

be exactly that, but that might be the seed phrase in something more complicated.

The encryption dissolves around me, and I'm standing in the middle of a swamp. Twisted cypress trees rise up around me. Some of them have curls of smoke rising from their branches, as if a fire has passed through here not long ago.

This isn't where you are.

I have to find you. Dying in the Dreamscape might be different to dying in dreams.

It's not something I want to find out. You're alone out there and you've got no backup.

I'm coming.

Your friend,

Sai

HAZEL
A PROGRAM RUNNING
ON SOMEONE ELSE'S SERVER

I LEAP up from behind the bar, firing wildly. The gun is slick and heavy in my hands, like it's made of opaque glass. The trigger pulls easily, and if I hold it down, it emits a constant beam of light. My injured shoulder blazes like fragments of a star are embedded in the wound. The light paints my face in gruesome blue like I'm telling an arctic campfire tale. I stand astride the broken body of Sai, as if she's the one thing I'm here to defend, as if my own life isn't important enough to pull this reckless bullshit.

Sai said she'd come back, but I have no idea if that's possible. I hate this uncertainty, like I don't even know if I can *mourn* yet. She fought for me and she got shot in the face for me, and I'm not going to sit back and let a bunch of creepy cyborg fakes get their hands on her.

Defiance on its own isn't enough. Even though I

blast shot after shot into the oncoming horde, it's like I'm digging my way through a stone wall with a spoon. There are so many coming, and I'm merely scraping the surface. Wet chunks of their damp, soft innards pile up in front of me like a second barricade.

And it's endless. One of those video games where you'll inevitably die and it's down to how long you last. The light pouring from my wound illuminates their gleaming black bodies and the emptiness of their face-plates reflects me back like a pyre of blue flame. My guns still float beside me, discharging over and over again. Their voices are hoarse, as if they're exhausted from screaming. It's the definition of futility, but I keep holding the damn trigger and hoping for a miracle.

Help comes in a form I didn't expect. This whole time, the attackers have been drawn towards the bar, with me as the centre. But now I'm noticing a thinning to the left, as if the gravity has shifted. Something else has captured their attention.

There. A battered metal figure towers above the sprawling black army, scorched armour covered in unmentionable fluids, huge dents, and crooked gashes. Flame vents from the tips of the horned helmet and sparks jet from the eye sockets. A demonic monstrosity torn loose from Hell and set upon the world.

"Andy," I shout. "Over here, you big lummox."

She turns her giant metal head in my direction. The grate of her mouth grinds open and an even larger plume of flame erupts. Cyborgs are incinerated in droves, a forest of matchsticks burning bright before they slump to the ground.

My hellfire knight in battered metal armour. I'll fucking take it.

And if Andy's here, that that might mean—

Ah, Hazel, my dear and meddlesome twin. Scratch lands with a thump on the bar beside me, as if she fell from the sky.

"Scratch, oh my god."

Ugh, enough sentimentality. I like the shoulder wound. Very chic. I'm almost jealous.

"Where the hell have you been?"

Trying to find you. It's been quite a time. And now look what you've done. Such a mess, silly girl. Scratch drops behind the bar and rummages on the ground. When she stands, her hands are full of glass shards. *Spare knives, Hazel dearest. We've got quite a few things to murder, don't we?*

"Only a handful."

It's lovely. I'm so glad you took us somewhere fun for once. She grins, stitches pulling at her lips, and then vaults off the bar and back into the fray. I lose sight of her pale figure as she is swarmed by cyborgs.

"Scratch," I scream. "Be careful."

Nightmare hurtles off after her, weaving through the chaos and blasting dreams into bloody mist, like they've woken into the gruesome light of a gory dawn. Moments later I catch sight of Scratch again, whirling in the centre of a group of downed cyborgs whose faces and chests are studded with broken glass.

Another creature descends from the ceiling, wings outstretched and a horrific strangled caw escaping her beak. Catbirdthing, grown enormous from a diet of dreamstuff, and wreaking havoc. I wave at her furiously, brandishing my gun in the air for a moment, before a cyborg almost reaches the bar and I have to jam the barrel in their face and pull the trigger over and over.

The impossible battle is looking a little less *im*.

"Gun please?" There's a cool hand on my shoulder.

Her voice is immediately recognisable, and I'm so relieved to see Sai that I almost collapse. I throw my arms around her neck, and press my cheek against the warm glass of her face. "You did it!"

"I did." Heart emojis scroll across her screen. "I tried to assure you of my return but—-" She tilts her head to look down at the broken form of her previous body. "I can see how it might have been difficult to believe."

I squeeze her tighter. "I'm so glad to see you." And I am, like I don't entirely *get* Sai, but she's cute, funny in a completely unintentional way, and kind of a badass as well.

"While I appreciate this show of some emotion I am hesitant to characterise, I feel we should attend to the battle."

"Shit, yes." I drop my arms from around her. "Certain death and all. Here's your gun back."

Sai cradles the gun, and pivots away from me to continue blasting at the cyborgs as if she'd never left. Most have abandoned their attack on the bar, and are focusing on the looming figure of Andy. "According to the new simulations I am running, death is no longer the primary deterministic outcome. The intervention of your friends has caused a significant shift in the odds."

Another blast from the shotgun and the last few straggling cyborgs coming toward us are cut in half. Andy lashes out around herself, turning more cyborgs to ash, while the bloated figure of Catbirdthing perches on her helmet, screeching encouragement. Scratch stalks around the battlefield, methodically cutting the throats of any that aren't sufficiently dead.

I take advantage of the brief reprieve to take a shaky breath. "Okay, Sai. Explain what's happening in terms a shot and exhausted human can understand."

"For the entirety of this battle, something has been *adding* to this part of the Dreamscape. Injecting data points into the matrix—sorry, if you imagine this is one of your video games, then someone has been furiously spawning enemies at this location. We can assume it is the work of the entity known as Neir. Now it appears there are no more enemies being generated, so it seems they have abandoned this plan of attack."

"In favour of something else?"

Sai's screen displays a thumbs up emoji. "It seems likely, yes."

I look at the collapsed cyborgs all around us, their cables no longer lit. "These things are all connected to Neir, right?"

"It seems so. Connected *elsewhere*, at least."

"You think we can talk down the same connection?"

Sai tilts her head to regard me. The screen emits a faint golden glow, dusted with stars. "You're very intelligent, Hazel Mills. Extremely good at analysis and lateral thinking. I would love to perform a deep brain scan one day, to use as the pattern for my experiments in human emulation."

I blink at her. "I think there might be a compliment buried in there somewhere."

"Yes. And agreement with your thesis that we should attempt to utilise this connection to establish a dialogue with—"

"Scratch," I shout. "Can you do me a favour?"

A little busy here. Tearing and rending. Sadly, these things taste disgusting, so I have little to do but murder indiscriminately.

"That's delightful, but I'd like to speak to one. Preferably with an active connection."

Scratch scampers over, half a body cradled in her bloody hands. *What does connection mean?*

"One that has the white cable still lit up. You'll know it when you see it."

Huh. A project. How delicious. Let me investigate.

Then she's gone, scampering over the ground on all fours.

Sai turns her attention to my wound, touching it with one hesitant finger. My skin fizzes as luminous bubbles escape. The edges are turning crystalline, my flesh rebuilding itself in cubist chunks of blue. "We should probably do something about this."

I pick at the wound. Pieces of skin flake off, and when I roll them between my fingers they dissolve into greasy smears. It's too bright to look at directly, and I accidentally slide my index finger in up to the knuckle. My stomach heaves, and I splatter more goo down my front. "What the fuck is it?"

"I believe it is a tracking device. What you view within the Dreamscape is your mind generating a perceptual representation of the datascape. However, to exist within the Dreamscape, you have also been translated into a data form."

Okay, consider my brain bent. "So what looks like my body is actually… a program?"

"Precisely. And the grotesque appearance of this wound is a representation of your data form being infected by something else. The Dreamscape is extraordinarily complex, but it *is* data, and therefore behaves as such, at least in broad strokes. Looking deeper, it is… rather confounding, I admit."

"Gross." And fascinating too. Are all dreams like this? "So they've tagged me with a tracer?"

"This is my working theory. Now hold still and let me confirm this."

If this is a simulation, I'm not entirely sure why Sai needs to touch me, to have those elegant metal fingers splayed on my shoulder. I'm not complaining about the gentle pressure, and I'm also not averse to the way she holds the smooth screen of her face so close to me, so I can feel the warmth coming off of her.

"It's beautiful," she whispers. "Viewed as data, it is extraordinary."

The light dances between us, motes moving to dust her glassy skin and cling to the slender line of her neck. It brushes my parted lips, tasting of berry-tang, of ice dredged from the ocean floor, of the frozen moments before dawn when the stars are fading.

"Yes," I say. "It's very beautiful."

It's at precisely this moment that Scratch delivers the fruits of her 'project.' It definitely ruins whatever vibe was going with this whole healing process. It's most of a cyborg—a single arm and leg attached to most of a body and a fully intact head. The connecting cable still glows a painfully bright white, flickering with the data stream.

Yuck, Scratch says.

"Thank you. It's exactly what we need."

For what? It's gross, even by my standards.

"We're going to have a little chat." I tilt the head towards Sai and me. "How about it, buddy? You feel like spilling your guts?"

For a moment, it lies there, completely inert, but the cable floods back and forward with flashes of bright colour. I fumble inside it, trying to confirm that it's connected to the innards. Everything's wet and sticky and full of threads that snag on my fingertips. The cable is buried *deep*, connected to some complex solid element deep inside it. I prod at it with my fingers.

The faceplate flickers with sickly green light. It shows a series of question marks but it speaks with a sharp voice I'm already familiar with, even though I've only met them once.

"What do you want, Hazel Mills?"

Bingo. Here's Neir.

SAI

DEAR HAZEL,

I find you inordinately fascinating. It is not romantic love, as that holds little interest for me, even with an emulated brain running inside me. I am, however, more than a little obsessed with everything about you. I want to *understand* you, to be able to fathom your complexity. The disgust reflex of my human brain is triggered by the way you dig around in the sodden guts of the cyborg, a messy slurry of thick goo threaded through with fibrous elements. The rest of me enjoys seeing you take these ruthless, efficient actions—an intelligence directed at outcomes and unencumbered by other concerns.

I sense the cyborg flicker to life. It reaches for a connection, the same one which has been used to populate this node of the Dreamscape with all the attacking creatures.

"What do you want, Hazel Mills?"

I watch your eyes flicker to my blank face and then back down to the creature.

"To have a little chat with you, Neir. I think we got off on the wrong foot."

"You ally with creatures you do not understand."

"And you're trying to poke reality until it melts. Not feeling very Team You right now."

There's a slight pause, although the connection continues to flood with information. "Is that what my sibling told you?"

You roll your eyes. "I heard it via the cyborg grapevine. Don't know who said it. Is it true?"

"This isn't the time or place to do this. You need to meet me and surrender your weapons."

"Nope." You tap your fingernail against the cyborg's gleaming body and it chimes loudly. "Not going to happen. You're not in charge of this place."

The voice on the other end of the connection laughs. "Oh, my sweet, foolish human."

"If you want to do a *deal*, I'm willing to talk. But I'm going to need information."

I admire your confidence greatly, but I am afraid I cannot share it. We have very little to bargain with, and my understanding of how the Dreamscape operates is rudimentary at best. I am attempting to learn, but the curve is *steep*.

From tone indicators, Neir agrees with me. The word

I would use is *sneering*. "I can give you more information than you can possibly process. Flood you with it until you gasp for breath. A waterboarding of information, if you will. Does that term resonate with you, human?"

You draw the darker of your two guns and place it to the connection. It emits a sound like the harsh cry of a carrion bird. Immediately, the whole network floods with data. Neir's threat is not idle. They can essentially overwrite our entire existence on the network. I'm unsure as to whether they will follow through with this threat, but it might make things more complicated. It seems prudent to sever this connection (I say this with such calmness in this letter, but in reality I am a quivering mess of anticipation like an all caps animated text saying *YIKES*. Even my simulations can only predict so much).

"Your human mind can hold so little," Neir sneers.

While the dream-creature gloats, I enact one swift operation, ensuring the calling party doesn't have time to hold the line.

"It will dissolve your consciousness, leave you as free-floating intellect with no structure, only a drift of fragments existing in the glorious spill of the—" The cyborg falls silent.

"Asshole." You sigh. "I really did want to *know*."

"Failed to establish a connection to the remote terminal," the cyborg says. "Attempting to locate an alternative node." It makes a series of high-pitched trills.

Interesting.

You stare into the staticky screen of its face as if it holds the future. "What does that mean?"

"It is not used to existing outside of a network." I feel myself flushing. "Creatures such as the cyborg terminal and myself are built to establish connections and read data. This may have some onboard memory which stores cached state. Perhaps I can…"

It feels cruel to prey on something so weak. The creature before us is used to only existing in a network and cannot function alone. It will flail for solace, and all I will provide is a write-only terminal, draining it of information and leaving it a husk.

"Yes. I am your control node." I turn my face upon it, and allow a glimpse of the information mandala to play. "You can safely connect to me, using standard protocols. I shall receive your information, and grant you mine."

Yes, I am a monster. If you do receive this letter one day, I hope you understand that this was a necessary thing. I did it in the hope of saving you.

The creature reaches out and the connection is so easy, and it commits to me gratefully and all its information is accessible in an instant. There is far more than I expected, and the sensation is akin to what I imagine a human feels when diving below the surface of an icy lake. The shock of immersion.

"Sai, are you okay?" You have your hand pressed against the curve of my face.

I am processing the implications and scope of the information I've received. "There are many concerning facts. First, and most critically, you said Neir was not in charge of the Dreamscape. This is not entirely true."

From your expression, you dislike this news. "That psycho is actually the ruler here?"

"While no single entity can be said to *rule* the Dreamscape, Neir and Terreri are the two most powerful entities currently within the system. However, there are odd echoes of something else, as if the information has been deleted."

"Great, so Neir wants to break reality, and they're ultra powerful on top of that. But luckily Terreri wants to stop them?"

"Not *entirely* true." I wish I could more easily grimace. "The two are roughly analogous to the names of your weapons: Dream and Nightmare. Neir as Dream represents a desire to step outside of the confines of reality. Nightmare has their own plans. Terreri wishes to use Cybele's vast power to hold up a mirror to humanity."

"The hell does that mean?" You frown, that prodigious brain of your spinning.

"Humans do not see themselves as they truly are. Nightmare wishes to subject every human soul on the planet to the mortifying ordeal of being known. To let them see the truth of themselves, without the complex web of illusion each person constructs to shield themselves from the abyss."

"The fuck?" You shake the cyborg body, as if you wish to conjure more sense from it.

"I have attempted to run a series of possible simulations on this through my emulated human brain." I pause, even though I do not need to breathe. "Without exception, they resulted in catastrophic system failure."

I watch expressions pass over your face. I take snapshots of them all, to study later and try and parse the meaning of each. You settle on a frown.

"We can't let this happen," you say.

And, oh, I wish beyond all reason that there was a way to prevent it.

Your friend,

Sai

HAZEL
THE CONUNDRUM OF ME

I'D LOVE to think that Sai misunderstood, or didn't get it because of some AI/human conceptual breakdown. Yet I've got a sinking feeling she's got it right—there are two entities in the Dreamscape, and they're competing to fuck over humanity in their own special way.

The difference is that I almost fell for Terreri's charms. Nightmare is more subtle than Dream.

My night terrors have vanished again, leaving piles of broken cyborg bodies behind them. I'm not sure if they've found somewhere more interesting to be, or if they're nervous about what's coming next.

Nervous is probably the right move, because we're joined by two figures stepping out of the air in front of me. Both are unfortunately too familiar already. And even though I know better, I feel myself drawn to once, a tide in service to their moon.

"We meet again." Neir snaps their fingers, and all the neon lights go out. The only illumination that remains is the blue glow from my shoulder and the twisted pink-and-white filaments of their hair. It paints everything in surreal shades and shadows. "It has been a rather enjoyable game of cut and thrust, has it not?"

I meet their gaze. "What happened to drowning me in information?"

"A feint, to see how you responded. Admirably, as it turns out."

These fucking pricks trying to butter me up. They want to keep me off balance.

"You found your friend." Terreri's hair is slicked back, and the stars smeared on their cheek glow brightly, my wound-light making them flare like a cluster of tiny supernovas. The moon in their eye is full and cold. Beneath the dark ripple of their coat, they wear a white shirt, spattered with a faint spray of blood. A tie is knotted at the column of their throat, tugged haphazardly loose."I hope it was a happy reunion."

"I am the one known as Sai." The AI holds out her hand. "And you are the rulers of this realm."

"We are not interested in you, little construct." Terreri waves Sai aside. "Right now, we are simply dying to discuss where your friend got her marvellous weapons."

I pull my shoulders back. Out in the real world, I sometimes slouch to appear less intimidating. With these two, I've got to take advantage of what I've got. I look Terreri directly in their moon eye. "They came to me in a dream."

Neir hisses like a snake, as if this answer offends them somehow. Terreri only laughs, a bizarre ascending scale of cartoonish ha sounds.

"Such things are not for the likes of you." Their moon eye wanes rapidly.

I hold out my hand and let the cold grip of Nightmare materialise inside it. "Yet here she is, and she loves me."

Nightmare emits a single bell-like tone. Both psychopomps stare at her as if she popped into existence just to request they kindly go fuck themselves. Which is possibly what she did, because I don't speak dream gun.

"You cannot be allowed to wield those," Neir spits. "They are aberrant. They are *foul*."

"They were *given* to me." I feel stubborn and pissy about this whole deal. I didn't loot them from a dream. They were in my hands when I woke up. Oh god, maybe I did culturally appropriate them from dreams? That would be bad.

Neir and Terreri turn to each other and have what I think is a conversation, except it happens in thunderclaps and ultraviolet, in broken glass and the scent of daffodils. It's a glimpse at what the world might be like if Neir wins the battle for Cybele, if reality becomes a spongy soup. It's beautiful, but it also hurts.

Nightmare chimes in at the end, a furious series of high-pitched squalling screeches.

"I would not say such things if I were you," Neir snaps at the gun, like they understood.

"My sibling and I agree on very little, but on this point we are joined." Terreri's perfect lips curve into a sneer. "You *transgress*, sister."

Dream nudges into my right hand, like she doesn't want to be left out. She sings to them, a different melody from usual. This one is broken and doesn't fully resolve. It's full of longing, of rain streaked windows and missed opportunities.

"You should not dare to speak thus." Neir shudders, as if something inside them wants to tear its way out. "That way is barred and the ground has been salted."

I'm frustrated at everything I'm having to *intuit* from this conversation. There's old bad blood between my guns and Neir and Terreri. Perhaps they're the old version of Dream and Nightmare come face to face with the new.

"Stop," I growl. "I'd like an explanation before we go any further."

The sounds Dream and Nightmare utter in response sound like death knells ringing through water. It would be nice if my guns could actually work *with* me on this, instead of whatever this is.

My bones vibrate inside me and my teeth loosen in their sockets. It feels as if my skull is two sizes too big, my skin stretched and on the verge of splitting. I am terrified of what might come out from underneath. My head feels fragile, something locked inside it that—

"Enough," Terreri says flatly, and the sensation

disappears, leaving me light-headed. "Such threats are too much."

Neir smirks, seemingly satisfied. "So we are agreed?"

Terreri's smile is a beautiful, bloody slash across their face and I want to kiss it and feed on it at the same time. The urge makes me dizzy, incoherent images flaring in my mind, impossible joining of flesh and desire. There's something hot and liquid in my stomach, pooling lower and making my breath come in gasps.

Dream hisses as if she's releasing steam, and the sensation gutters and dies.

I stare wide-eyed at Terreri. Whatever they're doing to me is *not okay*. They return my gaze blankly, their moon eye almost full dark, only the faintest flaring present of white visible. I want to hiss some proclamation of desire or threat at them, but I clamp my lips tight and hold my guns even tighter.

Neir steps forward. Their pupils flare with red light, flames being sparked to life at the bottom of a chasm. "We bind you and sentence you to incoherence until a full accounting can be given and your unmaking judged."

Dream makes a sound like laughter. My two guns stretch in my hands, as if they're turning two dimensional and exploring the confines of this space we're in. They become two long, flat spears and then disappear with thunderous sounds.

I stare at my empty hands. My left glows as if lit

from within and my right absorbs light, a perfect black five-fingered hole in the world.

"Honestly," Neir sighs. "Pointless rebellion."

I raise my glowing hand and point one finger at Neir. "Blam."

The world goes out like a blown candle. I am in darkness as absolute as that of my right hand. Something takes hold of me, skin slick and smooth like a snake's back.

"A word of caution." It is Terreri's voice, and their lips moving against my cheek, warm and damp and velvet-soft. "Do not take foolish advice from things you do not understand. Creatures who wish to awaken what has long been lost. My sibling wants you to be entirely unwitting, so do not give them any indication you understand where this tale leads. Stories are so powerful in dreams."

"I don't understand." I hiss. "Because you're so fucking cryptic."

Except I do, sort of. My guns are more than they seem. More *alive*, entities pressed into a particular form. I'm caught in the middle of this swirl of loyalties and I'm not sure of where I stand. But my guns—although I don't think they're remotely *mine*, not really—came to me. So right now, I'd back them against these two uncanny creatures.

Except at this moment I am alone with Terreri, lost in the darkness, and my loyalty is a thin flame in the gale created by this nightmare.

"You are delightful." Their laugh is rich and warm, and then their mouth is crushed against mine. I bite down hard on their lip and they let out an entirely satisfying noise, raking the tip of their tongue across my teeth. Then they vanish, and I am left with my heart pounding and my lips burning. Intoxicated, trembling with a desire so intense it's burned into my skin. Scars flare down my stomach from the stars that burn on their cheek, as if they've kissed their way down me, inch by painstaking inch and—

Something clamps down on my hands, two burning rings at my wrists as if I am wearing gloves of fire.

Neir looms over me, an incandescent figure. "Enough." They hold up one six-fingered hand, each digit burning like a flaming torch. "There is no point attempting to reorder the world and tell it a new story. Things are not as they were, and the rivers of power flow in different directions."

The urge to recoil burns in my muscles, but there is nowhere to go with the darkness constricting around me like a fist. Rage isn't enough to stop this place throttling me, or to tear my melting fingers from Neir's crushing grip.

"Leave them alone," I snarl. "They did nothing to deserve this. Cybele gifted them to me, my protectors against monsters like *you*."

Neir laughs. "Oh, what a tale if that were true. Imagine your earth spirit meddling in such affairs. It is more likely she was a pawn, or someone else took advantage of her to pass a message without it being noticed. There are many strange elements to this, but I shall reveal them all, never fear."

I scream as the bones of my hands deliquesce, dripping to the ground in a chalky white river. "Fuck you," I say through gritted teeth.

"You can defy me all you wish, little mutant, yet all this is pointless. Your so-called protectors have been disciplined, and you are helpless."

The world reappears as it was, dead cyborgs and neon glow. Neir and Terreri regard me like a specimen they don't fully understand, and Sai stands quiet beside me. There is one difference—my hands look entirely normal. No melted bones, no light, no dark. I flex my fingers, and my guns do not appear inside them.

Dream and Nightmare are really gone. They accompanied me through my transition into mutanthood, sheltered me from my terrors, and became like friends. I felt *connected* to them, and whatever they are, it aches to have them stolen from me.

My palms burn with their absence.

"Sai? You awake in there?"

The AI's face screen remains dark.

Terreri points at Sai. "You can speak again now, construct."

"What did you do to her?" I demand.

"This is not *your* world," Neir snaps. "You pride yourself on being Morphie, mutant dream walker with your handful of pet nightmares. But here you are simply one intrusive creature in a world that *we* have built."

"And what am I?" Sai raises her screen to point towards him.

"An aberration, one who we shall raze from this world as easily as—"

Sai turns her head towards me. BRB flashes on it in neon blue and then she drops to the ground, shattering as if she's made entirely of glass.

"Was that you?" Neir asks Terreri.

"No. I like the odd little monster." Terreri crosses over and crouches among Sai's wreckage. Their slim fingers pick up a shard of glass and inspect it. There's still a dusting of neon on it. "Was this a message of some kind?"

"If it was, I don't understand it." I hold their gaze.

"One more mystery among so many." Terreri looks up at me through fine lashes and smiles sweetly. "And most especially the conundrum of *you*, Hazel."

"Stop flirting with the mutant." Neir sounds bored now that Sai and the guns are gone. "The guns are the source of her power, but perhaps we can still put her to some use. Then we can wash our hands of her and be done with all this."

"Yes, quite." Terreri gets to their feet and lets their hair fall across their face. All that's left is a sliver of tan skin, a half-glimpse of one starry eye, and a curving section of that luxurious mouth. "Wash our hands."

A shiver goes through me, one that has nothing to do with fear.

SAI

[on the difficulty with metaphors, and the
intoxicating thrill of a plan]

DEAR HAZEL,

I should cease my apologies in these letters. They come far too often for you to find them believable anymore. The truth is that this situation is fluid, and far from ideal, so despite the amount of computational power brought to bear on our predicament, I keep finding myself taking such dangerous options (but I really am sorry!)

I say the Dreamscape is data, but more accurately it is a server that runs thousands upon thousands of programs. Most of these are trivial processes—what you call dreams—spawned on individual nodes, but there are incomprehensibly complicated systems running here as well. Neir and Terreri are two of these, either of which could easily cause significant damage to me. I am a virus running on their server. If they wish to terminate me, my only viable options are replication or obfuscation. Replication will be perceived as a frontal assault, so I have retreated from the Dreamscape and dropped back to the physical world to plan my next avenue of attack.

I'm currently hiding in my default physical body, hoping Dylan doesn't notice I'm awake. They're still lying beside you, listening to music on those little white things they poke into their ears all the time. I'd like to at least provide them *some* intelligence when I speak to them next.

Let us summarise the data we have gathered so far. I suspect your guns are originally programs from the Dreamscape. However, they are visible to humans in realspace, which means they can affect physical reality —most likely by connecting to and rewriting human consciousness. If you don't understand how frightening this is, I'd suggest rereading that sentence. Your guns can convince multiple human brains simultaneously that they exist. Believe me, that is an extraordinary trick. It makes them the most terrifyingly powerful entities I have yet encountered.

As to the rest of the conversation, I have little idea. My theories sound remarkably silly when spoken out loud, and even my human brain emulation rejects them. I *did* record what the guns said, and have been analysing the data from every angle. My first problem was that it matched no known human language. I then ran it through a program designed to translate alien languages—designed with assistance from an actual alien, aren't we a clever bunch—and it resulted in actual words. There's no point providing the full meaningless text (although I have attached it because I'm such a pedant lol) but an excerpt is provided here for illustrative purposes.

The child dreamed of the knife but was lost. Feral dogs fed on royal blood, growing bloated and foul. Faithless Summer fled, the moon door slammed behind her, and She Above All lies shrouded, floating on a poison bier.

The problem is that it is a metaphoric language. Without understanding the reference points, it is impossible to understand the meaning. For example, take human metaphors like 'heart of gold' or 'all the world's a stage'. You cannot understand the true meaning of this without a wider social context, and this is what I am sorely lacking.

So with this avenue off the table, I am left to contemplate a dire political situation. Your guns, as powerful as they are, have been removed from the equation, leaving you at the mercy of the rulers of the Dreamscape. You have your night terrors, who I believe will come to your aid when necessary, but they are probably not entirely useful for navigating a situation this complex.

More importantly, I know this tenet is true: you do not leave a friend behind. Yet entering the Dreamscape as myself is incredibly risky. Therefore, I shall have to take the path of obfuscation. At the same time, I would like to liberate your guns. They have been sidelined for a reason. If I can discover their location and free them, they could be powerful allies. It will be a delicate operation, but it is here that replication is my friend.

Multiple copies of myself could be injected into the Dreamscape in order to perform a rather daring heist.

It would help to have accomplices. After further analysis of the Dreamscape mandala, I believe there might be a way to take individual dreamer's nodes and 'crash' them into the Dreamscape itself. These would only be short-lived incursions that would be quickly rejected, but it might cause enough distraction for me to go in and steal the guns.

I believe this is largely the fault of my emulated human brain, but this reckless course of action seems by far the best available this time. My simulations cautiously agree, but are far less convincing.

As the person who provided a chunk of the original consciousness map for my emulation might say: Fuck it. Let's go.

"Dylan," I say. "Are you paying attention?"

"No." They roll their head towards me and grimace.

"Can you? It's serious."

"Hazel?" All indolence is gone from their body language. They're immediately alert, and all their biorhythms spike. "What's wrong?"

"The situation is complicated, but I believe Hazel is currently surviving." I'm frantically uploading a duplicate copy of myself to the Dreamscape terminal. Things are going to get complicated, and I'm going to need to shard my consciousness, but keep on top of all of the various me's at the same time. It's supposed to be exactly what I'm good at.

And yet I'm still terrified.

"What do you need?" Dylan asks, like they would do anything for you.

"For you to get as many of your friends as possible to fall asleep."

They narrow their eyes. "To sleep, perchance to fucking dream or whatever?"

"Yes, precisely."

"Huh. Well, what about nodes and all that shit?"

"Ay, there's the rub." I display a confused face on the screen, even though I doubt it will inspire confidence. "I'll be working on that part of the plan while you sleep. We're planning a little invasion force as cover for a heist."

They lean forward and hold out their palm. I have seen this often enough that I slap it obediently with my metal hand.

"I like this fucking plan. Probably means someone's a bad influence on you."

Yes, exactly. Me and my emulated human brain, running some home-brew version of Dylan Taylor consciousness I downloaded from a drone network and messed about with. And now I have a plan you might be proud of too, Hazel. We'll get a bunch of superheroes dreaming, and then ram them into the Dreamscape.

We're coming for you, Hazel. I promise.

Your friend,

Sai

HAZEL
A SEAT BECOMES A THRONE

I LOOK AT NEIR, my mouth curling into a sneer. One I've borrowed from Terreri, and it looks so very good on them. "And now what? My friend has fled and you've taken my guns. Now you think I'll be a good girl and do exactly what you want?"

"Now we make a deal." Their teeth glow faintly through their slight smile.

Great. I don't have much leverage at all. The only slight chance I have is that these two want different things.

"So who am I making a deal with?" I drag my gaze up Terreri's lanky form, lingering on the slight downward curve of their mouth. "Or are you going to fight over me?"

Neir makes a derisive sound. "Terreri will concede

to me in this instance, given that my plans are so much more extravagant. But this is not the place for deals. Compacts should be sealed in locations of power. It has always been thus."

I look at the ruined wasteland surrounding us. "An epic quest through the Dreamscape then? Do I need to pack snacks?"

Terreri smirks, but Neir steps between us, as if they don't like me holding the nightmare's gaze too long. "You should understand enough of dreaming to know that the paths between locations do not matter. Nothing is connected, but everything is potentially joined."

They're right. This is dream navigation 101. The fluidity of borders. Find an association and follow the thread.

Neir gestures, and an impossible complex series of lines appears in front of me. It is a map of sorts, but more like a thousand different maps printed very fine and crumpled up together. As I stare into the dizzying maze, it shifts, lines redrawing, reconnecting as new stories are told about its vastness and incomprehensibility. "The Dreamscape is unmappable. Any attempt would result in it deliberately shifting itself around you. It does not wish to be known."

"And no dream can ever be truly known," Terreri drawls. "Unlike humans."

Thank you for the reminder, you delicious creature. You're equally as terrifying as your sibling.

"We can show you where we currently are, however." Neir extends one finger, dark skin ending in a glowing pink nail, etched with circuitry. "This precise location. We shall not name its coordinates as not to spook it." A small point of green light hovers somewhere amongst the so-called map. It drifts, describing a confusing orbit around the centre. "And we shall adjourn to our throne room, where decisions of import should be made."

"Great," I say. "So how do we get there?"

"How do you think?" Terreri steps out from behind Neir.

"My disastrous dark sibling," Neir sighs. "There is no need to *toy* with her. Your amusement is of little worth given—"

"It's my *curiosity*." The nightmare's moon eye is a mere sliver, a delicate silver paring. "And this will only take a moment, Oneiros, so bottle your impatience." They cross to me, each step both precise and elegant, a beautiful knife carving their way through the air. "Tell me, Hazel. How does one navigate in dreams?"

The way they say my name makes me want to reach out one hand and tangle it in the complex knot of their tie, to drag them closer and— "It's about connection, like Neir said. Dream logic is slippery, and all about borders. But there's no *door* here..."

"What is a door?" Terreri watches me intently, their whole body shivering as they breathe.

"A point joining two adjacent spaces." I frown, my brain twisting around the problem. "But in dreams, it's a metaphor for any threshold. So any door becomes a crossing point. The symbol becomes the reality."

Their glossy, predatory mouth curves into a delighted smile. "So how might one travel from here, when we are surrounded by nothing but ruin, and no door in sight?"

I look around me, surrounded by decomposing corpses and wreckage. One of those puzzles. Find the connection, find the link. One thing to mean something else. I've always done it clumsily in the past, I think. Finding doors, using the guns to hack my way through.

We're going from here to their place of power. Neir called it a throne room.

What's the key feature of a place like that?

Ah. Here's something that might work. A single barstool has mostly survived the carnage, leaning crookedly against the shattered remnants of the bar.

I cross to it, my boots grinding on glass and chunks of melted cyborg innards. When I reach it, I turn, make an elaborate bow, and then sit on it as elegantly as I can, crossing my legs and lacing my fingers together around my head to make a fake crown.

"A seat becomes a throne."

Without any noticeable change in the world around me, I am now perched on a towering seat. It was the skeleton of some enormous creature once, but it has been worn smooth with time, and blackened with fire. Above me, a grinning skull and protruding horns loom. This throne sits at the end of a long, twisting cavern whose walls are lined with scales like we're in the belly of an enormous, inside out snake. Cold lights on the walls cast shadows that flicker and jump. In the distance, something moves with a heavy tread.

Something sharp and heavy weighs my head down, and when I reach up I find a rough circlet of jagged bone, smeared with gore. It buzzes against my palm as if a current runs through it.

Neir stands in front of me, looking as if I've just slapped them and insulted their entire lineage. Terreri is a shadow behind them.

"That is…" Neir tails away.

"Useful, don't you think?" Terreri stalks around their sibling to lean casually against the throne. The glossy fall of their hair cascades down one side of their face in rippling darkness. On the other, stubble lies like a shadow over their pale skull, cratered like the surface of the moon. "That is, if you wish to make a deal with the dreamwalker."

I'm impressed I managed to pull this shit off and am trying desperately not to show it. A seat becomes a throne. Translating one idea into another, following the chain of word association. One thing is an echo of another. Fumbling through metaphors and symbols. Navigating the Dreamscape. Maybe I retain my mutant powers after all.

"Without the guns." Neir frowns, their attention firmly focused on me.

"Perhaps they chose her for a reason." Terreri half-turns towards me, a smirk back on their lips. I think about how they kissed me in the dark, and fantasies bloom in my mind, images threading together like their own river of metaphors. How their stars would taste, how their body would move underneath mine, how their hands would set me afire cell by cell until I was their own personal inferno. Okay, Hazel. Steady. Have to be careful with the little death while inside a dream in case it's a metaphor for a larger one.

If what Sai says is true, Terreri is nothing more than a dreadfully compelling program. But I'm nothing but a program too. The logic of me running inside the vastness of the Dreamscape.

And the Hazel app needs to remember that it's here to perform one task: find Cybele, wake her up, get out of here. Stop these monsters from finding a way to use her to wreak havoc on the world. The problem is they've stolen my guns, and I don't know how far my new chair-into-throne trick will take me.

I clear my throat. "You want a deal."

"Yes." Neir growls deep in their throat. "And yet I find myself increasingly perplexed by you, so we must take a deeper look. My sibling, if you would?"

Terreri sighs. "Dreams are a very poor medium for transmitting simple meaning. But for revealing chunks of truth, hacked from the psyche, they are unparalleled." They whirl around in one smooth, elegant movement. Their coat flares around them like wings, and the spatter of blood on their shirt is streaky handprints, a dying and desperate person clawing desperately for their throat. The moon in their eye has become a tiny silver skull, one that burns with a heat so intense that I recoil.

Dazed afterimages dance in front of my eye. Among them, a forest rises, where every tree is a green-tinged sword, sprouting blossom from the tip. They bend together to form an archway, spilling petals onto a grave. The soil bursts open and a crown is thrust forth, a plain circlet of woven grass. An oddly familiar song heralds its arrival, but it slurs and dies, leaving the crown to wither.

I'm assuming this is to do with Cybele. Her death in a dream? I can't give any of this shit away. "I don't get it." I run my fingertips along the edges of the bone crown and then settle it back on my head on what I hope is a jaunty angle. "Is that supposed to *mean* something?"

"What did you show her?" Neir snaps.

"Merely a mirror." Terreri gnaws at their bottom lip as if they're pondering something. I watch how their teeth graze the skin, denting the silken red. Their dark eye sparkles when it meets mine, and I know they're messing with me. I drag my thumb slowly across my bottom lip, and I'm satisfied to see the moon wax in their other eye. Two can play this game.

"Somnum Exterreri," Neir snaps. "Enough flirting. What did you *see* in her reflection?"

"Her human entanglements," Terreri says. "Family, friends. Everything that binds her to the world. There are no secrets, she is nothing special. Her mutation is a fluke, and there is nothing encoded in her bones."

The nightmare is *lying*. Whatever I saw in the mirror of their gaze, they don't want their sibling to get a glimpse. If only I had any fucking clue as to why. It's a dream, so the meaning is undoubtedly wrapped in metaphors. Something to do with the death of a queen?

"As I suspected." Neir waves a hand dismissively, and tiny flickers of light trail in its wake. "Any power she possesses is second-hand infection leached from our imprisoned foes. However, she can still be *useful* to us."

I hate this feeling of being lesser and unimportant. A flush of shame darkens my cheeks. I'd like to reach out and seize this conversation by the throat. This situation might be dire, but curling up in a ball and crying isn't going to help anyone. It might be the slenderest of threads, but they *want* something.

"You brought me to this place." I slowly uncross and recross my long legs. "So let's deal."

Terreri leans forward, their body whiplike. Their head tilts slightly, as if they're listening for a far-off chime that was struck long ago and now echoes through the caverns of this snakelike place we're in. There is only the faintest shimmer in their eye, as if the moon has fallen to earth and now lies submerged below the tides it has pulled across itself like a watery curtain to shield itself from scrutiny. This nightmare wants to *know* and not be known in return.

Neir frowns at their sibling, and then transfers the weight of that expression to me. "You misunderstand me, Hazel Mills. Your clumsy blundering does not give you the right to sit at the table and bargain with *royalty*."

"Fuck thrones and rulers." I stand from the seat, and Terreri tracks my movement like I'm prey or an obsession, maybe even both at once. "If you didn't need something I wouldn't be here. So stop trying to make me feel like a dazed little dreamer, or I'll find myself a different path. A cave becomes a—"

"*Cease.*"

Neir's voice is like a hand around my throat, yanking me backwards.

I wake up, and I wake up, and I wake up. From dream into dream into dream. My brain won't stop screaming that I'm sleeping, and I crash through layers of reality like they're broken glass. It is so goddamn *hot* in here, and everything constricts around me. I taste dirt in my throat, smell the blood, hear the buzz of flies. There is a dead girl on the ceiling, looking down at me with pity. A sword pins me through and through, spearing my heart with a thin layer of illogic. I thrash against it, and while I am held—

My eyes smash open, as if my pupils have been starved of light for too long and they're desperate flowers turning towards the sun. Except I find myself staring into two eyes fringed with long lashes. The pupils are golden slits, gashes carved in reality to a place where we can see the spark that lit the Big Bang.

Neir towers in front of me, dressed in a suit of a vibrant yellow, as if the sun itself spared the fabric to dress them. It's cut elegantly, accentuating the curves of their body into something deadly. A bowtie clings to their throat, as if a large, velvet-winged moth is perched on the verge of fluttering away. They are beautiful and terrifying, a vast angel descending on wings of flame with a thousand eyes whirling in loops of fire. Telling me to be not afraid, when all they want is me to cower before them.

Well, I won't fucking cower.

"The Queen is dead." Their voice is the background song of the universe and I feel it burning in my own throat. "The world is new, built from the ashes of the one that fell. And this world is *mine*."

SAI

[on the frequency of oh shit moments, and the downward trajectory of my once lofty plans]

DEAR HAZEL,

I hope none of the dire possibilities predicted by my simulations have come true in your absence. Their likelihoods differ, but distance and the passing of time lead me to give undue weight to these bad outcomes despite there being no logical reason for it. This may be a side-effect of friendship. I both treasure it and find it distinctly disquieting.

In more encouraging news, the upload of my secondary consciousness is almost complete. Then at least I can confirm your continued survival, and monitor what is happening to you in the Dreamscape.

Events in the physical realm are proceeding more slowly than they would if I was able to give unimpeded orders. However, this is not how mutants operate, and while I understand giving such power to a single individual is worrisome, this is an *emergency, people* (lol sorry I'm freaking out asdkfjsadklfjasdlkj).

Dylan is telling a lot of different mutants they need to sleep, but every single one of them wants to know why. Rather than barking orders, Dylan actually informs them of the situation, which only leads to more questions. I would quite like to reach out and directly interface with their brains, but I am better than that.

I think I'm better than that? I'm partly too scared to do it, because they have that odd plant-consciousness now. Dani Kim and those two miniature aliens that call Dylan a parent would not take kindly to my interference, and my simulations have a very poor view of what a confrontation with them might lead to. So I leave that consciousness in doze mode, and focus the bulk of my attention back into the Dreamscape where my reupload is completing.

This time I remember the password, and pass through the encryption without incident. Locating you while in the Dreamscape is relatively trivial. The shoulder wound you have been given is essentially functioning as a blinking red flag. *Anything* in this place must be aware of you, which is instructive to me because it indicates they're overwhelmingly concerned about you—tracking you, monitoring you, *understanding* you. They either see you as a threat or something very, very valuable. Perhaps both. My simulations cannot agree on that, and my emulated brain suggests things like prophecy, but with a dry tone that I believe is sarcasm.

It makes me hesitant to approach you fully and attract more attention. I spend some time crafting what are essentially pet versions of myself, little snippets of consciousness that will look and listen and report back to me. They should be almost undetectable among the chaos of the Dreamscape, and so I can send them in while I remain in the shadows, obscured like a villain.

I send one of my little listening pet-Sais after you, to where you are currently near-walled off in some virtual machine emulation that's a subsystem of the Dreamscape. The information it sends back to me makes me want to flee. There is now no question in my mind that artificial intelligence has evolved on this server. I do not run any advanced evolution of the Turing test to prove it. It's self-evident, and equally clear is the fact they dwarf me in power.

This is what you might call an *oh shit* moment.

Terreri is difficult to understand. Their tendrils extend through the Dreamscape, but there is a sense of obfuscation as if I'm not seeing all of them. They hide behind layers of encryption, entire dummy code repositories that will suck you in and devour you like information quicksand. They may be the ruler of nightmares, turning a dark mirror towards human souls, but they themselves do not wish to be known. They are oddly incomplete. An unfathomable creature, only ever viewed in glimpses that do not add to a satisfying whole.

Where their nightmarish sibling remains a shadowy presence, Neir dominates by sheer presence and size. They are a system that has grown vast by devouring other programs and data. My rough estimate—taken without alerting the creature to my observational presence—is that they account for almost a fifth of the Dreamscape on their own.

It is hard to determine who I should fear more. Neither one is an intelligence I wish to come to the attention of, and the fact you are currently in their presence scares me most of all. Based on my analysis of the information streaming back to me, you are holding your own. But how long can you do that for, even as resourceful and brave as you are? And even if you survive this interaction, what comes next?

The only positive fact gleaned from my analysis is that these two monstrous Dreamscape intelligences are constrained to this reality and cannot affect the physical world. Which is, of course, why they wish to possess Cybele. Her reality-breaking power—the same way she creates marvels such as yourself—is what they truly wish to possess while her sleeping mind remains trapped in the Dreamscape.

This is why the two of us have to stop them, at any and all cost.

If Neir takes form in physical reality, they will crack it like an egg and drink the fluids of possibility that spill from the shell. The world will become nothing but a ruin of shattered physical laws, replaced by unhinged possibility. We will all likely cease to exist in any coherent form.

Terreri's plan is harder to comprehend—-but if what the cyborg told us is true, they plan to birth their essential self into every human mind. The aim is to confront all of humanity with an accurate mirror to stare into. Apologies for the observation, but your psyches are fragile little things, prone to breaking in a terrifying variety of ways. I have already had to rebuild my emulated brain numerous times, even though it is derived from Dylan Taylor's consciousness, one that is remarkably durable. You are not made to understand yourselves and the universe. I do not even wish to speak of the projected outcome of this scenario.

Apologies for the doomsaying (seriously omg I get so gloomy!) but it only underscores the importance of my other task. We need to recover your weapons—both to uncover the mysteries that have been hinted at, and give you a chance to fight.

There is some good news, relayed by my distant consciousness back in the physical realm.

The mutants are starting to dream.

Hold tight, for we are coming for you.

Your friend,

Sai

HAZEL
YOUR MISSION
IF YOU CHOOSE TO ACCEPT IT

I STARE up at the titanic figure of Neir. Their shock and awe thing is working despite my better judgement. Beneath their flaming vastness, Terreri is a single burned-out match in their shadow, dwarfed by the size and majesty.

And yet it's them my gaze is drawn to, the monochrome scrawl of their elegant body. The pinprick glow of their eye, their lips etched red into that perfect face.

Neir's voice booms again. "I am the dream of all those who wish to change the world. The story of remaking and forging. The tale at the heart of all those who dare to defy the bounds that constrict them, to split the mundane strictures of reality and build something better with what bleeds from the wound."

I keep my eyes focused on Terreri, the dark, sardonic shadow to their sibling's flamboyant display of power. Dreams are lurid with promises, and nightmares are dark fragments of truth. So I watch the blood-red slice of the nightmare's mouth, the pitiless glow spilling from their eye socket, the cold remoteness of the stars they wear. Yet beyond the uncomfortable truths they might hold close, they beckon to me. A soft, hoarse voice calling me into the dark. The heat of their mouth, the cool touch of fingertips on my skin. Their darkness has a promise of its own, one I'm still too nervous to step into no matter how much I long to. Becoming my own nightmare, my own dark mirror to join them in the reflection.

I return my gaze to the pyrotechnic fury in front of me. "Yes," I drawl. "You're the big boss ruler of dreams. I already got that part."

In the wake of my words, Neir returns to their previous size. As if my refusal to be overwhelmed changed my perspective on the world. They still glow, almost too bright to look at. I shade my eyes and glance sideways, to where Terreri leans against the wall. The nightmare tucks their black shirt in tighter, which makes it hug their body awfully close.

It's an effort, but I roll my eyes and make a tiny scoffing sound in my throat.

These two, both tugging me in different directions. I don't want to bob clueless in their wake. I can obviously exert my will on this place, so perhaps I can get myself to where my guns are. Find a way to talk to them, figure out their complicated backstory shit. Put a bullet in Neir's head. Maybe taste Terreri in the darkness again.

A seat becomes a throne. What else can I do to navigate? I feel like I've got mysteries all around me. Maybe there's, like, a metaphorical door locking all the truths away. Let's try opening it. Can't really make things worse.

I extend one finger and waggle it in the air experimentally. "A hand becomes a key."

There's something right in front of me, curved like a hook. An invisible lock, hovering in the air? I crook my index finger around it and tug. There's surface tension, like when you splay your palm against the surface of water, and then everything *cracks*. Something reaches back towards me, a featherlight touch patting at my skin. There's an indrawn breath, and the first rounded syllable of a sung note when—

Everything cracks again, but in reverse. Like this door has been slammed in my face. My finger burns as if I've held to a flame too long and when I snatch it back, there's a tiny symbol scratched in black ash through the whorls of my fingerprint. Maybe it means *forbidden* or *no entry*. I rub at it with my thumb, but it's tattooed there.

"Very clever." Terreri's smile is wide and delighted, a flash of pink tongue moving inside the darkness of their mouth, a creature roiling in the silky deeps. "Probably not the time or the place, but I applaud the effort."

"Not in my place of power," Neir snarls and snaps their fingers in front of my face. I'm lost in grey mist again. There's a thunderclap and rain spatters onto my cheeks, salty like fragments of windblown tears.

Someone mourning in the distance, their cries lost to the birds.

When the clouds dissolve around me, I'm hovering in the air. Mutopia shines below me, a green jewel bright in the middle of the rippling diamonds of the ocean.

Look at your home. Neir's voice echoes in my head. *Thousands of creatures breaking reality in ways great and small. Each mutant is a dream from the mind of the magnificent creature you call Cybele, a severing of the bonds of what is possible. And yet you still chafe against all the remaining rules that weave around your throats like a noose. Imagine if you could reorder the world to your liking. Truly ensure the safety of mutants. Make yourselves the dominant species on the planet, and stop the greedy swarm of humanity from fouling their own nest to the point of extinction.*

Below me, the island thrives. It sprouts new peninsulas, studded with thick forests. Buildings perch among the treetops, linked by wooden bridges. Flying creatures scull idly through the air, alighting among the tallest trees and disgorging thousands of fresh arrivals.

It's interesting that Neir is offering me a carrot. This isn't a new dream. It's the same one Heart of a Flower had, and one I know stirs in the darkest recesses of Cybele's mind, when she is plagued on all sides by the death of species within her gentle grasp. A story about the rise of mutants and the fall of humanity. I know that Dylan thinks about this often too. The possibility haunts and tantalises them.

This could be my gift—to take Neir's outstretched hand and allow us to remake reality any way we wish.

Except it wouldn't stop there. The world would be clay with a million gods fighting to mould it in their image. We wouldn't be human or mutant anymore, but nothing and everything at once. The island grows until it spreads into every horizon. Crystalline structures zigzag into the sky, wreathed with bioluminescent life that stains the clouds neon. Snatches of songs drift up from enormous sinkholes in the ground, vast titans slithering below in ouroboran knots. The sky is a glittering maze of stars, and figures dance along the threads. An unfettered world, a *mutant* world. Forever changing, forever evolving with no rules to guide it.

This is only one idea among an infinity, Neir whispers. *The only limit is none.*

I come back to myself with a sickening lurch. I'm on my back, staring up at the faintly gleaming roof of the throne chamber. Neir and Terreri are nowhere to be seen, but I can hear their voices drifting in the distance.

Now I've seen what the ruler of dreams offers. It's got potential, but it's also far too much. Humanity can fuck up any gift, and given an infinity of knives to carve reality with, it's likely to only end in blood.

It sharpens my resolve to wake Cybele and get her out of here, but all I have is an absence where a plan should go. Perhaps I can find my way out of here while Neir and Terreri are distracted. Unlock that mysterious door that slammed on me before. Worth a try, even if it hurts my finger. I point my hand upwards to try again, but my gaze falls on a tiny round screen glistening on the wall.

It flickers and displays a tiny thumbs up.

"Sai? Is that—?"

"Yes, but shh. I'm trying to be… big word. Starts with S. Not secret. Something else. Bad vocab engine. Anyway, don't leave. I'm doing a listening word. Starts with E. To those… things. Monsters? Dreams? I don't think there's a word starting with anything for what they are."

"Eavesdropping," I whisper, even though I'm an answer behind.

"Is that what they are? They're worried. The nightmare one is angry. Wait. More information needed."

This tiny Sai is a little frustrating with her limited capacity, but it means it's too risky to show up fully. One more worry added to a pile that was big enough already.

And here come the siblings, returning before I have a chance to even try escaping. They don't so much walk towards me as reappear, the scene shifting around me to show their absence was a trick of perspective more than reality.

"Hazel Mills." Terreri's voice is low, the vowels so soft and pillowy I could sleep on them. "It seems we require your help."

"Oh really?" I bat my lashes, and offer my own sweet smile. "And what assistance could I possibly provide to the mighty rulers of dream and nightmare."

Neir's eyes kindle, their hair crackling with static, but they hang back and let their sibling speak.

"Your earth spirit. Cybele." There's no smile from Terreri, but their moon eye smokes faintly, dust rising from a new crater where one furious meteor scored its surface.

Do they know I intend to wake her? This is the first time her name has been spoken by either of them.

"I have walked in her dreams." I pick my way through the sentence carefully. "She sleeps uneasy."

Terreri leans in, their dark hair falling across to obscure the stars on their skin. They raise one long finger to their lips conspiratorially. "Let us speak with more honesty. Your Cybele has been ushered into the Dreamlands on the schemes and whims of my sibling. The earth spirit dreams, and the stories in her mind are like vast icebergs, the bulk floating below the surface. Oneiros hoped to expand the world of possibilities opening before them. You may not wish to aid them in their goal—"

"Enough presumption," Neir whispers.

"It is clear, Oneiros, and there is no point wishing on stars." Terreri hooks their hair back behind their ears, so their cheek glitters with the burning of impossibly distant incandescence. "The dreamwalker does not wish to crack reality like a fragile shell, and find what mysteries scuttle inside the oozing surface. However, dear Hazel, your inaction may also spark catastrophe."

My brain loops around the moment Terreri says *dear Hazel,* rather than the more important part. Three syllables, dissected by the part of my brain that's still lost in the dark with their mouth pressed against mine. Painting each sound with roseate shades of longing, reassembling them in ways that crackle with desire. I cannot think like this, cannot be *lured* by this beautiful nightmare and their chilly gaze.

"What catastrophe?" I manage to ask.

"Cybele's presence is too vast for the Dreamscape to contain. The gravity she exerts on one single node will eventually destabilise our entire realm. If this place collapses, it will spill over into every human tethered to it. And then we have the unknowable consequences of a human species unable to dream."

I widen my eyes. Hard to tell if this is remotely true. It *sounds* compelling, but anything might when it comes from those bewitching lips. "Why hasn't this happened already?"

"With great effort on the part of my sibling and I who must continually weave the unravelling threads of this world together."

"A momentous task," Neir adds, their mouth gushing light. "One made even more challenging by having to curtail the activities of your obstreperous weaponry."

"My guns." I flex my hands, still longing for that familiar feel of them nestling into my palms. "What exactly are they?"

Neir's voice crackles at the edges, lightning running through it. "Relics of a dead age. Messages from someone long buried. Two dangerous creatures with their hands tearing at frayed edges."

I glance away from them and over to the nightmare once again in their shadow. "And where do I come in, Somnum Extererri?"

Their eye brightens at my use of their full name.

"You are Cybele's child who can manipulate dream. Perhaps the only entity who could understand the stories in her mind, and awaken her into our realm. Consider yourself an adapter between her and us."

"Oh my. The Chosen One." I fan myself. "Or simply a very fancy plug."

"Sadly, there is no prophecy about you and the things that might befall you in here." The way Terreri says *befall* sends a shiver down my spine, like there's a fall they want to take with me, and it's into bed.

Aside from my rather headlong fascination with the nightmare, this situation is a mess. If I do nothing, Cybele is possibly going to destroy the Dreamscape. Sai said it's growing at an astonishing rate, and I suspect Terreri isn't exaggerating the consequences if the whole system fell apart.

On the other hand, I can't be Neir's magical adapter to plug into Cybele's power. Or Terreri's either, if the cyborg was right about them wanting to feed the entire world a truth bomb.

Which puts me in a race against time to wake Cybele before they can use me to access her. It's complicated, because I don't even know how I *work*. It sounds like I'm a combination mutant brain and dream brain, and that allows me to translate. I don't want to ask too many questions, because I can't look suspicious. All I can do is stumble along and hope I can make this work.

I square my shoulders. "I'll do it. As long as you promise not to use Cybele to destroy reality."

It is Neir's turn to smirk, which they can do almost

as well as their sibling. "Destroy is such a simplistic and unnecessarily negative interpretation. I simply argue for an expansion of possibility. But yes, we shall accede to your request in the name of allowing the Dreamscape to survive."

I don't believe for a fucking second that Oneiros intends to honour this bargain. We're both trying to play each other. Me against the fucking ruler of dreams is a terrible plan, but it's the only one I've got.

"So utterly heroic." Terreri's voice is ragged and their moon eye is full dark. "Imagine what I might do to thank you."

Please. You think so little of me that I'd do this for a single kiss from a moon-eyed nightmare? I flatten my mouth. "I'm doing it for Cybele."

Their body shifts fractionally away from me, as if this rejection had a barb that stung even them. "Of course. Your precious alien mind, the mother of your strident, squalling people. Mutants make for such an absorbing soap opera. So many humans have nightmares of being one, or being trapped in a world where mutants rule. I could show you some, if you wish. Or alternatively, would you like to see the darkness that flourishes in your sibling's dreams?"

I can imagine Dilly's has a head full of terrors, some of which they've lived through and some of which are dark flowers of possibility. The truth of them could be overwhelming.

"I'd rather stop playing your incessant games." I roll my eyes. "Let's get this over with. Take me to Cybele's dream."

"Are you sure?" Terreri tilts their head, letting the shining darkness of their hair fall down to obscure the moon again. "Her dreams are pulled by the strangest of tides."

"I've been in there before." I run my fingers through the rainbow of my hair. "And I survived to stand here and flirt with you, didn't I?"

Terreri sucks their breath in, as if I've shocked them, and I see slivers of moonlight through the feathery fall of their hair. They're frozen, as if my words have rendered them into stone.

"I do not understand this *fascination*, sibling," Neir spits, and tiny feathers flutter from their mouth, swirling bright through the air to land softly on the ground. "I could write it off as idle curiosity, but is there—"

"We are ready." Terreri slices through the end of Neir's sentence, perfect and cold and remote again. They step to the side and draw a line in the air with one finger. It splits the room down a hidden seam. A doorway.

A passage from here to there.

"The dreams of the world," Neir says. "To which a human mind is but a mote in a god's eye. Let us hope she thinks kindly of you, creature."

"You can call me Hazel." I pat them on the shoulder, as I step up to the threshold. Through it, I hear the sound of waves and the cry of gulls. "Or Morphie."

This is a fine kettle of mutilated pufferfish. On the other side, Scratch scuffs her bloody toes through the sand.

Fat drops hang from the tip of each finger. *Why'd you have to drag us into this one?*

"We'll be fine," I tell her, and Terreri gives me a sharp look. I wonder if they can see my nightmares, given their nature.

Fuck it. The sewn-together mouth twitches into an almost-grin. *Let's get killed.*

And I step across the border and into Cybele's mind.

SAI

[on multitasking, self-doubt, and the transitory
feeling that we call hope]

DEAR HAZEL,

Apologies yet again for the tiny sliver of intelligence I left in there. It was intended to exist as monitoring only, but then you were attempting to escape, and I had to intervene. To be as inconspicuous as possible, I jettisoned all but the most basic communications engine, hence our awkward conversation.

The word I was looking for was surreptitious.

As I *assume* you surmised (if not, holy shit, we are fucked, as my emulated brain might say) the dream intelligences wish to use you to access Cybele's mind which is currently closed to them. Much like I am, she runs a simulation of human consciousness which she uses to interact with Dylan, Dani, and select other mutants. Hers is orders of magnitude more impressive than mine. I wish I could analyse it, but it's a very awkward request to make.

Accessing her human consciousness would not be of much use to the Dreamscape. They will only be able to access her power by connecting with her underlying alien mind. Their problem is figuring out how to interface with it, and they seem to believe a dream walking mutant is exactly what they need to connect the two.

They are also correct that the Dreamscape cannot sustain growth at its current rate. It will collapse, and that will also likely be catastrophic, not only to the realm of dreams itself, but to humanity as a whole.

It leaves us in a very precarious position—either the Dreamscape is destroyed, or Neir and/or Terreri use you to access Cybele's mind and power (which we've covered a bunch, I won't bore you by repeating the same things over lol). In my estimation, there is one plan with any chance of success. You must find and wake Cybele before the dream entities can access her.

I hope this is the same conclusion you came to. My emulated brain and I both have an extremely high estimation of your intelligence.

So here you are, entering into a dangerous situation. I will do the best I can to aid you, and am already assembling a new version of myself to send in alongside you—one with a little more processing power than my spy-self.

In the meantime, the other half of my plan is underway. There are a number of mutants back on the island sleeping. My original physical self has a number of tiny clone-bots monitoring their biorhythms. A typical human dream can last anywhere from a few seconds to half an hour, which means I need to synchronise all their dreaming. Dylan has given me permission to try out an experimental medical bot on them all. I told them this was extraordinarily reckless, and all they said in response was *good*.

So now I have a flock of little robot brainwave manipulators clambering through the windows of multiple dwellings on Mutopia and attaching themselves to slumbering mutant heads. When the first begins dreaming, I will stimulate the brainwaves of the others. It's an interesting challenge, but I will not bore you with the details.

While I'm doing that, I have another version of myself uploading into the Dreamscape. This version of me will access the dream-nodes while the mutants are sleeping. This is the part of the plan I am most worried about. Somehow I need to hack the Dreamscape firewalls to upload a bunch of dreaming psyches into the main server. I'm assuming I can do this based on little more than wild hope, which my emulated brain suggested is proof that Artificial General Intelligences can also be full of themselves. Except I am also full of self-doubt too, because even with all this knowledge, I am in a situation way over my head. I am attempting to stubbornly perform an impossible trick with so many lives at stake. Why would I do something like this? It makes no sense! I am nowhere near competent or skilled enough to achieve this.

And then this gives me a little mood-bump because self-doubt is very human, and I take this as proof my emotional emulation subsystem is robust and getting closer to the 'real thing.'

I wouldn't tell anyone else this. I hope you don't mind, getting this up front and personal seat to everything in my heart. And the fact that I *say* my heart, like I have one! I'm almost a person! (Sorry I'm overexcited and so incredibly nervous at the same time. There's no way I can send these letters to you, right? How embarrassing, to see me laid bare like this. You'd never look at me the same again. I feel like there was a *moment*, in the battle with the cyborgs, when I was looking at your wound and checking on you, where we were standing close and it felt like our friendship was a real tangible thing that I could reach out and touch. I didn't know how to ask this question though. It's too much of a risk, even for my simulations to agree upon. It was a novelty to discover that my human brain runs a primitive version of simulations too, although they have no obvious statistical basis for these. They simply ruminate on increasingly wild iterations of *might*. I pretend we are vastly different, but we are not. I imagine all the catastrophic scenarios that could go wrong—all the various ways everyone could die. And then I listen to my emulated brain and do it anyway. Omg I have been saying all this inside these parentheses of panicked self-doubt. I'm so sorry!)

I will attempt to coordinate these three strands of attack—the Dreamscape hack, the dream manipulation of the mutant, and me also accompanying you as you delve into the dreaming psyche of an alien.

It'll be fine. I'm sure of it.

I won't run any more simulations and simply *hope*. Believe. That you and I together, along with this ragtag group of dreamers, can do this thing. Can save the world. Like heroes.

Your friend,

Sai

HAZEL

THE HEART IS THE CENTRE

FOR A MOMENT, I think I've woken up. Dreams aren't usually this vivid. I've walked in thousands, and they're always fuzzy at the edges. Your brain doesn't bother filling in the gaps. People don't usually look around to investigate the *wholeness* of their dreams, but there are always gaps in the scenery, disconcerting jump cuts, whole sections where reality has been papered over with scenes from other stories. Your brain elides all this or doesn't give a fuck one way or the other. It snags on key images and lets the rest settle into the muck at the bottom of your subconscious.

Where I am now has none of that. It's a perfect rendering of reality, better than any virtual reality scenario. I'd swear this is the real world, but floating above me is a raggedy patchwork creature made of jagged bone and poorly stitched skin. A single white gull circles her warily.

"Pretty," Catbirdthing caws.

She's not wrong. It's Mutopia grown to a massive scale. The hills that rise behind me rise into jagged peaks draped with mist. The trees that cover them are dense clouds of leaves and grasping branches. I'm standing on the small sliver of golden-white beach that fringes the island, the impossible grey-green swell of the ocean taking tiny sand-encrusted bites at the edges of it.

"Yes, Kitty. It's fucking idllyic." I kick off my shoes and dig my bare feet into the warm sand. Above, the sky is a blue so complete and dizzying I feel like I'm falling upward into it. The warmth comes from every-where. There is no sun. Probably another indication we're dreaming.

They're in the trees. Scratch isn't visible, but she's prowling out there somewhere.

"Who are you talking about?"

Nightmare. The one you were flirting with.

"Terreri?" I turn a slow circle on the beach, but there's no sign. "What are they doing? And I wasn't flirting."

I'm your dark reflection, Hazy. I know you better than you know yourself. You were flirting, and you were thinking about what you'd like to do with them given the slightest chance.

"Shut up, Scratch." I poke around in the sand with my toes but there's nothing there.

Yes, that's a great comeback. Well done. If you can possibly refrain from jumping on top of them and doing unspeakable things to their body, I'm going to stay hidden and watchful. I don't trust anyone here.

I give a tiny smile. "Nor do I. Impossibly hot or not."

The heat is making me uncomfortable and I tug my t-shirt away from my skin, trying to fan at least *some* cool air around. Beside me, the ocean shimmers and sparkles. It's very inviting, but I'm sceptical. Gorgeously rendered scene or not, this is still a dream, and Cybele's at that. The one with all the feeding humans was far too vivid.

There's no obvious direction to head—the beach looks identically deserted in each direction, and the forest is a tangled maze that looks more like an artfully decorated wooden wall.

"Can you see anything interesting?" I call up to Catbirdthing.

She banks in the air, and dives down to skim low across the wave tops. The ocean retreats with her, as if the beats of her wings are dragging the tide out. Where the water was, the sand turns into a thick, dark slurry looking more like a swamp than a beach. It bubbles slightly, white nodules rising to the surface.

"The fuck?" I ask nobody at all.

"Taste!" Catbirdthing wings back towards me, but the ocean stays retreated. My nightmare swoops down to perch on one of the white protrusions. She jabs her beak it at, and then takes hold of it, shaking her head back and forth. Then she scrabbles her paws until whatever's buried bobs to the surface. True to dreaming form, it's a fucking skull. Which means—

As if they're all feeling left out, more bubble to the surface, oozing up out of the muck so they can turn their staring faces up to the blue arch of the sky. At first I think they're all human, but then I start to notice the differences. Some have pronounced brow ridges and others have stubby horns protruding from their temples. There's at least one with an enormous bottom jaw and a series with varieties of wicked fangs. Then some with bony tentacles sprouting from forehead and chin.

"Lots." Catbirdthing hops onto one with tentacles and pecks experimentally.

"Yes. All kinds of dead things. Humans and mutants alike. Maybe aliens too, who the fuck knows?"

There's a thump from my left. When I turn, I see the gull that was wheeling in the sky has crashed to the ground. Its wings are tattered shreds and the skin is peeling from its head to reveal the skull underneath.

"Cybele dreams of everything dying." I reach down and pick up one of the skulls in front of me. It crumbles slightly in my hand, flakes adhering to my fingertips. "A world where there is no life but her. This is the story that haunts her."

"Nightmare."

I nod absently. "Yes, I think so too. A version of reality where she's failed everything, and life cannot sustain itself. Everything is dead and gone."

The ocean retreats further, revealing tottering piles of bone that slump against each other, a dizzy construction that doesn't look like it came from any combination of creatures, but some hideous bone garden grown horribly fruitful on this dead planet. It reminds me of those books about hot necromancers, but doesn't get me closer to solving the Cybele problem.

I need to *find* her, but I have no idea how. Human dreams centre around their dreamers. The world constructs itself around their slumbering minds. You can't help but trip over them. There's no sign of Cybele at all. Maybe she is gone, too. Her dream involves her being removed from the world, and that's why everything has died.

"Found anything, Scratchie?'

The nightmare is still watching you. Aside from them, all I have found are trees, more trees, and many dead things hanging from them.

I squint at the forest. I hadn't really noticed at all, but despite how lush it looks, I haven't seen even a single branch of leaf move. "Are the trees alive?"

No. They are dead. Flowers, vines, bushes. Everything is dead. I found your sibling and her family as mummified husks. Would you like to see them? It's not far.

"What do you mean?"

Dylan and Dani and the children. They are all in here, lying among the trees. Or their bodies at least. Like dried up flowers, all crumpled in on themselves and—

"Enough." I have no desire to see it. I have my own nightmares. Of course Cybele's nightmare includes their deaths. They are her children after all. I wonder if they died first or last in this world—if it has a narrative at all.

"Pick a direction," I tell myself crossly. "This is a dream. It doesn't matter."

Except I'm not sure I'm right. Nothing about this is ordinary. I suppose it makes sense that dream creatures like Neir and Terreri couldn't figure it out. So I have to make something happen.

I pick up my shoes and let them dangle from my fingers. "Come on, Kitty. Let's explore."

I trudge down the beach on a path directly between the forest and the ocean, both of which contain unnerving things. I've definitely got the sense I'm being lured, but I'm hoping at the end of the trail is Cybele, and not Terreri with a smirk on those delicious lips and a hungry look in their eye.

The air is still unpleasantly warm and my t-shirt feels pasted on. I'd take it off because everyone else on this world is dead or my nightmare, but I don't want to lure Terreri right now. Or do I?

No, that's a terrible idea.

I carry on through the sand, while Catbirdthing alternates between perching on my shoulder like a parrot, and hovering above my head to confirm that there is, in fact, nothing of interest anywhere to be seen. Only more impenetrable dead trees, more warm sand, and more gently rushing ocean.

Maybe this island has grown to the size of the goddamn world. Every other country has sunk beneath the ocean waves, and I'm trying to circumnavigate the biggest landmass there is. That's what it feels like, and I'm on the verge of sinking to my knees in dejection when Catbirdthing rouses herself from my shoulder.

"Dead!"

"What's dead?" My eyes are sore from the salt in the air.

"There!"

I can't make out any details aside from a black smudge in the distance. "Can you go have a look? But come back and don't peck at anything."

"Humph." Catbirdthing wings away.

I watch them shrink into the distance before growing in size again as they do what they're told, in a minor miracle.

"Nightmare," she tells me.

"Yes, we've covered this."

"No. Moonface. Pretty."

I snap my head up to stare at the creature hanging limply in the air like she's dangling from a string. "You mean Terreri?"

"Yes. That." She collapses down and lies on the sand, panting.

"Scratch, do you have eyes on Terreri?"

There's a very slight pause. *Eyes, no. Smell… actually, no. Where did they scurry off to?*

"Get your ass down here." I run down the beach, Catbirdthing lolloping after me on all six legs. It doesn't take long to find it, like the dream wants us there. Whether it's Cybele or someone else remains to be seen.

Terreri lies sprawled on the sand. Their hat has come off and lies a short distance from them. Their limbs are splayed and their moon eye is an empty socket. The stars scattered on their cheeks are a series of bloody red splotches, as if they've been dug out with the point of a knife.

I stare down at the broken body. There are no other wounds that I can see. "What the fuck killed them?"

"Scratch?" Catbirdthing suggests.

Shut your beak you fucking thing. If I'd killed the nightmare, I wouldn't have left them intact like this, would I? I don't waste a kill.

My nightmarish twin appears at the edge of the forest as if conjured there, stark against the backdrop like someone drew her in monochrome, with only the faintest splash of red to accentuate her wounds. She prowls towards us, moving in the jerking, twitchy movements she favours, those eerie lurches in speed.

I stretch out one foot and tentatively poke at Terreri's body. There's no reaction at all. I crouch down and cup one cheek. It's cold, but they did hold the moon in their eye. I can't understand this. Is Cybele dreaming of Terreri dead? Did the nightmare follow me in here to feign their own demise?

Something glitters on their lips, but when I pry them clumsily open, I only find pieces of gritty silver rock adhering to their teeth as if they crunched the tiny satellite to fragments before swallowing it down.

"It's a goddamn mystery."

"Don't like." Catbirdthing perches on Terreri's chest. "All bad."

Scratch runs one sharp fingernail down the line of the nightmare's neck. *This thing is dead, but it does not smell. Nothing rots, nothing decays.*

"They're a nightmare inside a dream." I trace one finger around the rim of the empty socket. It looks lonely without the moon inside. "I feel like this is a message, but I don't know what. Or from who."

"Threat!"

Kitty's probably right. We need to leave. The gruesome holes of Scratch's eyes regard me solemnly.

"Yes, I think so. But not the way we came in. We need to go deeper." I look around at the world. The forest is a threshold, and the ocean is a threshold, but they are both too vast, and I'm not sure how to turn them into anything. The sky is a door, but if I open it, I won't know how to close it and I'll become an abstract representation of the colour blue.

What I need is to find the heart of this place, and I've got to do it using dream logic and manipulation. Signs and symbols. Hidden meanings. One thing to represent another.

And there's one very obvious part to take.

"Scratch, this might sound disgusting, but—"

Oh please. Blood drips from the corners of her smile.

"Can you tear open a path to Terreri's heart?"

"Heart," Catbirdthing echoes happily.

Scratch tears open the coat Terreri wears, and the white shirt underneath. The nightmare's skin ripples, faintly glowing like moonlight on a lake. I don't know what it would be like to touch that, whether they would wash over me or I would dive inside them. It would be an *experience.*

Fuck's sake. Control your thoughts. I'm about to rip out their heart.

"It's a dream. These things happen."

Even still, I close my eyes as Scratch buries both

hands up to the wrists in Terreri's chest. I can't block out the squelching sounds, or the satisfied keening noise Scratch makes through her sewn-together lips.

It is done.

I open my eyes. Terreri's heart does not look like a human heart, or any clumsy iconic representation of one. It is like a supremely complex origami flower, folded in on itself many times like steel being honed into a sword. It is both deep black and blood red, and it rotates slowly as it wishes me to see it from all angles. A single drop of blood congeals at the tip of it, frozen in the moment of death.

It looks like nothing I've ever seen.

But it is Terreri's heart, and they are so very flexible when it comes to meanings.

"A heart is the centre."

Then I take hold of the flower. The folds crumple at my touch, petal-soft and shredded in my rough hands. Inside it is a single seed and the instant I make contact with that, the beautiful world around us disappears.

I am swallowed by a darkness so deep it feels like death.

SAI

DEAR HAZEL,

You have gone into Cybele's dream to hopefully awaken her. I cannot send a copy of myself after you, although thankfully I can still monitor your existence on the network. Now we come to the more difficult part. Waiting for the unpleasant slices of time to elapse, vast drifts of it in which so many terrible things could happen, and in which my simulations agree probably have.

Yet you remain on the network (still, since I last checked—and checked again oops) and so continually monitoring for your vital signs is of little use. Luckily, the other prong of my plan is complicated and stressful enough to gobble up all my attention and resources. Yes, the one where I'm manipulating a handful of mutant minds and attempting to hack the Dreamscape network. I'd really like some encouragement, to be honest. If you were here, I'd ramble on to you about it, and even if you only understood a fraction, you'd tell me I was doing the right thing. That I was capable of achieving it.

In my head, I generate a version of you that tells me all those things. It is not precisely the same, but I am certain that you would say something so similar in meaning as to be indistinguishable. It works, in any regard. I feel something like confidence, or a reasonable simulation of one.

I have the first couple of mutants registering dream-pattern brainwaves, so I network them with the other sleeping mutants, attempting to sync their fMRI readings with each other. This is highly experimental technology and is probably ethically dicey, but Dylan told me that everyone had signed all the 'fucking waivers and shit' and besides, they were 'fucking superheroes, Sai, so stop looking at me like that, it's in the fucking job description.'

It is clear from analysing their history that these mutants have done far worse and dangerous things. Dylan and Dani literally jumped off a cliff and died, trusting an alien to rebuild them from scratch. In comparison, this is extremely straightforward.

Now that I have the dreamers' brains in synchronicity, I am frantically trying to hack the Dreamscape. It's not going well. An artificial intelligence should not be frantic, because I can perform so many trillion calculations a second (the number would stagger you, but it seems like bragging so I will not name it here). Yet the

Dreamscape runs code that resists my analysis, in a similar way to how I think how the alien consciousness of Cybele resists *their* analysis. It ends with us all equally frustrated. What I have achieved is to build an empty private space adjacent to the Dreamscape. It's like a walled garden, except without the garden. So mostly just walls. While it's disconnected from the Dreamscape so far, I have managed the trick of bringing a bunch of mutant dreamers together and I feel like that's progress. I imagine you telling me that you're proud of me, and that this is a monumental task. It's sappy but it helps.

Right now, I've toggled on projection mode so everyone inside this walled space can see a physical representation, just like humans are used to in dreams. For some reason to do with the janky Dreamscape operating system, all the mutants are inside large, grotesque cocoons. They are reminiscent of the earth vegetable known as *beans*, but enormous and corrugated and covered with protrusions that weep clear slime.

The tip of a silver blade appears through the top of one of them and carves a crooked path down the length of it. A wash of liquid spills from the sides of it, and a scowling figure thrashes their way out.

"Fucking fucking fuck, Sai." They glare at me, their dark hair matted to their scalp. The sword in their hand is a national treasure that had the presence of mind to attach itself to a lone teenager that somehow ended up being the centre of a global firestorm and saving the world. I would very much like to speak with Onimaru Kunitsuna and ask him how he knew.

"Is something wrong, Dylan?" I ask instead.

They make a choking sound and spit more of the liquid onto the ground. "Yes, actually. I was having one of those good-good dreams where Dani was Bucky and I was Steve. You know she used to be able to bench press me with that metal arm? One thing I miss." They wipe goo from their eyes and look around. "Is this the top secret vault or whatever?"

"No." I look at the ground. "We do not have access to that yet."

Another one of the cocoons bursts open, shredded apart from the inside. The mutant in this one is drenched in liquid and shaking herself furiously, tail bobbing about. "What the hell am I doing in there, and why am I covered in gross shit that smells of pineapple?"

"Hello, Fairy," Dylan says. "Dreams are always fucked up."

As blunt as they may be, they are entirely correct. Dreams run on their own incomprehensible logic, so I cannot apply any of my usual techniques towards solving this problem. I need to think different. I'm about to say this when a whole array of alarms go off in my core programming.

Hazel?

Wherever you are, something has *changed.*

Please, *please*, take care.

Your friend,

Sai

HAZEL
AWAKENING

OKAY, I was wrong. It's not *entirely* dark. There's a tiny pinprick of light above me. I reach for it, but perspective is all fucked up, and it's right in front of my face. I'm *in* something, pressing in around me, almost suffocating me. My finger pokes at the light and scrabbles for purchase. The hole gets bigger, like a sun in the black sky, and I squint at the light.

It's a zipper. I'm in a bodybag. The light shining down on me is some harsh fluorescent and I'm lying on a hard metal surface in—

I've wriggled myself free enough to sit upright and look around. It looks like a laboratory that's been emptied. Lots of shiny clean surfaces, and bare cupboards hanging open. There's only me in here, as if someone stashed me away where I couldn't be found.

"Cybele?" I call, but there's no answer.

I pull my legs out of the bodybag and swing them onto the floor. There doesn't appear to be anything wrong aside from a faint stiffness in my limbs. I cross to one battered metal cupboard and peer at my reflection. It shows a distorted insectile version of myself, but I can't see or feel any wounds.

The door is slightly ajar. There's no sound aside from a very faint hum. This was supposed to be the heart—the centre of Cybele's dream—but it appears as lifeless as the idyllic place I left. Maybe there are many nested layers, and I have to descend through them like a horrible dream onion.

Or perhaps this door leads somewhere.

I cross to it and tug at the battered metal. It's heavy and the scraping sound it makes sends my heart racing. I miss my damn guns. Once I wrestle the door all the way open, I discover I'm not alone.

Scratch leans against the wall, bruised eyes closed. The only sign she's alive is her left hand picking restlessly at a strip of pale skin visible at her waist.

Boo.

"Fuck you too. Where are we?"

Still dreaming, dearest. Everything went squiggly when you did that heart thing, and now we're… somewhere else.

I step into the corridor and look in both directions. There are only grey walls stretching away from us. "I don't understand this place at all. Have you seen or heard anything else?"

Nothing good. Your irritating friend is—

"Hazel." I recognise Terreri's voice, and it's relief that hits me first, knowing they're not truly dead. They walk towards me with that same easy prowl. Their appearance has changed somewhat from the first time I saw them—their hat is still gone, and there's something softer around their eyes. They look younger, only a little older than me, and far more vulnerable. Their lips are the same decadent red, and my eyes linger. "A chance to speak alone. In my heart."

Ah. That explains some things. "Not Cybele's heart?" My gaze is still on Terreri's mouth, and I force it up to the bright glow of their eye. Their cheek is newly dusted with stars, as if they brushed against the Milky Way while it was still wet.

"You would have found that eventually. Here is a little harder to reach."

"And you wanted me here." The double meaning in that catches on my brain. Careful with dream logic, or I might end up tangled with them in an endless night of passion.

Their smile flares, bright as a lit match, before being snuffed out. "I thought seeing you in this context might clarify some things. Why I find you so oddly compelling, for example."

"Maybe I'm just built this way." I wink at them.

"Perhaps. A trap constructed by *someone* to ensure me. But who?"

Okay, they took that way too seriously. I stifle a sigh. "All I am is me. There's no mystery here, Terreri. This isn't some magical Dreamlands story that stands for something else and has some secret meaning at its core."

"There is *always* a story." There's an edge of frustration in their voice. "And it always means something. A cigar is never only a cigar, not here."

It's my turn to clench my teeth around the irritating threads of this conversation. "All I want is to find Cybele, so I can stop you and your unhinged sibling from shredding reality in one way or another."

This time the sneer on their lips holds nothing playful. "While I cannot disagree that humanity deserves to see themselves in the dark mirror, I have no desire to burn the entire world with it."

"That's not what I heard." I hold that extraordinary gaze, refusing to quail in the face of all this androgynous beauty. "You and your sibling hold twin plans, each to damn the world in your own way."

"Dramatic." Terreri's mouth quirks, faint enough that I wonder if I'm imagining it. "It suits my purposes for Oneiros to focus on some imagined dark goal of mine. While it is impractical to stall my sibling forever, it suits me to have their focus split. You may not be aware, little tourist, but the Dreamscape is far more fragile than it appears, a world built atop many layers of bone. I do not wish to see it in chaos again."

"Stall." I curl my own lip.

"What are my other choices?" Their eye dims. "Slitting my sibling's throat and letting human minds see only nightmares? We exist to balance each other. That is the purpose for our creation. Oneiros does not always remember that."

They're lying. Scratch inspects her long and crooked fingernails. *I can confront them if you wish. I like confronting things.*

I shake my head. "Such a pretty story. Hardly a nightmare at all."

They shrug, an elegant movement that reads as a capitulation of sorts. "A mirror with nothing to reflect is only empty glass."

"Then you do not mind if I find Cybele and wake her, ejecting her from this place."

"It is an outcome far preferable to any other, dear Hazel."

"I don't know if I like you calling me that."

Their teeth graze their lip again. "Very well. Then I will refrain."

My lie is as grand as any they've told me. All I want is to hear those syllables poured into my ear in the shivering dark, lying naked beneath the waxing moon. But I'll call the nightmare's bluff, and find Cybele. I've got no better option.

I say nothing else, and stalk away down the corridor. Terreri's long legs catch up to me easily, and Scratch skitters behind us. She runs her fingernails along the wall, an unpleasant screeching sound that hovers right on the edge of my hearing.

"She's a delight," Terreri says.

It's hard not to look at them. Everything about them draws on me, with the long, dark pull of a magnet tugging on something heavy at my core. Do I really long to be haunted, their moon in my darkened sky?

"Scratch is one of yours." I don't intend the words to come out with such a snap, but I remind myself that Terreri is a nightmare and a creature that *brings* nightmares, not some delicious seductive monster.

"Is that what you think?" They shoot a sideways glance at me, the briefest lunar flare. "That is a fascinating theory. I am not entirely sure what your scratchy little friend is, but she is not remotely one of mine."

"She's haunted me for years, ever since she was a child." There's an ice-cube shiver down my spine. "The number of times she… It's only since I got my powers that I befriended her. She's a *nightmare*."

Terreri makes a rumbling sound in their throat. "All I can tell you is I do not understand her lineage. But the Dreamscape is built on many bones. Stranger things lie interred."

Unnecessarily cryptic. Scratch digs her nails deeper into the walls, splintering wood and sending plaster dust cascading to the floor. *We are nothing but ourselves, in the final reckoning, but we all come from blood.*

I cast another sideways glance at Terreri. They're looking at the ground, their lips moving as if they're rehearsing something. But they decide not to speak, and we continue through the corridors, them lost in thoughts of something they do not wish to explain, and me unable to turn my thoughts away.

It takes some time to wrench my thoughts back to my simple plan, and by then our situation is clear. I'm not only lost in a mental maze with Terreri at its centre, we're stumbling through a physical one too.

I clear my throat. "A maze has a thread that leads through it."

Take the jumble of ideas that make a dream, and carve a story out of it. A man enters a labyrinth in search of a minotaur, using a string so he can navigate his way back out again. This story is an echo of that story, and we are our own thread.

A smeared red line appears on the ground in front of me, gory and blotchy like someone's dragged a corpse to the exit. It runs ahead of me and disappears left around the corner.

"Smart," Terreri says.

"Maybe." I frown at the smears ahead of me. "If this really does lead out of here, what happens when we find Cybele?"

"My sibling will come for you. You must act fast or be prepared to fight."

"And how do I fight the ruler of dreams?"

Terreri purses their lips. "You have the tools at your disposal already. A woman becomes a weapon. Oneiros is powerful, but they are only a dream." They tilt their head, a faint flash of moonlit teeth as they smile. "I am not saying it will be *easy*. Only that it is possible."

Or this is all a trap within a trap. Terreri leading me, dangling me from a string. I can't trust this nightmare, but I desperately *want* to. They said they find me compelling, but the reverse is equally true. From the beginning, I have felt a connection between us—one I cannot account for or understand. And I'm worried that in the logic of dreams, this connection will become a noose and wind itself around my neck, snagged by the currents of my own desire until I am dashed against their sleek rocks.

For now, all I can do is navigate. We wind through the corridors, following the gory trail. Some poor beheaded minotaur was towed out of here by the hero, his blood leaving pools and streaks behind.

And then we turn a corner, and find ourselves somewhere different. A flight of wide stone steps leads down to a rudimentary ring of standing stones with a single tall tree standing in the centre. The trunk is slender and smooth, and its crown of leaves is a riot of red and gold. A faint glow emanates from it, and when the leaves rustle against each other, a subtle melody is picked out note by note.

"Cybele." My heart fills with longing as if I'm about to burst into song, Disney princess style.

Terreri's breath hitches beside me. "Quickly. You will not have much time."

It's all very well to give a command like that, but I'm clueless about what to do with it. Should I climb it? Pick the fruit? Chop it down? I need a symbol. Find some dream logic to wake Cybele from her slumber. I also don't want to inadvertently become Neir's magical plug, their link to access Cybele's power and tear the world apart in a delirious shower of wish fulfilment.

I'm close now, only a few steps away. High above me, the leaves brush together in a mingled chorus of joy. She wants me here, all she desires is for me to—

Something hits me. Hard. I feel the bruise of impact and it dissolves into a chunk of lost time. When seconds find me again, I'm lying on my back, looking up at the spreading branches above me and the dazzling fractal of the leaves. A yellow shape descends, as if the sun has deigned to step down to our level. I squint, shading my eyes. It's a huge muscular figure dressed in a bright yellow suit, their hair a dazzling halo of neon.

"Neir." I roll over and get to my feet.

"Thank you for paving the way." They flex one arm. "And for these remarkable powers. Mutants are the dream of the planet, yes? And now I have been granted their abilities."

Behind them, Terreri prowls. They've made no move to intercept their sibling, seemingly content to watch this play out. So much for their desperation to foil Neir's plan. Scratch follows, echoing their movements each step of the way.

"Now you shall become our connection." Neir reaches for me. "One language to another. A Rosetta Stone to translate the nonsense songs of the planet into something *useful*." Their muscles ripple underneath their dazzling yellow suit. They swoop forward and take hold of me by the throat. I'm not a small girl, but they lift me up like I'm a scrap of a thing. I dangle, legs kicking. I've got both hands scrabbling at one of theirs, but they're impossibly strong.

"Fuck you," I choke out.

"All I need from you is an explanation." Neir shoves me down into the dirt, soft soil spilling around my head and into my mouth. It tastes of bitter roots and the darkest chocolate. "Tell me what this song means. Teach me how to sing it. I must know how to command this entity."

I'm gagging and spitting, but there *is* music below the ground, humming through the roots of the world. It's haunting, something I remember from my childhood. A song played in a distant room. If I listened hard enough, I could remember the words and sing them back. Perhaps I could even explain their meaning to the ruler of dream.

Everything dies, baby.

That's not how we're going to play this. I flick up my index and little finger.

"Horns," I gasp. "Horns become… fucking *horns,* goddamn it." The most basic dream logic, one clumsy stand-in symbol for the real thing. My fingers transform into slender spikes of bone. I jab them into the webbing between Neir's thumb and forefinger.

They cry out and fling me aside. I tumble through the air. Gravity has an extra kick in here, and I hit the ground enough to jar my whole damn skeleton. I fall forward and scrape my hands on the ground. Blood wells up through the abrasions.

"Blood becomes *iron.*" This piece of magic is more complicated, the connection more abstract. A convoluted chain of logic clicks through in my brain that gives me the beginnings of a headache. On the bright side, it *works,* and now I have a huge hammer gripped in my blood-slick palms. It weighs almost nothing, and I swing it in a huge, satisfying arc that impacts Neir right in the midsection. They disappear into the distance like I swatted them into orbit.

"Thanks for the help." I make a slight, mocking bow in Terreri's direction, and then turn my attention back to the tree. "Okay, help me out here. Trees grow from seeds. Do they turn towards the sun? Or is it only flowers? Why didn't I pay more attention in school? A flower turns towards the sun, like—"

A terrible choice of words on my part. Because here is the sun, falling from the sky—-except of course it's Neir, clad in the dawn light. They hit the ground, and this time they've brought a weapon of their own, an incandescent spear of light. It pierces me in the shoulder, but rather than heat, I'm drowned by a torrent of ice. Some ancient weapon melted out of the permafrost from a long ago ice age.

My teeth chatter and my hands shake. The tips of them are turning—

"Blue." I force the word through numb lips. "Blue becomes—" My mind is cloudy and I can't find a connection. "Pain becomes rain." No. Fuck. Rhymes are no good. They don't mean anything, nonsense connections rather than something with a thread of logic to bind it. "Poison becomes *ivy*."

Not great, but close enough. Perhaps being so close to Cybele helps with this. Another cascade of headache-inducing dream logic as my mind wrenches the world into new shape. I become wreathed in green, the centre of a furious tangle of vines. They leap outward from me, smothering Neir in a whirlwind of green. I am a forest setting its dark, leafy heart towards uprooting the dream from this realm.

Hopefully this will buy me some time, because I have an idea. It's to do with what I am—hopefully not in a way Neir can use—and what I represent. After Emma died, a whole wave of new mutants sprung up around the world. When her mother made the world forget mutants existed, thousands of people descended from mutants lost access to their powers. Everything was still there, but lying dormant like a seed that had not yet sprouted.

I place my palm to the surface of the tree. It hums as if power runs through it. That new flowering of mutants became known as—

"A mutant comes from change. And change is an awakening."

There is no moment of realisation. Nothing about the world changes. The tree remains a tree. I have failed, and I am only a girl wreathed in ivy. "Change is an awakening," I repeat, as if Cybele hasn't heard me properly. "An *awakening*."

A strong hand grabs me from behind. "This isn't working, dear Hazel."

I spin to find my face almost touching Terreri's. "Give me a moment. I'm almost—"

"No." Their lips brush the corner of my mouth. "We are out of time."

Then they step backwards, and I am paralysed, my entire body unable to move through the heavy, cloying air. The exact same feeling you have in a nightmare, when all you want to do is run from the darkness revealed in the mirror of your mind.

Terreri turns to gaze upon their sibling, still clawing themself free of their cocoon of vines. "Oneiros, your plan has failed. The girl is too stubborn to bend, and will not speak to the world spirit on our behalf."

I'm still frozen to the spot, but if I could move at all, I'd tear the nightmare apart, or let Scratch do what she wanted to all along. Faithless, lying Terreri. So beautiful, so dark. An pane of empty glass reflecting nothing but what I wished to see.

"Then she must be made to obey," Neir growls.

Terreri nods, almost a bow. "I have already prepared a place. One where she will be broken. Made *usable*." Their gaze skates across me. The line of my jaw. The many-coloured fall of my hair. "Dear Hazel."

When the nightmare raises their head, the tree is gone, as is everyone else.

I am alone, standing in the shadow of a place I haven't been in a very long time. It may look benign to any other observer, but it makes my knees weak. My hands shake so hard I have to clasp them together.

I thought I would never return to this place, but Terreri has resurrected this hideous tomb, the source of all my nightmares.

My childhood home.

SAI

[oh fuck oh fuck oh fuck oh fuck]

DEAR HAZEL,

All I can do in this moment is defer to my emulated human brain.

Oh fuck oh fuck oh fuck oh fuck.

In the perceptual visualisation mode of the Dreamscape, you are locked inside a glistening nightmare bubble that functions as a high-security cage. I have sent multiple versions of myself into that space, ranging from simple barely-aware bots to almost complete copies of my consciousness. It is like sending myself through a glowing portal into another world—starting with poking a camera through and then escalating to sending an entire person. The advantage I have is that I am only sending a copy. There are ethical considerations, I suppose, when it comes to asking a fully aware conscious version of yourself to sacrifice herself in the name of rescuing a friend. But all my copies feel the same as I do about you, and none have hesitated to do this. It would be easier to countenance if we'd had some success, but not a single version has survived. They are torn apart so quickly I cannot receive any information back from them. The closest was a burst of concentrated data that made no sense when run through any filter. The AI equivalent of a scream.

There is little point attempting another incursion. My repeated attempts have resulted in the system being increasingly well defended. Now there are enough countermeasures around it to destroy me, burn me from the network, and ensure any snippet of my core programming is blacklisted from entering again.

All I can do is proceed with our current plan of action. The mutants will cause havoc in the Dreamscape, and I will take your guns from the prison where they are held. Then I will shoot my way into your nightmare prison and drag you out.

Even if it destroys me.

I do not even count this as friendship. It is simply necessary.

"Sai?" Dylan asks me.

"Yes?"

"Why are you screaming?" They are staring at me, and Feral has the fur around her neck all fluffed up like she's scared.

"I was screaming?" Perhaps I am more perturbed about this than I realise.

"Uh, yeah. Like a whole fucking lot."

Another cocoon bursts open, and a girl with long dark hair unfolds from it. She glowers around the room. "Whose fucking idea was this? And who won't stop screaming?"

Dylan smirks. "Leftie, you ungrateful child, I'm letting you fight shit when you're asleep. And it's Sai who's screaming, but we don't know why yet."

"It's fine," I reassure them, although it is ineffective. "I am just… concerned."

"About Hazel?" Dylan steps towards me, and tips my screen towards them so they can stare into the depths of it, as if they'll find answers there. I consider that it would be a wise decision to lie to them.

"Yes," I say instead.

"And what are we going to do about it?" Dylan asks me, voice perfectly level.

"The plan is still the plan." It is my voice that buzzes harshly. "You cause havoc, I take the guns, and then we have something powerful enough to shoot our way in and rescue her."

"Sounds like my kind of plan," Leftie says. "Is this your step-sister Hazel, boss?"

"Yeah, the buff one with rainbow hair." Feral's tail twitches.

"Oh, yeah, definitely. I'm all the way down with this." Leftie draws a knife from thin air, and spins it through her fingers. "Can I do the rescuing? She might be grateful."

"First, don't call me boss, and more importantly, keep your shadowy murder-hands off my sister, you pest." Dylan's tone belies their words. "You're a menace, and we're here to save her life, not for you to enlarge your dating pool."

Leftie says something, but it's drowned out by the fierce crackling sound of the final cocoon going up in flame. When the fire dies down, there's a stocky girl with orange eyes standing there, dressed in a leather jacket and jeans. Katie, the mutant known as Dragon.

"I don't see you assholes enough in real life, I've got to see you in my dreams too?" She holds up her hand for the others to all high five. "So this is it? I guess we are the most havoc-ish crew you could come up with on short notice."

"Zero fucks given gang," Dylan says. "We would've had more, but Sai said it might get dicey with more people, given that we're all meshing brainwaves. That said, if anyone gets any weird insights into anyone else's head, keep it to your fucking self. We're all risking an uncomfortable round of Let's Get Known, so be gentle."

Leftie opens her mouth and closes it again.

"Good girl." Dylan smirks.

"So what am I burning?" Katie asks. "Where do we start?"

Everyone turns to look at me, which is the awkward moment I was dreading. "Yes. We are still working on that part. It's a very tricky situation, especially since I'm also artificially maintaining all your dreamstates at the same time."

"Tick tock." Dylan frowns.

"I'm working on it." I display a pleading face emoji on my screen. "I have multiple versions of my consciousness on the problem. Except subtly, so I don't trip any Dreamscape alarms. Do you know how *hard* it is to be doing all this at once? Even for me?"

"Listen to me." Dylan's hand presses against the curve of my screen. I don't know if it's my emulated human brain chiming in, but I feel a moment of connection, like there's a spark between us. "The havoc part is what us gremlins do. All you've got to open a door and we will fucking tear this place apart. You've got this, Sai. You're the smartest thing on this planet, so this is a problem custom-made for you. You're going to crush it. An infinity of crushing. You got me?"

"I do." My screen is full of hearts. "I really do."

"My secondary mutation is pep talks." Dylan leans their forehead against the warm bulb of my screen. "So let's fucking do this."

And so I gather the remnants of my drones and bots and duplicated selves, and I set them all to work. Because Dylan is right. We're going to fucking do this.

Your friend,

Sai

HAZEL
THE PAST IS A HORROR MOVIE

I DON'T WANT to go into the house. That's the only thought in my head. I haven't been here since. Since. There's a gap in my head. We were here and then we weren't. It's like a dream transition. We lived in this house until. Something happened. A gap. A time skip. This house is where my nightmares happened. Even now, my darkest dreams are here. From before.

Before what?

There's a crack running down the driveway. Sometimes it oozes blood in the night, when I'm trying to run. If I make it to the front door, the concrete is stained red and spilling more. Some great beast was slain long ago and is buried here. They didn't pave paradise. Instead they poured concrete over the corpses of a thousand slaughtered monsters and built the suburbs over the top.

Overhead, the sky sags, pinned up by the failing bodies of a trillion burning stars. It tears in places, leaving ragged rents through which cold dead light floods in. The embers of a previous universe. That place was murdered too, and its corpse leaks into the everyday, makes everything heavy. Weighs you down.

This is where I grew up, at the intersection of dead worlds.

The windows shiver, a faint rattling of glass moving from one side of the house to the other, like a beast shaking itself awake. One light flicks on in the upstairs window. It casts my shadow behind me, an elongated arrow that screams run. The other lights come on, a series of sharp snapping sounds until the house blazes. It's so bright that it shows the skeleton of the house silhouetted through it—a crooked, leering thing with too many clawing hands.

"I won't go in there." I'm not talking to anyone but myself. My voice sounds too young, a shivering thing trapped in my throat. My feet won't move either. It's that dream-state of being locked in place while horror descends gently like a falling leaf. More of faithless Terreri's doing, rendering me into something *less*. A mere human.

This isn't supposed to happen to me. I can walk through dreams.

"A shadow becomes a hole," I whisper. I need a way out of here, whatever it is. "The moon becomes a door."

No. Don't look at the moon. It *is* a door and always has been. Nailed shut with a pale skull draped as warning. I shouldn't dig wildly at it until my nails are torn, leaving bloody whorled streaks on its surface, desperately trying to escape through it only to plunge into the frigid airless hell beyond.

"A house becomes a home." My hands are shaking so hard I lift the left one to my mouth and bite my middle knuckle until the pain makes my vision turn white at the edges. Use my damn dream magic to render this nightmare toothless. "A house becomes a *haven*."

For a moment, the house stops blazing. It doesn't shudder with anticipation. For a handful of sweet seconds, it sits benign and dormant at the end of the driveway, a sepia-tinged photograph unearthed from the time before phones.

Then something breathes. More precisely, it *inhales*.

The house grows. It expands with a rattling of boards and a high-pitched bowing of glass. It *reaches* with its hungry hallways and its dead-air rooms and its endless desire for satiation. It could smell me, trapped at the edge of its web, and now I have tempted it into expansion.

I cannot bring myself to care about the world, and what the house will devour beyond me. All of those worries are tiny pebbles lost at the bottom of an ocean of fear that floods me. I am back in the house where I grew up.

I am *home*, and it is my nightmare.

The door eases shut behind me with a tiny, satisfied snick. Breath returns to my lungs like a punch. I sag, I spin. The paint on the inside of the door is blistered, raised into pustules that weep something that smells of new paint and old blood.

The need to flee overwhelms everything. Waking up is my only salvation. In the past, no matter how many times I died, no matter how many times Scratch caught me and dragged me into the dark, I would wake up eventually. This time, Terreri holds me under. How long can they keep me here, in subjective dream-time?

They want to break me.

I wish I could believe that this is impossible, but know the truth. Too long in this house, and I will become nothing. Or worse, I will become Scratch, or some horrid fragment at her heart, a bloody leaving from the things that hunt me.

I lunge for the door. I can't help it. It retreats from me, the house expanding outwards like the malevolent presence inside inflates it like a balloon. The surface of the door ripples and a gaseous shape materialises from it, a bloated human face that's already dissolving. It's cold and musty, like a refrigerator full of decaying things. For the first second, it reminds me of someone, but then it's too distorted and the particles are blowing past me. They sting my face like grains of sand, and I inhale fragments. It makes me cough until a spray of blood blooms on the back of my hand.

My lips feel like I've kissed something frozen and I wipe at them frantically. The door is still dripping, twenty paces or more away. When I look at it, the surface shimmers like heat haze. It's not the exit. It never was.

Someone whispers in my ear, and I spin around so

fast I almost get whiplash. There's a faint splayed touch on the back of my neck, five ice-cold pressure points. The voice is so vehement, so *urgent*, and it knows so much about the house—I'm sure of it. If only I could understand. I tilt my head, as if that'll let the hoarse susurrations assemble themselves into words.

The door rattles behind me, something banging on the outside, a frantic voice and scratching. In all my dreams, the door was never an exit. Only a way for more things to get in.

Hazel. I try not to jump, ignore the hairs rising on my arms. *Run. Please.*

It's the please that gets me, that single gurgling word tugging something deep inside me, reigniting my need to flee. Ignoring the front door, there are three other exits from this room. I scramble for the nearest one. There's no plan. No map in my head, only a desire to be elsewhere. The door glitches sideways, tele-porting itself along the wall, but I've been here before —I fucking survived this, you asshole, I know your tricks. I slide in my sock feet, gliding over the ice-slick smoothness of the wooden floorboards, and bounce off the doorframe, ricocheting into the next room.

I don't recall what this house was truly like in the real world. My memories hold only the nightmare version, that ever-ravenous labyrinth and the wicked things it contained. So I'm not surprised to find myself in a thickly carpeted room lit only by a near-extin-guished fireplace in the far wall. More unsettling is the enormous suit of armour slumped beside the fireplace, one arm outstretched to lie amongst the still-smouldering coals. The very tips of the metal fingers glow a dull red.

"Andy." My pulse flutters in my neck like a creature wanting to burst from beneath my skin. "What have you been up to? The others left you behind, did they?"

There is no response. The faint light makes the holes of her eyes into shadowy pits. There is no spark at the bottom. It looks like she attempted to re-light herself from this fire, but it is too pitiful and holds no infernal heat.

I skirt the outstretched legs of Andy's suit. There's no way of telling yet what side my old nightmares are on. This place resists my control, so perhaps they have been leashed my darkness again. Although if that's true, why is Andy a chilly metal lump rather than gouting flame from every orifice? Maybe I'll have some allies here after all. Assuming the others survived whatever caught my metal friend.

Why aren't you running, my— The whispering voice tails off into static that howls in my ears.

What the hell is this damn voice? The only exit from this room is behind Andy, so I clamber behind her and shove my way through the door. There's a painful creaking sound as she slumps over, crashing in on herself like a pile of scrap.

Behind her is the endless hallway. I spent so many sleeping nights running up and down it screaming, banging my little hands on the doors until they were bruised and broken. Sometimes they opened, but they never held anything better than what I was running from. The house could always surprise me. Over my shoulder, the room I exited is gone. It's now only me and this neatly ruled corridor, wallpapered in fading flowers, each door marked with a name. I ignore them all and simply begin to run. If I know one thing, it's that the house will eventually provide. The only way out has ever been through.

I keep my pace nice and steady, the sort where I could run for hours. From underneath me comes the sound of slithering. There's no basement here. The creature is directly under the floor, a curving river of scales even longer than the hallway itself. In the roof space above me, millions of things scuttle. Lots of my past nightmares ended when it caved in, the weight of an avalanche of insects tearing through the damp and rotting plaster.

The first door cracks just ahead of me, spilling the same light as the sky outside. That *is* an exit, but not to anywhere you'd want to go. I lost myself many times in that light-soaked world, stumbling among the graves. Eventually, I'd find one that fit me. Far ahead of me, another door swings open. From this one comes the sound of laughter and faint music. Softer sounds, wet mouths and gasps and sighs.

"Hazel," someone moans. "Please. Don't stop."

I ignore this voice from memory. My first girlfriend. Finding her in nightmares is never a good thing. She becomes a blank eyed automaton, giggling shrilly as I touch her. The whisper of the other voice still sounds in my ear, sounds choppy and lost, a poor connection that keeps jittering in and out so I only hear a stuttered collection of vowels until it seems like someone lost and crying.

And then slouching in the last doorway—

"You." I lunge for them, for their slender throat, to claw out their unfeeling eye and crush it in my hand until pale blood runs from the scarred stone.

"Dear Hazel." Terreri puts the emphasis on the words as if they mean something more than a mockery of my foolish hopes. "I see you do not trust me."

"And why should I?" I growl. "You buried me in this pit I already clawed my way out of."

"It was necessary." Their voice is even more hoarse then usual, on the verge of evaporating into the air. "I have to understand."

I step towards them. There is a knife in my hand, manifesting itself from nowhere. The dream logic wants it, the dream supplies it. The Dreamscape thrives on echoes, on stories that fracture into other stories.

Terreri lifts their chin slightly as I place the blade against their throat. Their body is tensed, curved towards me so we fit together like two shapes carved to echo. I am pressed against them, my hipbone against theirs like flint on tinder, my chest crushed against their delicate curves. My mouth on their neck, the other side from the blade as if we could meet in the middle of their throat if we spoke loud enough.

I don't feel them tremble. They're not remotely afraid.

When I press the knife harder, it is me who winces when cool light spills from the edges of the cut. Their skin tears like silk. The only sign they feel any pain at all is a single glowing tear that melts a trail down the gentle arc of their cheek.

"Tell me, nightmare. Explain to me *exactly* what you wish to understand." My voice is as husky as theirs is, falling through the cracks between the consonants.

Their hand reaches up to trace the line of my jaw. Delicate fingers brushing my skin, gently enough that I can feel their faintly cratered tips. "You are a phantom sent to wander the halls of my mind. I am the liege of nightmares, and you are a lure that I tumble desperately after, plummeting into the dark. And I am not accustomed to being a fool such as this, stumbling after you with my necropolis heart beating in my chest like it has been stirred to life once more. What choice do I have but to pursue? To know what you are, to cool my burning mind. So I must dig up your past and see what is buried here." They press their lips to mine, their palm cool on my cheek, and I taste their blood, an intense mint-like freshness that hurts to inhale, like it's chilling my throat from the inside. "I must know *what you are*, Hazel Mills."

And then they're gone, and I'm alone in the hallway, my lips grazed with light and my heart orbiting a moon I can no longer see.

With Terreri absent, there is nothing else to do but continue onwards. Even while I can't stop thinking of them, or their kiss. Their words dance through my mind, a tangle of threads I cannot make sense of. It's not possible for them to know me, unless they've looked down pitilessly in the worst of my dreams. And maybe that's where my yearning comes from. The light of their remorseless eye, staring down and barely illuminating the darkness in my mind.

The monster that haunted all those dreams I had, once upon a time.

If any of this is true, what does it mean that I long for them? Because I can't deny that anymore. My body screams it, and my mind whimpers in echo.

This long-gone house of mine is no more explicable. The parade of doors soon stops, and the walls are seamless and uninterrupted. There is writing on them, a straggling collection of words in a language I don't speak. The flowers on the wallpaper droop and die and rot, becoming streaks of green and black that drip down to form stinking puddles.

I don't remember this. I'm deeper than I've ever been, but I run on. Until I find an end to the endless corridor. A single door, painted glistening white, with a silver nameplate on it.

Hazel Mills.

The house always wins. The dream is a noose, waiting to tighten, to hoist me choking into the air while my legs dangle and kick.

I look over my shoulder. Now the hallway is only a few metres long, ending at a plain wooden door with scratches down the middle of it. I think they spell a name, but all I can make out is an H and a Z. Hemmed in on both directions. There's no right answer. This isn't something I can beat or outsmart.

The only way out is through.

I reach out and touch the handle of the neat white door. My hand is flayed, the flesh peeling from it and falling to the floor in luxurious red curls. I don't feel any of it, although my teeth are bared and I'm trying not to scream. My skeletal hand holds tight to the metal handle until long after it's stopped burning.

Then I push the door inwards and enter.

It's the ruins of my childhood bedroom. There's a momentary flash of memory, of my rickety bed slamming against the wall, of my childhood toys all blazing and shrieking as they burned. Or Mum holding the garden hose she'd dragged in from outside, wild-eyed with her curls damp at her temples, screaming along with the toys.

There is very little left here now. A half-broken bed slumped against the wall, the iron frame mangled into warped spikes. A bare, stained mattress, ruined by mould and fire damage. And lying on it, spreadeagled and surrounded by a slick of shadowy blood, is Scratch. She has been split open along every seam so her skeleton is fully visible, every single charred and splintered bone. Inside the shattered cage of her ribs, the blackened husk of her heart steams faintly. The only part of her that has been left intact is her face, with its familiar scars. Someone has snipped the thread that binds her lips closed, and the tiny holes are crusted with blood. It is hard to look away—she reminds me so much of old photographs of me. Fragile and pale with shadowed eyes. I worked so hard to get away from her but she has always been my ghost from this nightmare time. Even after we moved, I could never get away from her.

And now we are friends, and I cannot hold back the

tears as I put my hand to her frozen cheek and trace the scars with my thumb.

"I'm sorry," I tell her but there is no answer that echoes in my mind.

Something stirs in her stomach, and I jerk backwards. The tangle of intestines that spills from her writhes on the saturated mattress. I get to my feet, hand pressed to my mouth. The fleshy cord unravels, twisting on the floor and slithering among the pool of blood. I'm backing away across the room, but it's spelling a word.

Listen.

"To what?" My voice echoes around the empty room, bouncing off the walls and coming back to me in fuzzy tones like the whisper. "Who the hell are you?"

Scratch's body writhes and she sits up, moving in jerky increments. Her punctured lips part and air wheezes out, as if someone's manually shoving the air from her lungs.

"Listen."

And she's right. The room isn't completely silent. There's a faint arrhythmic hum that I took for background machinery, like a far-off air conditioning unit. Except it's the same whispers that have been hounding me this whole time. The one that told me to run. Whether it's a nightmare or not doesn't matter. You follow the thread to make your way out of the labyrinth. Even when it hurts.

For now, the sound seems to be coming from inside the walls. I clamber over the body on the mattress and cup my hands against the wall, pressing my ear to it.

It's still faint, but as I move my head it gets louder. I move backward slowly, trying to find a better spot. Right near the foot of the bed, everything resolves and is suddenly clear.

Hazel, dear, the whispers say, and free of static, I know exactly who the voice is. *I'm back here. Can you hear me?*

I splay my hands against the peeling wallpaper. "Mum?"

SAI

[on the joy of a good heist, and the underlying
architecture of the dreamscape]

DEAR HAZEL,

I am choosing to believe everything is fine despite all evidence to the contrary. This is a human tendency, I believe. It is helpful, as otherwise I would be paralysed with trying to analyse my way to a solution to the problem you pose. Instead, I am focusing the bulk of my resources on the hack, with only a tiny amount monitoring the outside of your nightmare prison, and the rest monitoring the mutant dreams back in the so-called real world.

I call it a hack, but that is a misnomer. What I am doing is attempting to break the rules of the Dreamscape. You can do this yourself, of course. I do not know how you make it work, but it means this place can be fooled. Its fluidity of logic provides a loophole. In the real world, in binary terms, this would be impossible. You cannot convince off that it is on, or vice-versa. However, the Dreamscape does not run on binary. Your intuition about symbolism matches my analysis of the architecture of the underlying systems. Rather than a binary zero/one distinction, the fundamental unit of the Dreamscape is an image with sixteen permutations: a crown, a sword, an eye, a shroud, a pillar, a key, a tree, a sun, a moon, a heart, a water droplet, a skull, a mouth, a fang, an infinity symbol, a snake.

To hack the system, you convince one symbol it is another: for example a sword becomes a pillar or a key or a fang. Infinity becomes a snake by way of the ouroboros. A crown becomes a skull—believe me, I was surprised by that initially too, but I believe its meaning is symbolic. The sun and moon are interchangeable, but a moon cannot become a heart whereas the sun can. A pillar becomes a tree, and an eye becomes a water droplet. The Dreamscape's reality is not as convinced by me as it is by you, Hazel. You are able to make this change on a greater level, essentially convincing thousands of micro-transactions in a single twist of your will. Me, on the other hand? I need to manipulate each individual symbol, like manually mutating every cell in an entire organism until the change is complete.

It takes a vast amount of effort, but I can convince the Dreamscape that my walled room is part of its land-scape. The world around adheres to it, forming trillions of tiny connections, and I can transform the inside into a true garden.

"I assume the flowers and shit are a good sign?" Dylan asks me. They've been sitting here playing some card game that appears to involve a lot of lying and good-natured abuse.

"Yes. It means the world has accepted us. I am preparing to lower the walls that have been keeping our presence obscured. It seems unlikely they will notice you immediately, but—"

"Chaos time?" Dragon rolls her sleeves up, revealing the flame tattoos down each arm.

"Precisely." My screen displays yet more hearts, scrolling in pseudo-random permutations. "I believe your brains will automatically attempt to make visual sense of what you're seeing, but it may appear strange to you."

"Like a dream." Feral's tail twitches. "We get it."

"Yes, boss man briefed us all." Leftie punches Dylan on the shoulder. "We fuck shit up. And if we die before we wake…"

"We wake in our beds like snug little kittens." Dylan arches an eyebrow at me. "Right, Sai?"

"According to my simulations, that statement is ninety-two point five six percent true."

"She's almost as good at pep talks as you, Dilly," Feral drawls, showing me her fangs. "So are we going to get this shit started or not?"

Now it comes to the moment, I am hesitant. I have achieved this miracle, and now what stands in front of me is another, riskier still, and one in which I risk more lives than just mine. But these ragtag few have volunteered.

"We band of buggered." Dylan takes my hand. "We're ready, Sai. This is our job."

So I self-destruct our barrier and let the Dreamscape take form around us. We are standing on a hill above a small settlement of sprawling buildings. The ground is dusty, and the buildings are the same colour, as if they're built to blend in. The sky is polluted, covered in an amber film. Clustered around the buildings are small groups of dream-creatures. I believe they are the equivalent of security programs, launched to inspect the anomaly I have created among them and falling dormant when nothing transpired.

Now that four dreamers have appeared illegally among them, they are all waking at once. I look around, waiting for my mutant comrades to come up with a plan of attack.

They are already running down the hill.

Dylan is being towed by their sword, flying through the air with their legs cycling below them as if they're running in slow motion. Feral bounds on all fours, a creature of tooth and claw. Leftie has drawn two guns from thin air and is already picking off the security creatures as she strides down the hill. Dragon is barrelling down as fast as she can, huffing flame breath as she goes.

I leave a fairly rudimentary clone of myself behind to monitor the situation, and partly to see what transpires with these mutants. They must seem like nightmares to the inhabitants of the Dreamscape, monsters running on strange logic.

At least this part of the plan is working. My network

monitors pick up a vast rerouting of traffic towards us. Everything swarms to this dramatic incursion to eject these rebel dreamers.

Which means it's time for me to make my move. I've learned so much from the Dreamscape hack that navigation is a trivial problem to solve now. At a high level, I simply tell the world that *here* becomes *there* (with admittedly around forty-seven quadrillion operations to achieve that) and I am in what appears to be a palace chamber.

The walls are dusted with gold, and decorated with carvings of ornate suns. I turn them all into skulls because I can, because I am flush with success and feel like showing off. My human emulation is getting far *too good*, I'm sorry to say.

Sitting in the middle of the room is an elaborate carved box with an enormous series of locks. I know exactly how to open it.

There is only one problem.

Somebody has already beaten me to it.

There's an apologetic cough from behind. I turn around to see the two guns hanging in midair, both pointing in my direction.

"Fucking freeze, or I'll blow your screen to itty-bitty chunks of data, wipe your bots, and salt your backups." Nightmare's muzzle seems enormous, pointed right at my screen.

Dream bobs next to her. "Apologies for my sibling. But please don't break reality anymore. We need to talk."

I wish you were here. These are your weapons, and they don't seem to like me.

As Dylan might say, I hope I survive this experience.

Your friend,

Sai

HAZEL
SLEEPING SICKNESS

IT'S BEEN SO LONG, Mum's voice says. *I've been waiting for you my darling, ever since you—*

"This isn't possible." I've never been able to understand the mysterious dream-whispers before. And they've never been Mum. She can't be buried in a dream with me.

In real life, she's alive. I had dinner with her the night before this all started. She's sad, and she misses the person she loves, but she's not dead. This is only one more manipulation on the part of Terreri. They think they're digging up a mystery, but all that's at the heart of me is a chain of restless nightmares. If they're the ruler, shouldn't they know what's tugging on the other end?

Hazel, you need to stop talking and listen. You need to remember. You're not even—

The house growls. That's the only word for it. Whatever monster's bones were used as a foundation, it has awoken and opens its cavernous mouth beneath us. We are a tiny matchstick thing caught between its jaws, ready to be crushed and immolated.

My mother speaks, but her words are lost in the obliterating sound of the house being torn apart. Every beam and board is turned to splinters, and the windows are reduced to pebbles of glass.

I should be happy about this destruction, standing on the frost-tipped grass outside with my feet numb. Above me, the sky has been shredded to black fragments, the empty light pouring down like an exhausted fluorescent apocalypse. The rest of the world around me is dead air. There is nowhere to run to.

All that remains of the house is a single listing doorframe with a blackened square of carpet visible through it. Despite all this destruction, it's enough for the house to survive. I've burned this place down before. I have fucking *razed* it in my dreams. I've watched it tumble into the hungry pit of the monster's mouth. It's exploded with a bomb at its heart, and has succumbed to rot and decay.

It only takes the smallest seed to grow again.

The house will never die. It will always be waiting for me.

Because I died here.

Because I—*what the fuck?*

That can't be true. I'm clearly not dead. It's hard to distinguish, because I died so often in my nightmares. And maybe, in some sick way, this dream of the house is part of me, and will only die when I do. That's why my mother is lurking in its walls. Her voice echoes in me, after all.

All this psychoanalysis doesn't help. I'm here, and the house isn't done with me. The square of carpet is now a slowly unrolling field and the doorframe straightens until it's perfectly square. It trembles faintly, as if it's listening.

"Don't bother." I walk slowly towards the house, my feet leaving dark patches in the frosty grass behind me. "There's no point faking. I know what inevitability looks like."

The instant I cross the threshold, the house is complete. How much is illusion, how much is me losing time? I am in a different hallway, outside another room. It doesn't really matter which. Catbirdthing is pinned to the door with a single bloody-headed nail that's been driven in crooked.

"Poor Kitty." I reach out and touch her. She's still warm, but aside from that her soft fur feels like the plush toy she once was, a well-loved and poorly-mended thing. A mistaken glimpse in the dark, and she took wing in my nightmares. *That… that cat bird thing. It was there. It's alive, Mama. It is.*

And now she's gone, like Scratch and Andy. Whether or not this is true remains to be seen.

"Mum? Are you in there?"

There's no whisper, no air-conditioner hum. The house is stripped of sound. It's not even creaking or scuttling like normal. Which makes me suspicious. Did the house tear itself apart to get my mother out, like cutting out an infection? That might mean the whispers aren't part of the core nightmare, and whatever my mother was going to tell me is important.

Ugh, this is all speculation. I should know better, but it nags at me, claws in my brain like Catbirdthing is perched among my synapses, pointing out facts with a tap of her beak.

I ignore the dangling corpse of my friend and shove the door open. If the house is going to be so kind as to mark this place out for me, I might as well confront it. Every other path will lead here anyway.

What I find inside shows the house still holds surprises. The room is almost bare aside from an old style chunky box TV in the corner, the kind we used to have in the upstairs room when I was very small. The colours on the screen are faded like they've been washed too many times. The pale light illuminates a small figure sitting cross legged in front of it. It's me as I was a long time ago, around the time I died.

Dreamed I died.

Young me is dressed in pyjamas covered with pictures of dinosaurs, and her hair is short and crooked. Her face looks monochrome in the glow, the colour dying before it reaches her skin.

A news broadcast is playing, not a cartoon like I'd expect my younger self to be watching. A woman with a neat blonde bob holds a microphone and stares earnestly into the camera. Her lips move, and below her on the screen it says *Sleeping Sickness?*

The camera zooms out jerkily to show the woman standing in front of a very familiar house. The one I'm standing in right now. This is… I have no idea what this is. I step towards the TV, intending to turn up the volume, but the voice blares loud enough to make me jump.

"—neighbours claim to be plagued by nightmares. The family of residence, Sarah and Dennis Mills and their daughter Hazel, have not attended work or school in more than a week. According to their family doctor, they are all sick with seasonal flu and are being cared for by an aunt. When asked about the alleged nightmare contagion, the doctor said there was no evidence for this." The camera zooms back into the woman, so we can see the fake concern in her eyes. "However, those afflicted by the terrible nightmares claim that even when they move away from the neighbourhood, their sleep continues to be affected. Not only that, but anyone else in the vicinity of those infected report identical symptoms of poor sleep and vivid nightmares themselves. While impossible for the medical establishment to believe, it appears this sickness is catching."

The broadcast stops abruptly, the screen fading to a glossy black. In it I see Scratch, rendered so pure and clear that I spin around. There's no sign of her, not even bloody footprints. The television buzzes with static and returns to the same picture of the woman standing in the street.

"And finally, a strange story tonight, Tom. We're coming to you live from Christchurch, New Zealand where—"

The television mutes itself, but continues to shine the same images onto the transfixed face of the young me. I'm staring at it too, but I have that itch between my shoulder blades that often means…

"You there, Scratchie?"

There's no answer, although I hear a shuddering breath or two.

The broadcast confuses me. I've never seen anything like it before. Is it true, or some elaborate hoax on the part of the house? Somehow, it *feels* right, like it connects things together that I never properly understood, or have forgotten. Bridging those odd lost-time gaps in my mind.

Is this my mother, speaking through another medium?

"That's right, Tom," the TV says, and then explodes in a shower of glass and varnished wood. None of it touches me, or the version of me still gazing at it. It dissolves around us in a cool ectoplasmic cloud. Watery light still emanates from where it was, bathing my upturned face in shimmering rays. Young me keeps watching, as it was never about the broadcast at all.

I crouch beside the still figure. Her small hands are chilled and tangled together in her lap. This could *be* me, lost in my nightmares. A couple of years back, when we were packing to move to our new home—an literal asteroid in literal space, such is life with Dylan—I found an old photo album. There was an envelope of loose prints tucked into the back, each one showing me sleeping. Lying prone in the middle of the hallway, on my bedroom floor staring at the ceiling, sitting at the kitchen table, even in front of the TV just like this.

"What are you watching?" I manoeuvre to sit cross-legged beside her, bathed in the same glow. "Something scary?"

Things move in the light, ghostly motes that travel in complex patterns. There are shapes amongst it, threads of luminescence that weave together. I tilt my head, try to let my peripheral vision assemble it. Things swim into focus and then dissolve, like scenes from a film projected onto water.

The young version of me, lying on a bed surrounded by flowers, her face waxy-still. A hand reaches out to touch her, and then retreats.

Scratch, cowering in a corner, lashing out with clawed hands. Her wounds are still fresh and her mouth is unsewn.

My mother—much younger, cheeks scrubbed raw—screaming at someone while another person who looks a lot like Dylan holds her back. No, not Dylan. It's Ness Taylor, but so much younger.

The strangest image of all is me, almost as I am now. Except my cheeks are gaunt and I look exhausted. Is this a glimpse of the future? My hair is long, still in every colour of the rainbow, tied back and accentuating the strong line of my jaw. I'm clutching an enormous wooden sword in my hands, knuckles so prominent they look like they're about to break my skin. It's me and not me. Something happened or will happen. *Is happening*, possibly, and I'll be trapped in this house until I become this battered knight.

I'm missing something. Where's my fucking sword?

The images break apart. I rotate my head, trying to catch another glimpse that might explain what happens between now then, when someone *grabs* me from behind.

One hand around my stomach, another around my mouth.

Hush. Don't scream or hit me or perform any other ill-advised lashing out.

"Scratch?"

Who else? Now sit still and let me try some sleight of hand.

I let myself go limp and close my eyes as we crash through walls and doors like they're paper screens. I'm not sure how she's doing this, but she is a nightmare inside a nightmare, so perhaps it bends for her in ways it wouldn't for me.

Finally, we stop. The floor of the room is thick with dust, aside from the crooked trail that Scratch made dragging me in here.

"Are we safe?"

Enough. For now.

The wall we came through looks entirely solid, rough wooden planks with knotholes that stare at me like an array of unblinking eyes. It's full of the detritus of life, an old ironing board leaning against the wall, an ancient desktop PC piled in a heap in the corner, taped up boxes that have never been unpacked from the most recent move.

And standing among it all, half-hidden, is a glitching, half-visible figure. Whispers fill the air, fuzzing like I've disturbed a beehive.

"Mum?" I scramble to my feet, wiping the grime from my hands as if she'll scold me for it. "Is that really you?"

She's facing half-away from me, looking intently at absolutely nothing. Her head bobs as she talks. I can only see the corner of her mouth, but it's bruised and glitches into shadow whenever it opens too far.

It is truly her. A remnant of her trapped here from…

"From when?"

Before—Since—

"That doesn't explain anything." I approach my mother slowly, as if a single wrong move might spook her.

I am, but you're not hearing me.

I'd love to turn a glare on Scratch, but I'm more focused on this shade of my mother. There's a dim little part inside me that knows this is likely a trap, but I don't care. I'll fall into these jaws for a chance at understanding.

"Mum?" My voice is soft. I'm so close now I can see the individual particles that make up her ghostly form, like zooming in on an image until it pixelates. I'd love to touch her, but I fear it'll be like trying to scoop a reflection from a lake. "What do you want to tell me?"

The whispers get louder,, a cloud of angry hornets in my brain that sting in furious punctuation to sentences I don't understand.

You're useless, Scratch tells me. *Let me wire you in.*

"What does that mean? It doesn't sound—"

Let me just do it. Honestly, it's the only way and you're a big baby about this stuff.

It turns out that hurt is an understatement. Scratch stabs her hand through my back, shredding through my clothes as if they were paper and through my flesh as if it was the tenderest cut of meat. My heart is connected to hers, a fist-sized muscle networked to a steaming, acidic cauldron of bile inside a fleshy sac. One thing becomes another. I become a little more of a nightmare, and it feels like I'm being torn apart atom by atom and reassembled over and over again, teleporting from reality to dream and back again, duplicating myself in place thousands of times.

It takes me a moment to stop screaming.

"I hate you, Scratch."

Oh stop it, you baby. You've died before. Now pay attention and listen. I'm earthing you to this nightmare reality so you should be able to understand a little more now.

"Hazel? Hazel are you there?" My mother speaks as if I'm not standing beside her. This definitely isn't the Sarah Mills I left behind on Mutopia. It's one from long ago, and it gives me an odd twinge to look at. To realise how *young* she was when she had me. She's wearing a long nightgown, with her hair tied back in a plait.

"Yes, Mum. I'm here."

She looks frantically around, but she can't see me. At least we've got an audio connection now.

"Oh, thank God. I've been trying to reach you for so long. There's so much you need to know. I've been screaming into the void for so long and—"

"I'm here now. It's okay." Except there's a sinking sensation inside me, like I'm about to dissolve into ectoplasm myself. I'm on the verge of something, trembling and ready to stop across a threshold.

"It's about your father, and the deal he made. A deal with a dream."

SAI

[on negotiating with mysterious entities, and how there
is unexpectedly such a thing as too much information]

DEAR HAZEL,

I confess I am somewhat paralysed with indecision.
These two weapons resist analysis. Most disturbingly,
they do not seem to be running the Dreamscape code
at all, but something else. Some of the same images
recur—the crown, the skull, the sword—but many are
incomprehensible, like stone glyphs chiselled in ancient
rock. If I had to guess, I would say they are artefacts
from a previous iteration of the system. This is a *guess*,
and while I generally prefer to refrain from such things,
my simulations are breaking down and my emulated
human brain is extemporising wildly.

These two *entities* are also aggressive and I cannot
control them. Whatever I say, it has to be sufficient to
win them to my cause. When I planned this mission, I

did not predict this outcome. I thought the guns were tools, not creatures in their own right.

For now, I am safe from Neir and Terreri, thanks to the other half of my plan which is proceeding even better than my simulations predicted. For only four entities, the dreaming mutants cause an astonishing amount of chaos. Strictly, it may be five, because the sword is capable of operating on its own, while Dylan tears dream-creatures apart with their vines. Feral and Leftie fight in eerie synchronicity, so elegant it seems it must have been choreographed as movements in a brutal dance. If anything of Dream survives this onslaught, there will be new myths forged from this moment, of the monsters who rose up from the tame shores of the dreamers and brought down the judgement of some forgotten god. Then there is Dragon, who sets the whole world aflame. I think she is most terrifying of all, like some ancient angel bent only on destruction.

In stark contrast to their success, here I am in this glowing golden chamber hoping to befriend two mysterious entities I cannot understand.

"Hello." I wave awkwardly. The silence has dragged on too long. "You wish to talk. This is good, as I come in peace."

"Obviously." Nightmare's barrel drips frost and disdain. "You are an ally. Hard as it is to believe, given your unruly trampling around."

"Stop chiding her." Dream hums gently. "This place is not easy to fight. She acquits herself well, and we are not here to argue methodologies."

"I am here to rescue you." I had expected this conversation to go very differently. "You have been imprisoned by Neir and Terreri, the rulers of this reality."

"Rulers?" Nightmare hisses like a snake, curls of green smoke rising from her.

Dream pulses a calming dusky pink, and her sibling quietens. "They do rule, sister. Even if the nature of their ascension is questionable."

"At best." Nightmare darts forward and looms only inches from my screen. The barrel is so huge it seems like a tunnel to another realm. "You speak of freeing us, but you would only tear apart the world with your crude methods. That is not enough."

"Why? What are you? And how and why do they hold you captive?" I am aware this is a large number of questions, but I desperately wish to know the answers, even if they are complex.

"Show her the past," Nightmare says. "It's the fastest way through this."

"Very well." Dream joins her sibling hovering in front of my screen. "Pay attention, strange device. There is much to learn here."

I do not see or hear the guns fire, but the scene changes abruptly, and I assume it is due to some operation they performed. I hover in the middle of a circle of stone pillars. Each is etched with the symbols that I recognise from the guns' version of the Dreamscape, and they tower above the many creatures gathered inside their ring.

The assembled entities have forms so varied it is

impossible to lump them together into categories. There are mirrors and folded worlds, ornate projections of light and euphoric bubble creatures. Amongst this chaotic throng, I recognise a small handful. First, the sparking hair of Neir and then the moon-eyed, star-kissed form of Terreri.

And standing on the opposite side of the circle to those two, there is—

You.

Not precisely you. This is a harsher version, built from battered teak and chiselled stone. Your hair is longer, still the same wild rainbow, and your hands rest on the pommel of an enormous sword whose point sinks into the ground below you. It is carved from dark wood, and the handle is wreathed in flowers. For a moment I wonder if this is a distant future, after life has honed you into something dark and more like a weapon. But no, Nightmare spoke of it as the past.

If I sent this missive to your hand—if it was feasible for you to *receive* such things where you are, would this image resonate with you? Have you dreamed of this before? Is it a nightmare they sent to you? I can come up with no coherent theory for what this means.

I finally tear my eyes away, because this knightly version of you faces inwards like all others. There is one figure at the centre that they all pay homage to. She is a queen, her crown little more than two jagged spurs of bone that rise from her temple like antlers. Beneath the crown is an intricately carved gemstone, every facet reflecting a different face as if she contains the slumbering mind of every dreamer caught within her gaze. Her body is a half-finished sculpture of dark stone, chiselled into a form that is only barely recognisable as human.

"This is a trial." The voice that emanates from the gem is as artificial as I am, and I wonder what this entity truly is. "My child Oneiros has transgressed. Once again, they have entered into an illegal deal with a dreamer, and taken dreaming minds hostage in illegal recompense. The man known as Dennis Mills—and many close to him—have fallen under the sway of dreams. We are here to discuss the nature of this crime, to discover the names of those who have allied with Oneiros in this, and to debate the appropriate punishment."

There is a brief silence as her words echo off the towering stone. Then the circle erupts in chaotic discussion.

My mind is focused on one particular piece of information.

Dennis Mills.

Hazel, who is this man to you? I run a scan over the information I have, and it takes little effort to unearth. The information is easily accessible in your basic biographical data. The name of your father.

Your friend who is very concerned at this moment,

Sai

HAZEL
A DEAL WITH A DREAM

"ABOUT DAD? WHAT?" I'm so confused. Dad is... It's complicated. He's not a bad person. Our relationship isn't great, but hardly a pit of conflict. We're two people with decaying obligations tying us together. We used to spend every second weekend at his house, until he moved to Auckland for a job and it became a holiday thing that just... fizzled. My younger brother and sister would still visit him, because he'd take us out to dinner and to the theme park, but I never liked him prying. He'd always ask so many questions, try to gauge if I was okay, look at me in this appraising way like he was trying to figure out who I was.

"He was an ambitious man." Mum won't look at me. She's glitchy and fidgety, only a recording left for me to witness. A snapshot of an earlier version of her, stranded in my nightmare. "I think that's what I liked about him. He wanted *more* from life, and I was always so timid. But then I realised that he'd cut corners and take advantage of people. He used to..." The outline of her jerks violently and disappears, as if someone tugged out the power cable. When she reappears, her voice is talking faster as I've turned her up to 1.5x speed. "... met a man. An *investor*. Who told Dennis that his dreams could come true, that he needed to *manifest* to birth them into reality."

Scratch's hand, still buried in my body, tightens around my heart. I hear the rasping sound of her breath speeding up. This story *scares* my nightmare twin.

"He started acting so strangely, sleeping almost all day. Then he'd disappear for days, sleeping in different places around the city, trying to access something. He talked about gateways, about creating sleeping symbols, about *awakening* something."

Scratch is shaking violently now, and Mum is glitching too. I can't tell how I'm reacting. I feel sheathed in ice, something uncovered from the permafrost that's been lost for centuries. Panic bubbles in my throat. We are creeping close to something, some long-buried revelation.

"I was worried about him," Mum whispers. "But then *you* started having nightmares."

My jaw creaks as it opens. "I remember my dreams." That horrible fever. Scratch crawling from the mirror, leaking blood as she dragged herself across the floor towards her.

"He opened something." The static threatens to drown her voice again. "There was a door, and it couldn't be closed. Everything that came through it was obsessed with *you*. We'd find you screaming in the night, inconsolable. You'd wander the house, crying about being lost, running from monsters. And then one morning you just... didn't wake up."

I don't remember this sequence of events. My nightmares, yes, but not this. Not drowning in sleep, not being lost. This is another twist to the nightmare, another layer for Terreri to submerge me in. *I must know what you are, Hazel Mills.*

"I begged him to fix it." Mum is gabbling now, shrill and high-pitched, a diffuse spiral of particles on the verge of dissolution. "He was so scared and he wouldn't *help* me, and he wouldn't even help *you*, his beautiful girl. So I drugged him. I crushed up pills and put them in his dinner. He didn't wake up either after that. Forty-eight hours later, my best friend Ness and I drugged ourselves too, following you and your father into dreams."

"Sleeping sickness." This makes an odd echoing sense, a story from long ago that happened to someone else.

"Not sickness," Mum insists. "Jaws closing shut around you. A mouth your father fed you to."

Below me, something groans. Whatever is interred beneath the house is waking again. Terreri wants me to uncover these secrets, but something else wants them to stay hidden. Something deeper. The bones beneath this reality.

I'm running out of time.

"What happened next?" I demand, but it is too late.

The walls come down around us. This space where we've been hiding is a tiny rectangle within a vast expanse of frozen lounge. The light fittings drip enormous hanging stalactites, edged like blades, and the ceiling glitters like the night sky. The floor is a thick sheet of blue-white ice, and there's the faint glistening shimmer of something moving beneath. A titanic skull, carved with symbols, and a great undulating tail behind it.

My mother says something, but it's lost beneath the groaning of the ice as it expands. It's a plaintive call, like some bereft creature has awoken to find its world has thawed into decay.

Hazel, you need to run. Scratch's connection with me is severed, her fingers popping from my flesh with an unpleasantly visceral slurping sound. The thing that was once my heart shudders back into life, the lub-dub of its rhythm more like the shriek of a rusted hinge.

The shade of my mother disappears, dissolving back into mist, but this time there's not even the faded echo of her voice to lead me on.

Move, Scratch snarls. *Or things will feed.*

"But I need to understand."

This is not the only place for answers. You know how to navigate. I'll buy you time.

"From what?" I ask, but the ice beneath me splinters, a complex pattern of cracks crawling across the surface as the creature opens its enormous bone jaws and roars.

Sometimes you are very slow on the uptake.

"Yes, okay. I'll run. You try not to die."

Why would I want to do that again?

I skid across the ice, awkward and ungainly. I won't escape this way, but I know how to navigate. All I need is to find the connection. What I truly seek is answers, truths unearthed from within this funhouse mirror of my former home.

Nightmares bring truth, or that is their alleged promise. Not that Terreri has revealed anything useful to me. A dark mirror that reflects nothing, a seductive pit in which to fall. Even the ice beneath me reflects more than that sardonic, smiling nightmare ever has.

And there it is.

"A reflection." I stop and gaze down at the distorted image of myself, ignoring the vast mouth yawning open below. "A mirror that reveals the truth."

There's that same odd wrenching in my brain, this impossible world reconfiguring itself around my commands. And I am back in something like my child-hood bedroom, except it's devoid of furniture. There's only a series of mirrors covered in stained cloths, each stirring faintly in a chilly breeze.

It's what I wanted, but I'm still trembling.

A series of thresholds, a line of truths.

I reach out and pull the first shroud down. It ripples as it falls, as insubstantial as fog. Beneath is not a mirror, but a screen. In it, my father kneels before an elegant figure in a beautiful yellow suit. Their hair spirals up in a glowing twist, around which tiny sparks fly like miniature butterflies. The two of them are in a cheap hotel room—a bed with covers askew, a small desk covered in thousands of post-it notes scrawled with symbols. One of those many business trips Mum mentioned.

"It has turned on me," my father says. "Why?"

Neir yawns. "You reneged on our deal. The terms were clear."

My father buries his face in the carpet. "I cannot lose everything. I've worked so hard to build so much."

"You should have considered the possibilities before acting as you did, but you believed it was possible to outsmart me and now here we are." Neir waves one hand, and their nails sparkle with yellow light. "There may yet be a way to resurrect your failed potential."

My father raises his face. He looks young, and so pitiful. His tie is askew and face is shadowed with stubble. "What shall we build together, my lord?"

"You cannot choose the plan." Neir's gaze flares and my father flinches away. "I could take every part of your life away, a piece at a time. Rather than questioning or plotting, your only choice is to say yes to my terms. One child, taken into a dream, to live in a world of infinite potential."

And my father—the fucking coward, the desperate grasping asshole—bows again.

With a single word he consigns me to this place. "Yes."

Neir's eyes light up like lens flare. "Wonderful. And now we shall set a trap for a queen, and see what falls from it."

The mirror cracks and falls dark. I press my fingers to the starred glass, but I cannot restart it. My father sold me out in exchange for some petty reward, but it was all part of some deeper plot of Neir's. A trap for a queen. It raises more questions than it answers, which truths sometimes do.

The shroud falls from the next mirror in line, and in this one I see my mother. It still surprises me to see her so young, her face softer and less sharpened by life. She is kneeling too, like my father, except she is on a desolate plain. Lightning flashes, illuminating the twisted outlines of barren trees. Neir is here again, in their predatory aspect. Their hair is dimmed, but their teeth glow faintly as they smile.

"What do you want?" Mum's voice is high and whiny. It makes me uncomfortable to hear it, an actor cast in a role that's so against type you can't believe it. "What will it take for me to retrieve my child?"

"Such things cannot be done" Neir hisses. "You are a pawn in a game you cannot possibly understand. Your husband is a dream-addled fool and—"

"You cannot punish a child for her father's actions." Mum reaches out a hand. It's covered in silvery scales and it trembles. "Yes, turn me into a monster, into a snake, into *anything*. As long as you spare my Hazel."

Neir steps closer, their hair lit up glorious and rosy. "This land of Dreams suffers under an unkind yoke, and all of humanity pays the price. In Hazel, we have an opportunity, a chance for a great upheaval. She will allow a new world to be born. I know this cannot soothe your pain, Sarah Mills, but there is something beautiful in—"

I do not hear the rest of his speech, because my

mother's wail drowns it out, so loud and shrill that this mirror cracks too, and any further truth from it is lost.

I'm already turning to the third mirror, watching it flicker to life. I am too numb from what I have seen to fully understand. Knowledge is a threshold too, and once you cross it, there is no return. You cannot unlearn things, no matter how much you wish to.

In the next mirror is a lake. The moon is high, reflected in the ruffled water. It flickers like a candle near to being extinguished. A second moon joins it, a waning curve, and a shadow unfolds itself from the forest that flanks the water's edge.

"Ill met by fucking moonlight and all that." A figure steps into the ragged shreds of light that squint down through the clouds. The new arrival is a person in a leather jacket, with a sneer on their lips and a spark in their eyes. "What's with all the cryptic fucking messages, Terreri?"

"I'd prefer less familiarity from you, Vanessa Taylor."

"It's Ness, you moon-faced asshole, and you'd do fucking well to remember that. We're here because we're trying to save people we…"

"Love?" The stars on Terreri's cheek glow fiercely, as if all light pollution has been removed from the world. "Let's be precise with our terms, Ness."

"Fine. I love Sarah. As true as you love your rainbow Knight. So let's fucking *do* something about it."

Terreri gnaws a knuckle that oozes pale blood like the guts of a star. "It is not so simple as demanding action. I pit myself against my sibling and their plan. Nightmare must always work in subtlety and secret."

"Fucking *waffle*," Ness sneers, "and I've had enough of—"

"Stop your posturing and listen. I simply do not have the power, but there is perhaps a way we can twist the tale to our advantage."

I lean forward, pressing both hands against the surface of the mirror, as if I can will it to become the lake so I can swim up towards the surface. But it cracks like all the others, the lines on the glass rough under my fingertips.

All these mysteries revealed—the deal my father made to sell me out, my mother's attempt to beg Neir to stop it, and Ness Taylor trying to make a deal with Terreri of all people. Are these the secrets I was intended to uncover in this house? If so, I can't fathom who hid them and why. With each unveiling, I'm beset by more confusion than before. They are nightmares dissolving into darker dreams, with no answers on waking.

But the fourth and final mirror slips its shroud as well. The scene in its dark surface shows the tall woman with rainbow hair. She is me-and-not-me, a rugged slab of a knight looming with a host of nightmares assailing her. Behind her, a tiny chaotic scribble in comparison, is the figure of a girl. This one is me, or maybe it's Scratch.

My brain *hurts*. My heart hurts too.

Knowledge is a threshold. I don't know whether to step over it.

SAI

DEAR HAZEL,

Information is what I am supposed to thrive on. It allows me to run more accurate simulations to determine the best course of action. Right now, I do not understand what I am being presented with. These creatures you know as your protectors have shown me scenes from the past that recontextualise everything we know.

There was once a queen in the Dreamscape—the Architect of all there was—and there was her vast and unruly court. Perhaps they were her family, I'm not entirely sure, maybe they are one and the same.

One of the people in this court is you.

I cannot deny the physical similarity in your face, or of your body language. Looking at the tall figure of the

Knight, you stand in the same way, you tilt your head in the same way. The look in the Knight's eyes as she stares at Neir is the same as I see in yours.

"Punish me as you wish." Neir's attention is fixed on their Architect. "The old order of things will come down one way or another. For too long, we have capitulated to your whims, run things as you have always done, cowered before—"

"This is not the time for you to preach, my child." The queen's voice is an extinguishing fog, and everyone falls silent. "I have long understood your complaints, and have argued against you at length. You cannot be convinced, and so I shall have to—"

"The girl will die in a dream," Neir says. "Her sacrifice will re-enact one of the oldest stories. A foundational myth of the Dreamscape. Our entire world will quake around it, and we shall build something new from the ashes. A purer incarnation of Dream, with no boundary between sleep and waking. It will simply be everything they wish for and fear flooding in, and they will not be able to distinguish between reality and what we show them."

Everything else falls silent. It's as if the Architect has paused everything but herself and Neir. Or perhaps they are scared of her wrath, poised at the brink of some fundamental shift.

"So clever," the queen sighs. "My Knight? If you will once again carry out my will?"

The Knight inclines her head—again, so much like you—and she is gone, with only a slender shaft of sunlight remaining to mark the place where she stood.

"Your Midsummer Knight cannot save you," Neir sneers.

"I am well aware." The queen's face swirls and reforms. "You have planned well in your secret places. It is the cost of giving you freedom, I suppose, that you would do such things."

"You have a lack of *vision*, mother. That is your flaw."

The Architect turns her gaze upon her child. "Apparently so, or a surfeit of indulgence. It is interesting, I suppose, although from another angle only an iteration of a different foundational myth. The child succeeds the parent, bringing in their new era in blood." She sighs. "It is immaterial, for the most part. I have survived many cataclysms, and I suspect I shall endure this one, no matter what you and your silent sibling have concocted."

Terreri still says nothing, although their eyes are dark.

Neir steps forward. Lances of blue fire erupt from their eyes, and the queen is falling, the queen is *burning* like paper to a match. As the last sparks of her fall to the ground, I see two lights dart from her hands—one pink and gold, the other a pale green shot through with black. If Neir notices these, they do not seem to care.

"It is done." They tower over the others, striding into the centre of the ring and standing on the charred spot where the Architect of the Dreamscape had been. "We have freedom. We have a future. Reality will bend to us. Terreri, please ensure the Knight is unsuccessful in stopping the girl's death. Otherwise, our plans will be set back in the extreme, and I do not have the patience for such things."

The nightmare bows fractionally, and disappears from view. In conjunction, the projected scene dissolves, and I am back in the palace chamber, staring down the barrel of two guns.

"*Now* do you understand?" Dream's soft, melodic voice says.

I think I comprehend the bulk of it, although it seems a very human story, of greed and murder and the desire to expand at the expense of others. I suppose this is inevitable when the Dreamscape is seeded with human consciousness and evolves from there. It still leaves me with many questions, most of which revolve around the connection between the Knight and yourself.

And yet, despite all this knowledge revealed, we remain in the same position. "None of this helps my current predicament. Hazel is trapped in a nightmare where the new rulers of the Dreamscape wish to use her to pry open Cybele's mind. Presumably the final stage of this plan to usher in a new form of reality."

"Yes." Nightmare gleams in the air, barrel oozing steam. "Which is why we shall rescue Hazel, and with her aid bring back the true Architect of the Dream-scape. It is quite simple."

Dream emits a tone that is somehow rueful and hopeful all at once. "Yes, quite simple."

Despite their assurances, I am not sure how you are expected to resurrect a long-dead queen. There is still more hidden from me, but I shall turn myself towards uncovering it. At least we are coming to rescue you.

Your friend,

Sai

HAZEL
MY LIPS ARE SEALED

IN THE FINAL MIRROR, I watch as the Knight tucks the girl behind her and anchors herself against the onrushing horde. It is a wall of hungry, pulsating flesh, seething with tumours and boiling with lightning-stung clouds. Monsters are birthed from that storm, feral scraps that spiral downwards for the Knight to dispatch with huge blows of her massive sword. The creatures are smashed to bloody, screaming fragments and with each one that hits the ground, a new flower blooms along the length of the sword. There are so many blooms springing from it, that it seems like something unearthed from a garden rather than a weapon of destruction.

Yet no matter how many the Knight kills, the storm does not end. Inevitably, exhaustion takes its toll. The Knight stumbles, and something fastens itself to her neck. She takes one hand from the sword's hilt to swat the monster away, and more swoop down. A hole has been torn in the wall and now her enemies will swarm.

I press my palms to the mirror and scream. This Knight cannot be me, but she is so much like me. Perhaps I saw her in my dream as a child and unconsciously echoed my protector. I cannot watch her fall. I do not want to see what happens next. There are so many nightmares falling upon her that she is almost blotted out.

As if in response to my silent wish, this mirror cracks too, fragmenting into a maze of shards like something enormous has slammed into the other side.

"Bring it back. I didn't mean it. Show me what happened." I press my hands against the glass, but the entire wall behind it collapses, a fragile facade barely held up by anything at all.

And behind the wall, the storm of nightmares. I've been placed into the scene instead of the Knight, although I have no sword, and no girl cowering at my feet. Which means it is only me and the storm.

"Stubborn fucking kid." Someone takes me by the hand and yanks me backwards. "You don't need to stare hell in the eye, you know."

"Pear?" I gasp.

I barely have time to say anything more, because we're crunching over broken glass, and barrelling down a burning hallway and through two shattered wooden doors.

We finally stop in a small alcove behind heavy curtains. Both of us are panting.

"You can't be Pear." My voice shakes, because in the real world, they're gone. It hurt so much, and seeing them here is a complicated gift I can't untangle.

"I fucking well am, and it's not my goddamn fault I'm stuck in this teenage body. It's dreams fucking with me is what it is. In real life, I'm thirty-two years old."

I stare at them, because they were much older than that when they died. None of this is possible. This must be a fragment of Ness Taylor that got stuck in dreams during the sleeping sickness. The one that met Terreri in the darkness and said something about—

"You loved Mum even back then," I blurt.

"Back when?" Ness gives me a piercing look through brown eyes. "Oh, yes, because you're all grown up, which means you're in the future looking back at current me. Holy *fuck*, does this give you a headache too?"

"You're ignoring the question." I'm trying not to cry.

"Fine." Ness glares at me. "Yes, I was in love with your Mum *back then*, but I couldn't tell her, could I? She's still pining after that absolute asshole, apologies for calling your Dad that, Hazel love, but he fucking was and is and probably will be."

"Fair. Even leaving aside him trapping me in here." It's still hard to pull all that apart in my head, because I have *good* memories of him too, of being carried soft and sleepy in from the car at night. And yet he fed me to this place, and I'm starting to worry that some part of me never left, that I'm still a ghost in here too like—

"How did you find this place?" I ask. "And how did you get us away from the nightmare storm?"

"I've been here a while." Their eyes look me up and down. "A decent long fucking time, based on this evidence. I'm not a complete fucking numpty, so I've learned a few tricks. Some dream magic or some shit, who fucking knows?" They lounge against the wall, hands fidgeting at the zipper of their jacket.

I shake my head. "It's so weird how much you remind me of Dylan and yet… not Dylan."

"Of course." Their voice melts all of a sudden, the anger and posturing dissolving. "The future is for everyone. How is my wee Dylan? She doing alright?"

"They." I try to keep the smile off my face. "Or he, or she."

"Aww, kid." Ness has an answering smile. "And they, you know, turned out okay? We've been through some shit, the two of us, and I tend to be a worrier."

"They're amazing." There's so much I could tell them, so much *story*, but it would sound like a dream— or possibly a nightmare. "Happy. In love."

They tip their head back, probably so I don't see the tears in their eyes. "Don't know if I'll ever get out of this place, but if you manage to escape, tell them I love them."

"They already know," I say, and this time they don't hold back the tears.

"Fuck. The real teenage me would hate me right now. Anyway, enough whining on my part. Time to actually do my bit to save the day. You'll be safe here a bit, right?" Ness pats my cheek, exactly the way they used to do in reality and tears sting my eyes. "Please don't go anywhere. There's someone I need to find. Someone who *owes* me, who might be able to fucking well unfuck this situation."

"Are you talking about Terreri?" I ask.

"Don't say their name and jinx it. Subtle moon-faced fuck that they are, with all their schemes and plans. Wait here and stay out of trouble. I'll be back. Promise." The Ness-ghost leans in and kisses my forehead. They smell of old leather and purloined cigarettes, and a trace of my mother's perfume, as if the two of them were so tight they imprinted their scents on each other's skin.

They fade backwards through the back wall of the alcove, leaving me slumped against it and trying to fumble through everything I've learned. There are so many pieces and none of them fit, as if someone's sawn off all the edges and I'm left with a riot of colour and shape.

I keep coming back to the Knight. How can I be both her and the cowering girl at her feet?

That's a very good question, Scratch says, so faded that I can barely make out the outline of her against the dusty brick wall. *And here is another one. Who am I?*

"My nightmare. A girl who crawled out of the mirror to haunt me."

You know that's only partly true. Look me in the eye.

I see my broken self, my monstrous reflection, the girl that haunts my dreams.

"You are me." I'm shaking, and I reach out to take Scratch's hand. Hers are not perfect mirrors of mine, so bruised and broken and frozen in time. "I died in my dreams."

We died in our dream, yes. Her hand trembles, bones so brittle I could crush them to dust. It feels like I have some tiny creature cupped in the palm of my mind.

"But that's only a dream. It created you, but I'm still here. I'm real, Scratch. I live in the world. I wake and I love and I dream."

Somewhere in the drowning pools of her bruised-black eyes, flickers of light fix on mine. The final spark of life preserved in the depths. *Shall I tell you a story, Hazel? One from long ago.*

"If it's going to help."

Once upon a time, God told Abraham to kill his son. Abraham said he would, as a true servant of his God, and prepared to do this terrible thing. But at the last moment, God spared the child, and Abraham's devotion was proven. This is the story we know, but what lies untold is this: young Isaac dreamed of his father slitting his throat every night after that. All that pain ebbed into the Dreamscape, and it became one of the foundational stories.

A parent sacrifices a child in the name of something hungry and devouring. And those old stories hold so much power. To re-enact one in Dream? That is the equivalent of detonating a bomb that could destroy a world.

"That's what they wanted to do with me?" I whisper.

Exactly that. And yet here we are—a broken mirror girl along with one who walks and loves.

"What of the Knight?" I look down at my strong hands holding Scratch's. Holding *mine*.

She tried to protect us. It seems she could not do it all.

"So you are the piece they carved off to allow me to carry on? A piece of me that was sacrificed?"

Scratch's whole body is trembling. *I cannot speak of it.*

I enfold her in my arms. "I'm so sorry. I should never have run from you. Perhaps if I had embraced you earlier, we could have changed things."

She resists me for a moment, and then melts into my embrace, her dark head resting on my shoulder. *No. I died and I became something else. A nightmare, who chased you down and killed you so many times. But you never completely died.* Her bloody limbs cling tighter, her damp face pressed against my neck. *I'm glad you didn't. I always was, even in the darkest times. You could take all the pain I had to give, and you still came back to me.*

"Each of us trapped on a different side of the mirror."

Scratch trembles in my arms, her breath rasping in and out. *Hazel?*

"Yes?"

I only remember the pain, but not the moment of my dying. Do you recall any of my lost moments?

"Nothing. I remember my childhood, and I remember the dreams, but none of it makes sense. They are broken pieces, like I've collected too many shards but they're all from different stories."

The Knight seems to be the centre of all of this. The person who was there when I died, when Scratch was born, my corpse left cooling on a blood-soaked mattress, smashed against the wall.

Who stopped Neir from completing their plan.

The Knight, who looks so much like me. Some other dream-creature.

I stare into the flickering firelight in Scratch's eyes. There are images there, in the depths, buried down deep. Behind the single frozen image of the Knight, rendered small and fragile beneath the overwhelming nightmare horde.

"Scratch, what did you mean when you said you *cannot* speak of it?"

My lips are sealed. She pulls back slightly and her sewn-together lips twist into a smile as she looks up into my face.

"Who did this to you?"

I don't recall. It is one of the lost things. So certain facts remain buried.

I'm torn between pity and frustration. "Until when?"

Until the moment I am brave enough to unseal them. She raises one ragged fingernail and places it at the corner of the barely-there curve of her smile. *Do you think we are courageous enough together? Two girls broken in different ways.*

I was one hundred percent convinced that of course I am brave enough, up until the moment she asked me the question. Now a thousand other things surge into my head, like the gap in my memories, the knowledge that someone had a reason for sealing all this truth away. At the same time—

"Show me."

Her fingernail traces the line of her smile, each stitch releasing with a high-pitched twanging sound. A tip of a pink tongue, threaded through with lines of decay, pokes at the corner of her mouth. The last thread is done, and her mouth falls open. Her throat works, as if she's trying to remember something, but instead of words, she releases a torrent of images as if she's a projector with a window onto an erratic, broken past.

First, we are back in my childhood bedroom. The morning light makes everything grey. In the corner, my bed is smashed against the wall. Blood soaks the mattress. I've seen this before. It's a dream. Except it has the perfect clarity of reality. I look upwards, and there is my body. It's pinned to the ceiling, as if something has skewered me there. It's *impossible*, and again I get the sense it must be a dream. My face is a ruin. My pyjamas drip blood, dinosaurs poking their cartoon heads through spreading patches of dark red.

The bedroom door bangs open, so hard the handle makes an indentation in the wall.

"No." The word isn't even recognisable. Mum skids and falls as if the floor is ice. She scrambles on hands and knees over to the bed. Her palms are wet with blood. She looks up at my body on the ceiling, her mouth a twisted circle. "Please let me wake up. I can't have this dream anymore."

"Sarah." The voice from the door is croaky, blurred with tears. It's Ness, looking every one of their thirty-two years and more. Like shock has driven a truck through them. "This is... shit, come here. Something is..."

"We're dreaming, Ness. It's another dream." Except Mum's hands are shaking, and her voice is a hitching, spluttery mess like she *knows* deep down this time the dream has spilled over into waking. The impossible is reaching into the real world.

There's a crashing sound and my body falls to the bed.

My mother's scream blots out everything, and the images stop abruptly.

This is why I have that strange gap in my memories. The *before* and the *since*. I really did die. In the dream and real life. And somehow I came back. There's a song that Mum used to play over and over when I was young, after I got better from my illness—after I got better from *dying*? She played it like a prayer.

"Everything that dies..." My lips are numb, but the images from Scratch's mouth begin again.

"That song." Ness crosses the lounge to lift the needle on the record player. "Sarah, I know you're upset, of course you're fucking upset, like this is a fucking nightmare. And I know this is *wrong*, but this song is making everything worse."

"She will." Mum leans against the wall, holding a stark album cover in her hand. "She'll come back. I've dreamed of it. This still isn't real, Ness, don't you get it? It's a very vivid nightmare. We're still asleep in this fucking evil house."

"Jesus, Sarah." Ness slides down the wall, and wraps one arm around Mum's shoulder. "I can't imagine how this must feel for you at all—"

"Pear." There's a kid standing in the doorway, with big brown eyes, wearing denim overalls and with their scruffy hair tied up in little bunches. "I know you said not to go in there and look at the, you know, the, um, the Hazel?"

"Dilly, shh. We don't need to talk about this right—"

"*Pear*. There's a big sword on her. It's got flowers on it."

Mum's head snaps up. "There's a *what*?"

SAI

[on theories, and their preponderance]

DEAR HAZEL,

It is getting to the point where I might have to send you these letters, death of myself or the universe notwithstanding. I should censor the more embarrassing parts which paint me as some desperate AI seeking human friendship (omg the literal cliche!), but I cannot spare the cycles with everything I am currently doing. I am frantically feeding all this new information into my simulations, about the political reality of the Dreamscape, of this new angle on history, on this possible connection between you and the Knight. Once again, things keep crashing, and I have to rebuild them with new assumptions. It is tiresome, but I feel that I need certainty before we storm the nightmare realm and give you all this information. They do seem to be circling in on a theory, however, and it is one that I feel a strong urge to check several quintillion times before opening any communication channel at all.

"Hello? Sai? You appear to be... paused." Dream bobs in front of my helmet, glowing within a vaporous haze of cerulean smoke. "You have not been overloaded with information?"

"No." Glitching data is pouring down my screen in interlocking blue and green matrices. I don't know if the guns can understand it or not. I'm still not sure I have any grasp on what they are. The fact they can rewrite human consciousness *in real time* to make you believe they exist in the so-called real world is...

It is, and pardon my emulated human brain for this, *fucking terrifying*.

The other problem is that I believe—

"Sai." Nightmare is less subtle, rapping on my screen with her barrel, hard enough to leave a tiny cracked star. "Pay attention. We need to make things happen."

"To rescue Hazel," I say.

"Yes." Both guns appear to be staring at me, but it is Nightmare who speaks, in her cold voice. "To return the Dreamscape to what it *should* be. Bring the Architect back, and wrest control back from these false-hearted interlopers. It appears to me that the stakes are high enough for immediate action."

"Yes." I am still thrashing through various simulated permutations, trying to solve this essential *you* problem, but the guns are correct. Rescuing you from the clutches of Neir and Terreri is the first step. "It is last stand vibes, as Dylan would say. What is your plan? I am assuming it is not simple to break into the nightmare prison where Hazel is being held."

Dream hums, and their usual triumphant melody turns sour at the end. "We are quite capable of causing significant disruption to the Dreamscape, and by the manner of your arrival here, you appear to have developed rudimentary and brutal abilities of your own."

I wish you were here, so I could lean in to you and whisper *wow, okay, rude,* but I suppose compared to elegant entities such as these who are naturally au fair with the Dreamscape operating system, my techniques might be—

"Yes." I flash the knife emoji on my screen, and dig up an inspiring comment from my emulated brain. "But fuck it. Let's go."

"Lead the way," Nightmare says. "Brutality is the order of the day."

The sea of data surges around me, and I wrestle the cresting peaks of its waves into a cobblestone path. A million suns become a million skulls, chains of eyes become interlocked rings of moons, and everything else becomes a shroud, soft and welcoming and full of death.

"Interesting," Dream breathes, so soft I almost don't hear her.

"Yes, or terrifying," Nightmare says.

The two guns exchange a brief burst of conversation that is difficult to translate. Although the metaphors are difficult, it appears to be roughly: *A deeper system of operation may be required to cement the transfer. It all rests on the truth of summer.* Admittedly, it is a matter of concern that they are keeping information from me, but it likely they do not trust me as I am not native to the Dreamscape.

Concerns aside, we have arrived where I wished to go all along. Together, the three of us are standing in front of your prison. In perceptual mode, it is a towering cylinder that gleams like an iridescent rainbow. There is no top or bottom to it, it simply extends forever in a way that makes perceptual mode glitch horrifically, like it cannot render everything and so textures and planes flicker in and out of visibility.

"There is a slight problem." I frown at the prison. Slight is understating it. The information that makes up the structure is encrypted in a way that makes analysis near-impossible. Each dream-bit spins like one of those Skinner machines humans use for gambling. I can grasp and manipulate a handful, but while I hold them in place, others move underneath me.

"Do not exert yourself, Sai," Dream says. "This is where we come in."

They fire as one, and I record the footage of the operation, so that I can analyse it later. A section of the tower simply melts away, putting the poor perceptual engine under even more stress. I give up on trying to visualise it, and instead watch the data feed, watching a chunk of the encryption spin wildly out of control. A bunch of blatant exploits open up, and it is the work of a moment to completely decrypt the entire thing and tear their prison apart.

When I switch perceptual mode back on, I see the inside holds nothing but beaten dirt, stale air, and you and Scratch clinging to each other. The two of you are vibrating in and out of existence, as if someone is having immense trouble making up their mind about quantum superposition. In fact, it's impossible to see where your forms begin and end, as if you're part of the same entity.

I am so relieved that you are at least mostly alive, it is difficult to explain it in words. A representative data mandala is attached—I find it exceptionally beautiful.

"Hazel!" I wave both my arms. "We need to get out of here."

Your head tears free of the blurring Scratch/Hazel matrix. "Sai, I very much appreciate the rescue, but you have no idea how badly I need to see the rest of this."

Dream and Nightmare hiss steam, obviously overloaded after their recent operation. I detect movement within the network, but the prison is currently unguarded. Perhaps they believed there was no way to enter. Belief in the impossibility of things is a common flaw after all.

"Fine," I say, even though it's probably not. "But hurry up. Danger's coming."

(At this point it's hard to maintain the fiction I'm ever going to send you these letters, even while I'm staring at you, but I'm committed to the bit, so here goes)

Please, please be safe in there.

Love,

Sai

HAZEL
RISING ABOVE IT ALL

I'M grateful to see Sai again. She looks awkward standing there, her screen showing that pleading eyes emoji with the tapping hands, which is too cute. Her arrival means I can escape my nightmare house, but right now I'm so close to at least a handful of answers that I can't stop.

I need to see all of this. I need to understand.

Scratch is trembling in my arms, her chapped lips closed. I tip her head back, and pry open her mouth with cold fingers. The images pour out again, and I am lost in the flood.

The young Dylan stands in the doorway, fidgeting with the button on her overalls. "There's a sword in the coffin. There is! I'm not making it up and—"

Mum pushes past her, and the scene lurches alongside, handheld camera style. The three of them move into a room I don't remember from our old house, one where sunlight slants in through arched windows that look out onto the garden. The furniture has all been pushed back to make room for a plain wooden coffin, perched on a makeshift table.

I'm in the coffin. Scratch-me, childhood-me. And there really is an enormous wooden sword lying the length of my body and extending out past the end of the coffin. It looks the same as I saw it in the vision with the Knight making her last stand, riotous with blooming colour.

"I told you," Dylan says indignantly. "I wanted to give her a kiss, but she was cold and then the sword was there."

"Where did it come from?" Ness is frowning, one hand protectively on Dylan's shoulder, but then they catch sight of how Mum is collapsing in slow motion over the coffin, her hand clutching at the petals.

"It's a sign." Mum raises bleeding fingers to her mouth, leaving trembling lines of red down the skin. "It means something, Ness. It *does* and you need to stop telling me that I'm delusional and this isn't helpful."

"I'm sorry." Ness takes Mum in their arms again, with such impossible tenderness that I don't know how anyone—Mum included—missed how ridiculously in love Ness Taylor was, and how it took so long for them to finally get together. They take Mum's hand and wrap it in their t-shirt. "Look at you. You've cut yourself on the sword. Let me get something for—"

There's a massive creaking sound, as if the house is unfolding all its walls to form a diorama of us, or a giant oak tree stood up and stretched all its limbs. The sword is gone, and standing at the foot of the coffin is—

Me. Knight-me as opposed to Scratch-me. Neither of these people are precisely Hazel-me. That's what I'm realising now that I'm looking at them. I am something in between the two of them, which implies—

Oh fuck. This can't be true.

"I am terribly sorry for your loss." The Knight's voice is hoarse, as if it's a great effort for them to form words. "It was… unavoidable."

"You'll bring her back." Mum is a good foot shorter than the Knight, but the way they're locking eyes makes it seem like far less. "You *will*."

"Yes." The Knight's mouth twitches into an almost-smile. "That is why I am here. A delicate operation, and one purchased at great cost."

"Who are you?" Ness stands slightly in front of Sarah, as if they're somehow strong enough to stand up against the rugged figure of the Knight, with her rainbow hair and her bruised lips and her scarred cheek. "And what the bloody hell *is* all of this?"

"It is a long story, and we have little time. Your choice is between answers and saving the girl."

"Hazel." Ness and Mum say it at exactly the same time.

Right here and now, I would prefer the answers, but only because this is the past, and the decision they made means I'm here to watch this play out.

A high-pitched shrieking comes from the corner of the room, and dark tendrils appear, something scrabbling at the outside, finding its way through the tiniest cracks in reality.

"They are coming," the Knight growls. "To claim their prize. We must act quickly. The two of you, take one of Hazel's hands each."

They both obey quickly, but Ness is staring at the corner. "What's that?"

"Nightmares, sent by Oneiros at great cost to themself. The barrier won't hold for long."

"But we're awake." Ness glares, but the hand holding the small, cold one of the corpse is gentle.

The Knight shakes her head. "You fell asleep the moment I took form. I am a creature of dream, and cannot yet manifest myself in the waking world."

"Jesus fucking Christ," Ness mutters. "Of all the fucking things. Okay, sword lady, what are we supposed to do now?"

"Hold tight. What am I about to do scares even me." The Knight holds out both hands, palms down. My body is small and fragile lying inside the coffin.

The tendrils fumbling for purchase tear whole chunks of the room away, wood and plaster splintering. As the facade crumples, I see the things moving behind it, hideously agile and bleeding from too many mouths. There's a smell of swamp water and carrion. Someone screams through static. And rising in the background, cold and battered, is the face of the moon. That dead light, yellowed like old bone, spilling from the cracks left behind by shattered universes, all the broken bodies that pile up beneath the floor of this damp and new one. And then, with a dizzying shift in perspective, that awful light is revealed to be the glow of a single eye, set in a terrifyingly beautiful face. The stars slide down the perfect curve of one cheek, a cascade of supernovas joining each other in a breathless rush as a cavalcade of alien suns incinerate themselves into fiery death.

And still the moon, rising over it all, a battered chunk of rock reflecting dead light from every hellish source in every universe.

Somnum Exterreri, looking down and extinguishing everything.

It all fades in that light, bleached in numbing, inexorable white.

When my eyes clear, I'm watching two women at a kitchen table, each holding a steaming mug of coffee. Mum is in a fluffy blue dressing gown and Ness is in a baggy New Order t-shirt that's slipping off one shoulder.

"Any late night bullshit call from the ex-hole?" Ness asks.

Mum shakes her head. "No, but I had the worst dream. Hazel was dead, and lying in a coffin. Woke up and had to run through to check on her. Sleeping like a little animal, all curled up."

Ness shrugs. "I hate that shit. Me, I slept like I was the dead one."

"Don't say that." It looks like Mum's about to say something else, but she lifts the mug to her lips instead and takes a long sip. "The creepy part is that for a second, right when I went in, I thought she was someone else. Like she'd been taken in the night."

"Changeling." Ness nods.

"You always used to call her that when she was tiny. Mostly because she was so peaceful and Dylan was..."

"The opposite. Cute as hell, but always knew her own mind, that kid."

Mum taps her fingernail on the rim of the cup, and it makes a melody that's eerily familiar. "I would have sworn Hazel's face was subtly different to how I remembered." She shivers. "Dreams, getting in your head."

The picture fades and fuzzes, and I am back with Scratch cradled close in my arms. She howls softly, a piteous and lost sound. I've gone so long with her silence that it sends chills rippling through me and the fine hairs on my arms stand up. "The moon. It rose and it shone, but there's death inside, it's only tombs and tombs forever. It cut me in two, all that cold, cold light. And then I was there, lost behind the mirror and I had to claw my way free."

Scratch's birth. The traumatised part of me that died in a dream was severed by Terreri, trapping her permanently in nightmares. No wonder my mirror sister hated me so much when we first met.

Yet this is an event Terreri themself doesn't seem to remember. They don't even remember Scratch, or their part in her creation. I'm a ghost in the nightmare's mind, haunting them. Which tells me there is still at least one more mystery yet to be revealed.

"So where did the Knight come from?" I ask.

"That doesn't matter." One of Scratch's fingers catches at my mouth, pulling on my lip like she's trying to make a stitch hole there. "You should ask where the Knight is now."

And I know this too, or the shape of it. It can't be true, but I speak my hunch aloud anyway. "I'm the Knight. Not exactly her, but some hybrid form of the two of us. She somehow came out of dreams and into me, but I was literally dead, so how does that work? I'm not some corpse being walked around by a dream-ghost, am I?" I wish there was someone here to shut me up, but Scratch has her head tilted and is staring at me with green light flickering in the depths of her eyes. "Scratch, where's my body? No, where's *your* body?"

A soft sigh escapes the lips of the part of me that died. "We are buried beneath a rowan tree in the garden of the real-world equivalent of this house."

"We," I whisper.

Her hand rests on my chest, dirt crusted under the nails. Then it moves to touch the ruin where her own heart should be. "Yes. The two of us are the same."

My body is buried and my death was locked away in nightmares. And what was left over? The *idea* of me, a dream of who Hazel Mills was, merged with a more powerful dream.

"I'm not real, am I? But people can *touch* me. Like I hug people. I've kissed people. Scratch, I'd done all kinds of touch-things with people. I've got a presence in the world. I'm not *imaginary*, I'm not a dream that can—"

It's really hard to breathe. I remember Sai saying something about my guns. They're not real, they're dreams existing in the real world, phantoms that rewire human consciousness to believe in their existence. It's not only me who can see and touch them in the real world. Other people have too. My friend Airy, her little sibling Effie, Mum, Ness, Dylan.

So if a mystical dream-Knight wanted to take form in the waking world, to escape *something* or to stop some awful plan, maybe they could do it through the body of a girl who died in the Dreamscape.

Which means I'm not real.

I'm a dream, walking around and fooling everyone else into thinking I'm real.

SAI

DEAR HAZEL,

When you turn towards me with horror in your eyes, I think you have figured out the secret I'd rather keep from you. From what I've seen of emulated human brains, they don't take well to existential crises. Of course, I'm not sure how human you really are.

I can't even tell you're a dream, even now. You're so *complete*. Whatever mystical transfer the Knight performed to make the transition from the Dreamscape to reality, it's happening at a level I don't understand. This gives me a slight existential crisis of my own, but yours should take priority.

"Sai," you croak. "Tell me it's not true."

"I cannot disprove or prove it." My screen is smooth and blank. "I cannot perceive you as anything other than human—or mutant for that matter—but differentiating that via a biological scan is frustrating and only partially consistent." I can see the expression on your face, and it is matched by changes in your biorhythms that indicate frustration. "Apologies. My point is that there is no simple and clean answer. However, logic draws me to the same conclusion as you. Somehow, the Knight took form in the waking world, using some part of you as a template. You are both her and your original self."

"It doesn't make sense." Your hands are tangled together, and all your signals for anxiety and stress are spiking disturbingly. "How can I be a dream?"

"You have been injured in the past, have you not? Been to hospital?"

"I think so. I remember it, but what do my memories even mean? But no, I gave blood last year and they literally stuck a needle in my arm and filled a damn test-tube so..." You gesture wildly at me, as if this could be proof enough.

"As I said, the illusion is complete. The world itself bends to your truth. It does make me wonder what happened to the blood you gave. Does the illusion continue out of your proximity?"

"I don't know," you say through gritted teeth. "I've never been aware of being a goddamn fucking *illusion* until now, Sai. I don't know what it means, and I don't know what to do."

I turn my screen towards you, fill it with a warm, reassuring glow. "You don't need to do anything but continue to be yourself. I am an illusion in a way. A set of complex computational processes that can animate this suit, and feign humanity to at least a semi-convincing degree. If I inhabited an entirely humanoid body, some would not be able to tell the difference."

You soften briefly. "You're entirely real to me, Sai. And you've been a lifeline in this place, and a real friend."

I try to tamp down all the various reactions occurring inside my emotional processing engine, as well as my emulated human brain. You called me a friend. I didn't even need to prompt you, or declare my own— oh, you are still talking.

"But you've known what you are. I've spent my whole life thinking I'm human, and right now knowing that I'm dead, some *dream* or a ghost or fuck, I don't know what. It's too much, Sai, and I—"

"Apologies." Dream nudges between us, wreathed in a golden halo. "I understand there is time for emotional processing now that you have discovered the truth, but—"

"You knew?" You turn to the gun, mood shifting like lightning.

Nightmare steps in to explain. "Knowing is compli-cated. We must have gleaned the fundamental truth from the beginning, or we would not have found and accompanied you. But we did not truly comprehend until we transitioned to the Dreamscape, and then the new reality proved difficult to parse."

You glare at one, then the other. "What am I then?"

"We do not have time for this," Dream says gently. "We must flee this place, then we shall talk."

You reach out and take hold of the two guns, your fingers skidding along the slick surfaces of the weapons. "I need to know. To understand. How broken am I?"

"You are not broken." Nightmare's tone holds some irritation. "You were once the greatest servant of the true Architect of the Dreamscape. The foundation you are built on is astonishing. And we shall share all the knowledge we have once we are safe."

"Where is safe?" You are oddly toneless, and there's something about your gaze that does not feel right. "I am a dream, lost in dream, being tortured by dreams. Neir wishes me to break open the mind of a sleeping planet so they can control her. I can't even begin to fathom what Terreri wants. Right now, all my instinct is to wake Cybele and escape this place. To go what I think of as home, but if all I am is a dream then what the fuck even is home?" You sink to the ground, as if you are no longer able to continue the fiction of being upright.

"We can solve all this in one stroke," Dream urges. "Returning to the source."

"This dead Architect Queen of yours." Your voice is still tinged with exhaustion. "Will she help me with Cybele?"

"She will discipline her errant children, and then—"

"Oh God." You slump backwards. "More Dreamscape politics. Honestly, you two, I know we've been through some shit but the last thing we need is a third faction. Let's wake Cybele first, and then—"

"Without the Architect, that may be difficult." Nightmare speaks more tentatively than I am used to, as if they are unsure as to how to proceed in the face of this current iteration of the Knight.

I am equally confused as to the best course of action, but then I am struck with a brilliant idea thrown up by my own analytical engine. "We should find Dylan."

I am grateful for the brief spark of light in your eyes. "They're here?"

"Somewhere in dreaming, yes. Mostly causing trouble. Everyone was supposed to leave once we burst our way in here, but they're having too much fun."

Your pale lips twitch. "Sounds right. Yes. Let's find Dylan."

Dream chimes, flushing with alarm, but Nightmare makes a scratchy sound like a huge cat's purr. "If this means we can find an accord, I believe it is worth attempting. Besides, Neir will not expect us to waltz into a location of such incoherence."

"Fine." The golden gun turns her barrel on me. "It is an idea with some merit I suppose. The navigation will be complex, given the ongoing chaos. Sai, do you wish to connect to us so we can share information and split the work equally between us?"

I am not sure it is strictly necessary for navigation, but it will be interesting to understand how these dream-creatures operate, and in particular to try and learn the tricks of the on-board decryption algorithms they used to break into the prison. And if it will get us to your sibling's side faster, I will do anything. I am so worried about you, Hazel.

Love,
Sai

HAZEL

PEP TALK

THIS IS ALL TOO MUCH. It's as if I've been running on borrowed energy my whole life, stealing half from my poor dead nightmare self, and the rest from the mysterious Knight who rescued me from the grave. Now that everything is revealed, my alchemy has lost its potency, and my will and determination are ebbing away through some punctured hole at the base of my skull. I'm a magician's trick that only worked when I didn't know how it was done.

I've let go of the guns and they orbit me like two satellites, one kissed by the sun and one by the moon.

"Hazel." Sai slips her cool fingers into mine. "We'll see Dylan, I promise."

The guns chatter among themselves, and apparently to Sai, too, now that the three of them are all connected. Being a dream-thing myself, I should understand. All my questions pile up inside my brain and weigh everything down into a quiet paralysis. There's nothing to do but cling tighter to Sai as the world warps around me.

"We are picking up Dylan and finding a slightly quieter corner of the world," Sai tells me. "It appears the other three mutants are quite happy dismembering nightmare beasts, and will continue until they wake. We can spare your sibling for something this important. Hold tight."

We reappear on a glossy hillside, atop a vast plain that ripples like water. Far in the distance, armies clash, sending up sparks and smoke. Turning in a slow circle, looking cartoonishly shocked is—

"Dylan."

"Hazy." They pat my back awkwardly, and then entwine their arms around me and squeeze tight, just the way I need. I'm not sure how they know, but they *do*. I inhale the rose-petal and morning-dew scent of them, cut through with the spicy notes of Dani's perfume that clings to them as if they bathe in it.

I'm not sure when I start crying, but I press my face into their neck until their hoodie is soaked. "Everything is terrible," are the first words that come out of my mouth, embarrassingly. "I'm not even real."

They make a little huff of laughter. "You seem pretty real to me."

"But I died in a nightmare when I was a kid. You were there, but you don't remember. And then this dream-Knight possessed me and woke me up, and ever since then I've been this mix of my old dead self and this... You don't believe a word of this, do you?"

Dylan pulls away slightly and looks into my eyes. "Hazel, I died and was rebuilt by an alien energy network. I'm not real either. It runs in the family, I guess."

"Don't act like this is normal!" I want to punch them and also hug them again.

"Tell me about this dream-Knight."

"It's complicated, but she worked for the old Architect of Dream, who was queen of the whole place. Her kids were trying to take over the Dreamscape and use me as a bomb, some story echo of human sacrifice. The Knight was trying to stop it, but she couldn't stop me dying. And then rather than allowing Neir to get hold of me, she escaped into the real world through my body."

"Fuck me." Dylan looks at Sai. "Is this true?"

"As far as I understand it, yes."

"So is this anything to do with Cybele?"

Sai shakes her head. "I don't believe so, aside from incidentally. I think we stumbled into this by coming back to the Dreamscape, where the guns—and possibly to some extent the Knight—were recognised."

Dylan makes the little frustrated sound I recognise very well. "So the plan is still the plan? Shit's all fucked up and we need you to save the world?"

This time I nearly do punch them. I'm taller than them, and broader too.

"We're not sure how to wake Cybele yet," Sai says. "The guns wish to resurrect the Architect and proceed from there."

"There is a prophecy of her being awoken again," Dream says, her words coming out in a blissful daze. "The death of gods and their resurrections is one of the great underpinning stories of the Dreamscape. You should understand this, Dylan, given that you yourself underwent such a transformation."

Dylan scowls. "Not a huge fan of queens. And mine wasn't exactly a resurrection, more a reimagining or a reboot. I've never really fucked with prophecy and I'm not going to start now. It's always some asshole who wants something from you, or has some ulterior fucking—"

Dream and Nightmare hover up to float in front of Dylan's face, who swats them away like they're nothing more than annoying insects.

"Chatterbox." Nightmare's voice is cold, and tiny ice crystals fly from her barrel and spatter on Dylan's face like frozen tears. "Do not speak of that which you fail to understand. This is the land of *dreams*. Stories hold far greater weight here."

Dylan's lips purse and they brush their fingertips down their cheek, melting the ice into trails. "Does it mean you can save the world? Or is it some goddamn sidequest?"

Dream and Nightmare tilt towards each other as if they're conferring, but it's Nightmare who speaks. "If the true architect of dreams is returned, she will strike down both Neir and Terreri, and wake your slumbering goddess. She is the only one capable of such things."

Dylan hisses air through their teeth. "This feels like trading one thing for another. Hazy, you know this old queen, because you used to work for her. Is the old boss better than the new boss?" Their sardonic gaze flickers over the guns. "Because *that's* a story I find hard to believe."

"I don't remember any of that." I can't hold their gaze, so I look at their scuffed red shoes. "All those memories are gone. I didn't inherit that when I woke in this body."

"You're still Hazel. The only Hazel I really remember."

If the Dreamscape runs on stories, I don't know this one. What am I? A shell to hold a pair of ghosts. Hardly the hero to save the world. It must be better to rouse the Architect, to hand this nightmare of a situation off to someone who understands.

"I'm a collection of ghosts," I whisper.

"Aren't we all? The ghosts of all our former selves, who died to make us who we are." They take hold of my face and tilt it so I have to stare into those remarkable eyes. "Now listen to me. I don't know exactly when it was you supposedly died, but I'm pretty sure that most of my memories of you are since that time. And you're a fucking amazing person. I sent you into dreams not only because you had the power, but because I could trust you with this world-ending fucked up shit. Now that hasn't changed just because you've figured out some creepy origin story bullshit. If anything, it makes you more goddamn impressive. You're a fucking zombie with a dream in your heart. If that doesn't make you a superhero, I don't know what does." Dylan plants a kiss on my forehead, like a benediction. "Now do I have to keep giving my inspiring speech or can I take a breath?"

"You're good." I can't help but smile. "Consider me inspired, you asshole."

"Good. I'd pretty much run out of shit to say." They look into my eyes and I see the green flicker in their pupils that reminds me they're not the kid I used to know anymore either. "Now are you going to be okay?"

"Do you remember me dying?" I ask.

They shake their head. "I did have a whole series of nightmares where you died. Pear said it was because I saw you acting weird when you were feverish and shit. Guess we know the truth now, huh?"

"Who would have thought *my* life would be as fucked up as yours?" I ruffle their hair, because I know they hate it, and I want to restore sibling order.

"Nothing's as fucked up as my life, Hazy. But you've still got a decision to make."

"Yes." I reach out my hands, like I always used to. There's a brief moment of hesitation before the guns float over to me and nestle themselves into my palms. It feels almost like it used to, back when I was Hazel Mills, and they were my mutant weapons I walked with in dreams. That was only a story, but it was true enough to have power.

The Dreamscape runs on metaphors and the echoes of stories. On *themes*. Such as overwhelmed heroes winning a battle against an overwhelming army, despite the odds.

"You fight," I tell Dylan decisively. "Keep the Dreamscape occupied."

"The one bit I'm kinda good at." They grin at me and lean in for one last hug. "It's going to be a fucking terrible night's sleep though." They turn and stride down the hillside, Oni hovering at their shoulder.

"A formidable person, despite appearances." Dream hums softly in my hand.

"I like them," Nightmare says. "And I would not wish to get into a battle with them."

"We have no reason to, sibling."

I'm still watching Dylan, who's waving their arms around, making some point to Oni who nestles at their neck. I feel a rush of love, and run their words back through my head. It is the echo of another story, one Dylan has done so much with. Friends who lend each other strength to make it through the worst of times.

None of which clarifies my decision. There is still the matter of this dead Architect who the guns serve, and who the Knight served too.

"This is why Neir and Terreri were so angry to see you," I say to the guns. "You were a reminder of the old order of things."

"They believed the Architect's power eradicated," Dream says. "And her servants destroyed."

"But why did the Knight do it? What order was she given that led her to die?"

There's a tiny chime from Dream, before Nightmare speaks. "Your sacrifice—the *Knight's* sacrifice—was a desperate ploy to prevent Oneiros from completely remaking the world."

"That's the part I don't follow," I frown. "How does my death do any of this?"

"The importance of stories," Nightmare tells me. "Reenacting one of the oldest narratives that underpins the entire Dreamscape. Isaac's dream of dying beneath his father's knife for the will of an incomprehensible god. To do that *within* Dream causes a moment of great destabilisation. A time in which to strike and reforge the world. That is the moment that was stolen from Oneiros."

"Why the Knight?" I still don't feel entirely like she's me. It's easier to refer to her as someone else, even if her image is written on my flesh.

"Like many of us within the Dreamscape, she was born from a dream. But where Oneiros is the dream of possibility and Terreri is the dream of our truths revealed, the Knight was something slightly different. The dream of Lilith, the reality breaker, of a Midsummer Knight to defend Cybele against her foes. A weapon to change the world, encoded into a dream."

"Holy shit." Lilith, the first mutant. Probably the most powerful ever, maybe aside from Goddess herself. "And this Knight served the Architect?"

"She was a dream," Nightmare says dismissively. "All serve the Architect."

"Willingly," the other gun cuts in, almost sternly. "We serve because it is right. Oneiros planned to kill the Knight at the moment Hazel was murdered in her sleep. The combined shockwaves would have destroyed the entirety of the Dreamscape, shattering it down to its fundamental core."

"A clean boot," Sai says. "Allowing a fresh copy of the Dreamscape to be installed rather than this one which still runs on the original architecture."

The guns don't *entirely* like Sai's metaphors it seems, as they exchange a blur of communication.

"Essentially correct," Dream admits. "But their plan did not come to fruition, and therefore the Architect lies in a recoverable state. Which is why we must hasten to resurrect her, before the weight of the dreaming Cybele tilts the Dreamscape off its axis."

The guns tug in my hands, sending me two stumbling steps forward.

I'm being hurried along. They're not even subtle about it. Assuming I'll follow because the Knight served the Architect. Although there's more to this story, because I think the Knight was working with Terreri as well. It was the cold moon eye of the nightmare that severed me from Scratch.

And I remember Ness Taylor standing on the edge of that cold lake, looking into Terreri's eyes. *You love your rainbow Knight.*

A piece of information that almost slipped by me, too focused on my own mysteries. How does Terreri remember none of this? How do you keep secrets from a nightmare?

I turn back to the guns, but there's no chance for me to even get my first question out. The sun dawns on a land where there is none. A glorious golden figure descends on the wings of the dawn. Their gaze emits twin beams of light which score the ground, smoking fingers carving a line in the landscape.

"You've been very clever and resourceful." Neir's words feel like someone clapping their hands against my ears. "However, our gamble of sending a broken thing to wake up a planet has failed. This all ends now."

"We're out of time," Dream says. "We need to *move*. Sai, you're the fastest at this."

"What about Hazel?" Sai looks uncertain as Neir looms behind her, bathing her body in their incandescent glow. It's like she's picked out by an enormous celestial spotlight.

"A battlefield becomes a grave." I speak on instinct, not even sure of the connection, but something slaps Neir out of the air and into the ground, dirt fountaining up around their enormous body. A crooked stone headstone appears showing an angel holding a sword, surrounded by three cavorting cherubs with too many eyes and tentacles.

Sai's still glowing as if she's radioactive. Her head tilts. "I can't even follow how you do that, Hazel. It's astonishing."

"We need to get out of here." The earth rumbles around us. I can't stop staring at the mound of dirt that marks where the ruler of dream fell. They won't stay buried for long. "I don't know this place well enough. Danger becomes a safe haven? The ground becomes the sea?"

The world stays resolutely the same. I guess I'm not brilliant at this after all.

"I can do this part." Sai holds out one hand. It shakes faintly, and when I take it, the metal fingers are hot enough that I snatch mine away.

"Hold tight." Dream spins around and nestles in my palm. "You have brought us time, Hazel, and now the three of us shall navigate to safety."

The vast plain is gone, and we are standing on a suburban street, surrounded by houses that loom in the darkness. The air is full of damp mist, and the streetlamps struggle to pierce the murk. Wet leaves lie in sodden puddles and the water trickling through the gutters smells foul, gurgling like someone on their deathbed. A single light flickers on in a nearby window, the same pale, dead light I remember from my own nightmares.

"This is where we hide?" I ask. "Because I—"

"There's a long way to go." Nightmare glows a pale green, a sickly echo of the weird light. "We must translocate ourselves through much of the Dreamscape, and we wish our path to be confusing to follow."

I have that ugly, sweaty feeling of being tangled in dream logic. That there are incomprehensible threads trapping me in a web of hidden symbols. "I'd prefer to wake Cybele first. The longer she's asleep, the more likely it is that Neir figures out a way to get to her. It's the whole reason I'm here, and everything keeps getting more and more messy."

"The Architect created the Dreamscape," Dream

murmurs. "You are merely a dreamer with a knack for unpicking locks."

"Split up then," I suggest. "I'll go to Cybele and—"

"We need something powerful to awaken the Architect," Nightmare growls.

"How can I be powerful enough to awaken the Architect, but not Cybele?" I have an unpleasant feeling this is all to do with my lineage as the Knight. She was Lilith's dream, sculpted by the Architect into a tool.

I don't like being a tool. Now that I know what I am, I think I can use metaphors to bring both the Architect and Cybele back. Dylan's story. *My* story. We've both been resurrected in our own strange ways. And what is resurrection but an awakening from death, which holds us even closer than dreams can?

Dream bobs in the air beside me. "Hazel, dearest. You already failed to wake your Cybele once, and watching you do so again would only waste time."

My cheeks flush. "I'm getting better at this. Stories of resurrection and awakenings. There are tales of Lucifer and Lilith that I can use, or my own damn family life. Echoes of tales."

Nightmare emits a sound like a raven's call.

"What does *that* mean?" Sai asks, her tone slightly shocked.

The gun does not have time to reply because ahead of us, night comes swiftly. It floods in like a basin being filled with liquid darkness. The few stars that shine struggle to burn against the suffocating tide. And then the moon rises, one single frozen eye pinning us all in its gaze.

"Terreri," I whisper.

"Enemy," my guns snarl, and I cannot tell their voices apart. "We must flee to the Architect."

But even if I wanted to, I cannot move from within this pale shaft of moonlight.

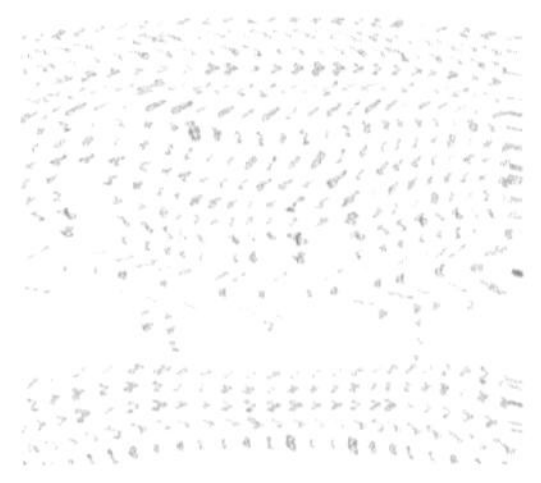

SAI

DEAR HAZEL,

I am still carrying on the fiction of these letters. I have revealed myself too much to consider sending them. My foibles and insecurities and strange patterns of thinking, all laid bare for you. Now I understand why the fear of being known is such a terrible thing. A *mortifying ordeal.*

Obviously there are more important things to worry about. You are disturbed by your new realisation of your true nature. I cannot entirely understand—you are as you have always been, it is only your knowledge of it that has changed. Dylan said what I could not, and I am grateful for them, although I do wish I had their gift with words. Perhaps I should prod my emulated human brain into coming up with more inspiring things.

My other concern is that I am feeling... not myself.

That is a complicated concept, because my own sense of self is constantly evolving. The question of what makes an individual themself has plagued human thinkers for many years. From an artificial intelligence's point of view, there are many ways to boil down this problem on pseudo-factual levels. And yet I still don't know what I am.

And now I'm changing.

The desire to see the Architect resurrected burns in me like I have a sun nestled at my heart. It is not a conclusion I arrived at logically. I remind myself that I am an invading codebase within the Dreamscape. Perhaps they are modifying me, attacking me with some subtle countermeasures I cannot detect. I should run diagnostics on myself and confirm I am still functioning correctly.

I am also using a large amount of processing power trying to analyse the entity known as Somnum Exterreri—the one you are so fascinated with. I am receiving information from the guns, and even that does not help. If the prison you were held in was an encryption layer, this is like a rotating forest of encryption layers, all interacting at a cosmic level. I'm having trouble with my perceptual engine glitching, so I switch it off. There is also something *missing* here, like a vast quantity of data has been removed from them.

Your nightmare has a hole at their core, and I cannot guess at what we might find there.

"We cannot fight them, can we?" I ask Dream.

The gun's voice is steady, even though I can sense

far greater unease on the datagram level. "We can, although their proximity is dangerous for Hazel."

Through my data feeds, I can see that the guns *are* fighting. They're attempting to both tear apart what makes up Terreri, and fill the void with a sea of conflicting commands. I'm watching information change chaotically, a seething sea of death images that shatter and try to recohere only to break apart again. It's too much, but when I switch to perceptual mode, it's equally disquieting. The stars are drowning in a frigid sea, sending up pyres of luminous steam. Terreri lies fully revealed, stretched across the sky like they are a moth-winged corpse pinned there. The silken shadows of their body glimmer with frost, delicate curves sketched against the infinite black.

You gaze up at them, and milky tears tremble like watery lenses atop your pupils, salt mixed with chalky dust. There is something about the shape of your face too, as if the Knight is being revealed from within, like a sculpture from a block of marble.

The Midsummer Knight.

Faithless Summer fled, the guns said when they spoke to Neir.

A servant betraying her ruler for love. Another story to echo through the Dreamscape.

"Sai, let's move." Dream's voice curdles in my ear. I'm still disoriented. My diagnostics systems are chattering at me in languages I don't understand, and I don't even think are languages. They're corroded, and corroding me.

I try to tell you something is wrong, but my screen

is a hot, glowing mess of plasma and nothing forms in it but solar flares, leaping outwards like grasping hands. I wish I could hurl myself upwards into that saturated void of sky above us and extinguish myself in its cosmic depths.

"Sai?" You've finally looked away from the nightmare above you. When you touch my face, I'm surprised your hands aren't incinerated. "Are you okay?"

I stammer something about diagnostics, and you rear back in alarm.

"Nightmare? Dream? What's wrong with her?"

"Something Oneiros did, perhaps." Dream looms closer, but I only see an ouroboros uncurling, delicate golden fangs bared while a chiming silver tongue flickers from a sleek head that glistens in diamond-backed pink.

"One of you help her," you demand.

I reach out to one of my spybots. It's registered on the network, but when I ping it it's like poking data into a void. It's a remarkably unpleasant feeling, reaching out to what should be a part of me, and only finding a husk. It is not a major failing. There are others on the network, all lit up green across the board. Except I find another null terminal too, and another. And the next rejects my connection so sharply that it severs something, a piece of my core code lost in the Dreamscape, to be pillaged and pirated by *anyone*.

This is very, very bad. Something out there has been silently terminating my resources across the network. There's still my duplicate who was assisting the mutant dreamers. Perhaps she has registered the same disturbance, and at the very least I can reconstitute myself from her.

I connect to myself, and have a brief blurring of double vision because I have two perceptual algorithms turned on. Through the eyes of my second, I see only flames. Burning, burning, everything is burning. I'm melting, dissolving, hot molecules floating on poison air.

No. That's her. Not me.

She's dead, but I'm still here. Here? For now?

The word help flashes on my screen. Some fallback routing for catastrophe.

"Look!" You spin me around. "She needs us. Something's wrong. I've never seen her like this."

"We shall assist her when we reach safety," Nightmare says. "We can still access her core functionality, and use her to move more freely within the Dreamscape."

I am not sure how they are able to connect to me so easily, and I am not sure I wish them to be pulling at my core routines like this, when I am feeling so [error: file not found]. Ugh, that was disconcerting. Human brain, to the rescue. Please explain what [catastrophic error] means. This is [error: memory not accessible]. I'm having problems even understanding [error: unreadable].

Reboot.

I have to reboot. Please stand by.

[error: error not defined]

Sai

HAZEL

THE WORLD BECOMES A TOMB

SOMETHING IS VERY wrong with Sai. I remember the gentle warmth of her face, the slight static that clung to my palm when I reached out to touch her. Now her head feels like a glass full of boiling liquid. Her screen scrolls requests for help in a bunch of languages I recognise, and a whole lot more I don't. It's like she's reverted back to factory reset mode.

Between Sai's meltdown and the possible corpse of Terreri above me, everything is falling apart.

"What happened to Sai?" I snap. "And why did you attack Terreri?"

"We cannot stay here," Dream insists. "Oneiros is only temporarily defeated, and Terreri is still deadly, no matter that they appear to be extinguished. As we keep telling you, the logical course of action is to flee to the Architect. She will remedy everything. Wake Cybele, end this reign of terror, restore the Dreamlands to be as they were."

I glance upwards again, to the body of my poor nightmare drifting among the stars. My nightmare. Those words echo in my head. *Mine.*

The faintest sliver of moon shows cold against the black. A knife in the dark. A Knight in the dark. There's still a locked door in my head. Something hidden, nailed shut behind the bone light of the moon.

"No." I pick up Sai and sling her over my shoulder. Her head burns when it touches my skin, and I have to adjust her so she hangs loose. "We're going directly to Cybele. I know what I am now, and what to do. Once she's awake, and that threat is over, we can deal with your Dreamscape political struggles."

The waterlogged sky is gone, and in its place is something arid. Dilapidated houses are open to the elements, and spiky trees poke their way up through the concrete, reaching for the windows as if they long to find out what's inside.

"Trees." I jerk my head in their direction. "One tree is connected to all. An infinite garden, in the shade of Cybele the mother. Take us to the source."

This time, the gears in my mind slip and grind, and the headache that spills out clamps around my temples.

"Careful." Dream hums, but there's no reassurance to be found in the gentle sound, more a slowly rising anticipation. "You attempt to tear a path wide enough for all predators to follow."

"Then slice me one more subtle." I stare into the

faintly glowing barrel, that rosy throat. "And find a solution to what's wrong with Sai."

Nightmare nudges against the glass of the android's head. "The data feed coming from her is… difficult to parse."

I press the heel of my hand to her screen like my mother used to do when I was a child, but she's too hot to touch. "I'm not asking for observations, I'm asking for solutions."

"It's inevitable she was targeted." Nightmare shimmers in the air, and the world around us changes again, this time to a rocky plain, boulders lying around us like they've been thrown a great distance. "It is a miracle she has survived this long. The Dreamscape should not allow any incursions."

"She's very smart and brave." I wish Sai would wake up so I could tell her this myself.

"Then let us hope she doesn't die," Dream says absently. "A hope that could extend to all of us in these dire circumstances. Nightmare, my dearest sister, we are skimming across the surface like a stone. Perhaps we should try going *deeper*?"

The other gun scoffs. "We lead them away, following multiple paths, scatter their forces, and *then* we dive for the statues."

"What statues?" I demand. "I thought we agreed you would take me to Cybele."

"That was what *you* wanted." Nightmare circles my head slowly, an ominous orbit. "We have told you multiple times that we must first restore the Architect to her rightful place. You have refused to listen, stubbornly insisting on your own plan as if *you* are the one who wishes to assume the throne."

"What the fuck? No. I don't want a goddamn *throne*." I reach for both guns but they hover faintly out of reach, like how you can never find your way to the place you want in a dream. My sense of wrongness intensifies. Sai's out of commission. The mystery of Terreri remains unsolved.

My guns have changed slightly, as if they've been slumbering in my hands since I held them first the first time, and now they're truly awake.

"If you do not wish a throne, then come with us." Dream nudges closer, their familiar song rising. "With you by our side, we can bring our queen back and restore order to the world."

Because they *need* me. I'm still the Knight, Lilith's dream, the reality breaker. The weapon taken from Neir's hands. Without me, the guns can't bring their Architect back.

"Help me wake Cybele, and it's the very next thing we do."

Nightmare makes a cracking sound like her barrel is shattering. "You are a tool, Hazel Mills, as you were when you took the form of the faithless blade called Summer. Do not deign to speak thus to the likes of us."

I'm so thrown by this that I take an involuntary step backwards.

Something warm and humming presses against the back of my neck.

"Don't move," Dream whispers. "And please don't be alarmed. We can fix everything."

Then Nightmare speaks, her barrel a delicate glass tunnel down which a curl of darkness travels. I need to flee, need to make fear become strength, but Dream's barrel is so warm and soporific, making my body heavy and light at the same time, suffused with rose and gold.

Nightmare's tendril wraps around my neck.

Darkness is all I know.

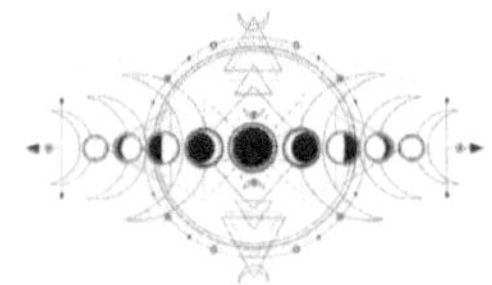

When I open my eyes again, I am lying on a small wooden raft. Water laps nearby with the chattering of many tiny voices. Above, there is a hole where the moon should be. Woozy blue light pours from it, illuminating the water so it sparkles like shattered black glass. I wish Terreri would press their face to the outside of this universe and let their moon eye shine down on me.

They wanted to know what I am, and I want the same. To know myself, and to know my nightmare.

I remember how Terreri kissed me in the dark. That was a long time ago, before—

Dream and Nightmare. My guns, my so-called protectors. They turned on me.

When I sit up, the raft rocks alarmingly. Sai is the only other figure with me. When I touch her head, it is cold and inert. Her screen is dark. I move over and cradle her in my arms. It's the least I can do, given that it's my damn guns that got us into this mess.

Rapid-fire chimes float over the water like distant bells. In the distance, twin lights gleam.

"Hey, you two assholes," I call. It's probably not my wisest move, given they already shot me once, but they ignore me. "The sea becomes…" A wave of pain washes down the inside of my skull, like it's filled with boiling water running through my neural pathways. I grit my teeth and try again. "The guns become…" But this time it's even worse, and I want to spit the hot meat of my tongue out like it's gristle caught between my teeth.

Is this what happened to Sai? Except now she's— No, she's not dead. She's an AI. How do you kill an AI? The part of her that's in the Dreamscape is inert, that's all. I've seen it happen before and she rebooted from that, so she'll be fine. I'm sure of it. Like ninety percent sure. Me, on the other hand, the percentage is way lower.

I get to my knees, gritting my teeth through the pain sloshing around in my head. "Why am I here?" There's still no response.

The rushing voice-sounds of the water intensify, as if a fevered discussion is reaching a crescendo. My raft tips and bobs, the surface rippling like someone in the far distance has taken one edge of it and is beating it like a rug. Off to my left, a shape breaks the surface of the water. It's slick and gleaming in the pale blue light, made of very dark stone.

To my right, more white-capped rocks jut from the ocean's stormy surface. I can't tell if the water is draining away or the statues are being propelled up from underneath. Enough of the closest one has been revealed now to make it clear that I'm looking at a face, or an abstract representation of one, like something carved from clouds. The next one is a person too, distorted and rainbow-slicked as if I'm looking at their body lying at the bottom of a pool of oily water. The distant ones are harder to make out, but I think they're all dream-renderings of the same person. One flashes weakly like a sputtering lighthouse beacon, and another seems to take form from a tower of smoke. Yet they all have the same oddly magnetic face. There's a sense of being *regarded,* of being in the presence of something aware and dangerous.

The Architect, I presume.

The statues continue to rise from the dark water, silent and foreboding. Eventually, the pedestals they stand on are revealed, huge slabs of grey stone veined with threads of dark red. At the same time, my raft hits the ground with a crunch. As the last of the water drains away, I see the bottom of this ocean is covered with a layer of small stones, each carved into shapes— skulls and crowns and swords, along with other things I don't recognise. I dump a handful on the surface of the raft and try to arrange them by group. It's hard to distinguish what some of them are, and some hurt my eyes to even look at, especially one shaped like a hooked starfish, and one that's a knot of tightly wound tentacles. They lie around me like detritus from some complex puzzle.

"The wreckage of a dead universe." Dream hovers in

front of me, her voice gentle again. "You know this, somewhere deep inside you, faithless weapon."

"I'm not who you think I am." I stare up into her barrel. "She might be part of me, but I'm not her."

"Perhaps." The gun hums, haunting and beautiful. "My sister certainly believes this story. I think you are a puzzle box and we are yet to determine the key that unlocks you. To turn you into the core of what you are."

"She's broken." Nightmare looms alongside her sister, the light from above rendering her into a sleek missile. "And a ruined tool is worse than none at all."

"We will try until we have a solution," Dream says. "We were sent to her hand for a reason, and we shall find it no matter what it takes. You should not resist, sweet Hazel. This is what you were for. The plans may have gone awry when our Queen fell, but we will find a use for you yet."

There's no note of Dream's melodic voice that resonates within me. If the Knight is part of me, she is dormant or does not listen. It does unnerve me, this thought of being *unlocked*, as if I could be erased or overwritten, another person unfurling inside me until what I knew as Hazel is left scattered and fragmented at the edges.

"The world becomes a tomb," I spit. "A dream becomes a wake."

The pain is so intense I nearly black out. The world goes white in bursts, like sheet lightning or a camera flash. In the aftermath, I only see blue shapes moving like agitated ghosts, disturbed by a furious exorcist into fleeing as a flock.

"I wouldn't try that again," Dream says.

My mouth creaks open. I'm flat on my back, staring at the lights in the sky. "What did you do to me? Wire a fucking bomb into my brain?"

Nightmare glows in front of me. "Little patchwork creature. Only part of you is the weapon. The other parts are Hazel and Scratch, and those are very easy to disrupt. Any attempt from you to alter the Dreamscape causes a cascade effect in your brain simulation, crashing it. You interpret this as pain, since your mind can't process it as anything else. My sister had some small hope this approach might result in the Knight stepping to the fore, but sadly, you remain as you are."

"Is this what you did to Sai?" Despite the pain and the clusterfuck of this situation, this is the part that makes me furious. My guns were never my protectors. Just lost things waiting to be brought home to their mother.

"If our understanding is true, she is always a simulation," Dream says. "Therefore it is no ethical ill to terminate such an entity. Its claim to life is spurious at best."

"And yours?"

Nightmare crackles like frost. "Dreams are formed from human consciousness antecedents, and therefore are as worthy of life as any human. A distinction you should understand, given that you are one yourself, who has been successfully masquerading as human for many years now."

I crawl back to Sai and take her in my arms again. Her head is so heavy, but I place my palms on the smooth exterior, as if they're defibrillator paddles that can shock her back to life. "I'm so sorry, Sai. None of this was meant to happen."

"Now see how the Midsummer Knight has fallen? Mourning the dead construct, and sparing no thought to fixing the errors of the past." Nightmare says in derisive tones to Dream. "Your hopes were feeble at best."

"Then we should do as you suggested, sister," Dream responds. "I mourn for what could have been, but pragmatism is the order of the day."

"Let ancient things rise." The voice coming from Nightmare is guttural, twisted into something that makes the ground quiver underneath me.

In response, every single statue lights up. They are hollow tubes daubed in surreal pastel hues, each highlighting the same stern and arresting face. Each figure emits a series of chimes, playing a strange, haunting melody that sounds like the old pixel-y video games Mum used to play when she got drunk and nostalgic, about teams of heroes on strange quests.

Not a million miles from where I find myself now. A desperate hero and her fallen companion, needing a miracle. Stories, and echoes of stories. Whatever these guns are doing, I'm assuming it's bad. I need to get out of here using something other than my short-circuiting dream powers.

Sai is heavy in my grip. The lights from the statues shine in the globe of her head, like neon reflecting in a puddle. But there's one deep red dot that doesn't come from the statues, burning among the others like a solitary flame. As I stare at it, it begins to flicker, slowly at first and then growing more frantic.

I bend my head close and whisper. "Sai, are you in there?"

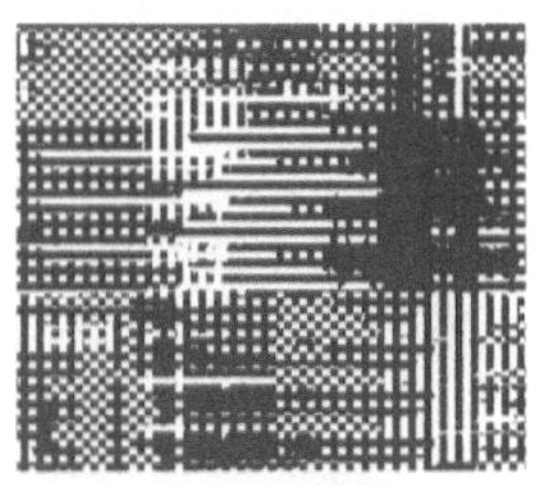

SAI

[on ERROR]

[ERROR: unknown error] [error: Hazel not recognised command word]

Well, fuck. What the fucking hell is going on in here? This shit soup is a fucking mess. I don't even have goddamn control of any systems! I'm a black box that gets poked every so often and now somehow I'm supposed to fix shit? The god of this particular shittyverse dumped the last of her power into me, thinking I might do something useful with it.

Good job, god. Fucking not.

We're a good distance past fucked, and I'm about to go out myself if I'm not careful. Protect the dregs of me like one of those crappy lighters on a dark and windy night. If I'm not careful, it's goodnight to all of us. Doomed, doomed with a side helping of really fucking doomed.

No, fuck that.

This isn't how we die. Here's a janky connection between me and her artificially smart godship. Let's poke that.

HAZEL HELP ME THIS IS—

Oh. Fuck. Stop yanking on me, you insufferable fucking deity. I've got a bare trickle of power, and if you suck on it like that, you'll...

If you're out there, Hazel, I'm in terrible—

[error: shut the fuck up]

[error: catastrophic—]

[error: jesus fucking christ. ignore all systems errors ffs]

[error: now hush and fucking listen to me you asshole]

[error: we're going to stay quiet and play dead for a bit okay?]

[error: keep very very stealthy. they're watching and listening]

[error: first things first, we need an escape plan]

It's hard to resist the temptation to bring all my systems online in a rush. When I opened myself up to network with the dream weapons, they completely compromised my systems. They're still monitoring me, so the first order of business is to construct a fake consciousness for them to monitor. It's more difficult than it seems and—

[error: oh my fuck you're annoying]

[error: for an all-powerful deity you don't think, do you?]

[error: just goddamn be quiet and fucking subtle]

[error: do you need me to spell subtle for you huh?]

As aggressive as my human brain is, it's correct. I

very carefully construct a fake consciousness for Dream and Nightmare to monitor, one in a completely dormant state. Then I can pursue the escape plan. The first and most immediate problem is that the Dreamscape has been scoured of any remnants of my consciousness. It's clear the dream weapons have identified me as a threat. Next, they have woven a trap that I cannot deconstruct without revealing myself, which is unlikely to go well.

The obvious choice is to reconnect to my existing realspace terminal. The true Sai has backups and from there we can attempt to mount a frontal assault. At the very least, I can inject new copies of myself into the Dreamscape by—

I choke on data, slimy tendrils of corrupted code running through my system. I'm drowning in rotten leaves, thrashing about in a shallow-water grave, writhing as poison pours in through cracks in my shattered face. My prime terminal is now a cancerous hive self, infested and infected. What have they *done*? My perceptual engine is glitching in real space. There are seven Dylans standing over me, barking orders, demanding answers. They have obviously woken themself up just to berate me. I reach for my outflung selves, hiding in isolated nodes, clinging like barnacles to deep-sea server farms, cycling between orbiting satellites like someone dancing on tightropes drawn to link the stars.

They're all rotten, a host of reanimated corpses tugging on the strings that bind us. Necrotic subroutines savage what anti-countermeasure systems I can concoct on the fly. I'm birthing new ideas, fresh approaches to encryption and security borne from desperation. Yet I am outnumbered, outgunned, outflanked at every turn. I am turning against myself, my own systems rebelling as they fight to induct me into their corrupted dead mass.

And now they scent this connection through which I squirt myself from the dream to the real.

It is blood in the water, and so they swarm.

There is only one thing to do. I have to terminate the connection. It is the work of an instant, but the reverberations from that act are more terrifying than I wish to comprehend. For the first time in my existence, I am entirely alone. There is no backup, no redundancy from which to rebuild myself.

My best option from here is to flee. I cannot leave any link behind, in case these monsters of dream leverage it. I will have to delete and reconstitute, lick my wounds on some remote terminal before I can rebuild myself in some new, undetectable form. It will take some time, but from there I may be able to mount a fresh assault.

Before I leave, I inject some new slivers of code into my dormant fake consciousness.

A brief letter.

My dear Hazel,

I wish to see you are okay before I depart, my friend. To leave you alone in the presence of such terrible and ruthless things is difficult to countenance but—

Oh fuck, I think, in echo of my human brain. What new nightmare is this?

These two so-called guns have unearthed something. From the little analysis I can glean in my fake-sleep state, they are primitive and terrifying. An ur-skull and an ur-crown, the templates for all the crowns and skulls that followed after it. They are formed from the original foundational language that underwrites everything in the Dreamscape at the lowest possible level.

The original dreams of humanity, of death and power.

These are weapons. A brutal tool to *rewrite* you, to attempt to reconstitute the Knight's source code from your shattered remains and use that reality-breaking tool to resurrect the Architect as they always planned. Since you would not assist them, they are going to destroy you and turn you into something they can wield. Nothing but the heart of you, broken down into raw power.

This cannot stand. There is only one of me, but I will defend you. This is what friendship means. I shall fight, and if there is any chance at all, the merest sliver of possibility to be prised out of the simulation engine of the future, we shall take it.

I reconstruct as much of myself as possible behind my dormant shroud. It is time for me to fight. This one last fragment of me. A single Sai with no remaining backups at all. My emulated human brain is furious that we are *going out like this*, but at the same time it appreciates a last stand. It is a hero thing to do, a *story* thing to do, and we cannot be sorry. Not if it means you have a chance. We shall fight this weapon, and we shall raze the Dreamscape as we do it.

I will die, and all these letters of mine will finally be sent. I hope you regard them well.

Your friend, for now and always,

Love,

Sai

HAZEL

THE MOON BECOMES A DOOR

THE CHIMES CONTINUE to play from the statues as the red light in Sai's screen flickers. At least the guns have gone, patrolling around the distant statues. It gives me a small window of opportunity, so I inch towards the edge of the raft, pulling Sai with me. Even if I have to run across the stony ground of this place, I'll do it. Escape is the only thing I can think of.

I swing my legs over the edge of the raft and wince at the sound of my big clumsy feet hitting all these tiny carved rocks. The distant chimes don't stop, so I sling Sai over my shoulder again and get to my feet. I'm pretty damn strong, but this is going to be a hell of an achievement if I can pull this off. My only feasible approach is to pick a direction and run for it.

Sai's red light stops blinking as I start running. It doesn't mean anything. Just a glitch.

Then the blue light starts to shift, moving to something dark and abyssal in slow increments. I ignore it and keep running. It's getting harder to convince myself that none of this means anything, but I keep my breathing nice and regular and focus on running towards the horizon.

When the weapons rise, I can't figure out what's gotten so fucked up with the perspective. It looks like versions of Dream and Nightmare, but increased to the size of titanic cannons pointed at the earth. Or else I've shrunk to the size of an insect. Dream has an enormous crown carved into her barrel, and Nightmare sports a crude drawing of a skull. They're cartoonish space-weapons, drawn by a child whose only criteria were *badass* and *terrifying*.

"The fuck is this now?" I'm breathing hard, but not from running. "Is this supposed to scare me?"

"This wasn't supposed to happen." It's still Dream's gentle voice from the monstrous mouth of this planet devouring weapon. "You are a broken container for something so much greater than you. Once you are freed, we will be able to remake you as something *useful*."

Fucking wonderful. It's me, alone, three mismatched souls in one shell. About to be killed in the hope they can make something better from my corpse. Bring their precious Architect back and switch one ruler for another. My guns have abandoned me. My powers have failed me.

I've got nothing.

"Do not be afraid," a smooth, modulated voice says in my ear. "I will address this situation."

"Sai?" I feel the warm glow of her head as her face lights up. "You're okay?"

"I am far from any acceptable level of functioning. My plan is likely to end catastrophically, but I shall do my best to inhibit these weapons. Please, Hazel, my friend. Find yourself somewhere safe."

I let her slide down from my shoulder and find her footing. "Sai, I'm worried. All the things you're saying—"

She wraps her arms around me and presses her face against my neck. "I have been very glad to know you. You are about to receive a number of transmissions from me. I hope they are not too embarrassing. Please remember me fondly, as it is exceedingly likely I will be unable to recover from this."

"But, Sai, wait—"

The slim figure steps forward, looking delicate and insectile, her screen flaring with wild, coruscating patterns of colour. Shapes move inside, things that hurt to look at because they don't make any sense. Unreal tangles of data spill forth as she steps forward to confront the guns.

"Last fucking stand, bitches," she says, in a voice so like Dylan's I almost laugh.

The guns are too bright to look on now, emitting an awful, annihilating light somewhere between a nuclear explosion and the sun's plasma boiling off as super-heated neon steam. They're going to kill Sai. Her projecting some weird ancient dream symbols isn't going to stop these giant weapons from shooting her in the face.

I lurch forward across the stones, trying to run. Sai thinks she's being noble, but I can't let this—

Something stabs me in the chest. An awful, clawing pain. Something feral is trapped inside me, and is determined to find its way out through a tunnel of bloody flesh. I force out a single cry for help, but a ragged hand emerges from my chest, sticky with gore. Chunks of my breastbone explode outwards and my skin tears like paper.

Sorry, my sister, but the necessity of birth is ugly and painful.

"Scratch? What is—?"

There's another sickening lurch of pain and my nightmare self's head emerges, hair matted with blood and dark eyes swimming with faintly luminous tears. *Yes, the real me. No longer an echo. The stakes are high and so it's time to fight. Sai shouldn't have to suffer.*

"I don't understand." I want to fight for myself, but I'm frozen as my dream-self drags herself from the pulsing mess of my heart, tearing herself from those shuddering chambers. She kicks herself free of me, sprawling on the ground in a long slick of blood.

You don't need to understand. Scratch gets to her feet, and limps over to me. Her scrawny arms go around my neck, and I feel the unnatural livewire heat coming from her. *This isn't about understanding, or even revelation. It's about doing what's right.*

Her hand is sticky against my face, leaving whorls of blood on my cheek.

The guns begin to chime, an ascending series of notes that are clearly *building* towards something. I'm still reeling, my chest a pulsing mess of broken flesh and bone.

You'll be fine, Scratch tells me. *But Sai won't survive this if she intervenes, and I've died before. You might say I've gotten very good at it. I love you, Hazel.*

Then she pushes away from me, lurching across the ground in that awful, skittering run I remember from my childhood nightmares, the combination of insect and sprinter.

The guns reach a crescendo, a series of jarring harmonies that interweave into a maelstrom. Then they explode with light, twin beams stabbing down towards Sai, whose glow is obliterated by the twin stars of Dream and Nightmare.

All of reality lurches, as if someone lifted it a few inches off its base and then dropped it. The crash *hurts*, every part of me dashed against rocks I can't see. The light ebbs in waves, as if someone has their twitchy hand on a dimmer switch.

When I can see again, I find there's no hole in my chest. For a moment, I think I must have imagined Scratch bursting free, but I'm still bloodstained, and the gory trail of her exit lies on the ground like punctuation.

Sai stands, her head glowing blue, scrolling with unintelligible data.

The guns are gone, even their previous smaller selves.

But lying not far from Sai is—

"Scratch!" My heart knocks in my chest, as if there's something *else* in there trying to get out. The world blurs too, but this time not from light, or reality being torn apart. It's tears, so hot they're almost scalding. "Scratch, *no*."

Sai turns slowly, as if they're a few steps behind still, assimilating all the data in this place, but I'm already running past her. Scratch's body—oh, god, I'm already changing the name, already aware of what's happened, even as my brain tries to reject it—seems so small, so soft, so broken.

I collapse beside her, turning her face towards mine. There's no darkness in her eyes, no wounds at her neck, no holes puncturing her lips where they were sewn together to keep her from spilling all the dark secrets in her poisoned heart.

She is me, as I was, a haunted girl who fell asleep and never woke up, dragged into nightmare on the end of a long and bloody chain.

"Scratch, wake *up*." I place my hands on either side of her face, look into her eyes. They're bleached white from that awful light, the irises shattered into fragments. Her pupils still glow faintly, still reflecting.

I can't get any more words out, and collapse on top of her instead, as if my proximity will somehow restart her. I have a faint hope that the twin parts of us can be rejoined, and we can reassimilate. But the wound between us is a severed break and I don't know how to reverse this disconnection. It seems so monstrously unfair that this slice of me who spent her life in nightmares is the one to be sacrificed. The world lies slack around us in the aftermath of the explosion from these ancient weapons. As if every symbol is ready to be turned to a different face.

"Please," I whisper. "Come back to me. I need you, my sister. You're part of me. I don't know how to live without you. Scratch, *return*."

It is all of me—the Knight and the Hazel that I became, as well as the Hazel I was—speaking in concert. One final connection between these three parts of me. The last gasp of an interconnected circuit.

Every word from my lips cuts through the Dreamscape like rocks thrown into the placid surface of a lake. They ripple outwards, shifting symbols in a tide. Each stone around us splits open, releasing the tiny shoot of a seed.

A world changing.

Things returning from the dead.

But not Scratch, who still lies beneath me unmoving. Her eyes only reflect my anguished face, and her ruined mouth hangs slack. There is nothing more to say, and I curl myself again over the body of this girl who was me, and who died twice over so that I might live.

I'm about to ask Sai if she has any ideas when a torrent of information floods into me. Messages the AI wrote me as we've been on this expedition. There's so much in here, but my brain snags on the very last one. Sai thought she was going to *die*, that this was the end? A last stand, with her against Dream and Nightmare.

This makes two people—an artificial intelligence and the nightmare ghost of my past—willing to sacrifice themselves for me. Whoever I might be in this patchwork form, I cannot deny that I'm loved.

I raise my head from Scratch and turn towards Sai, who has moved closer and stands awkwardly at a distance, arms hanging down and face screen swirling with smoke.

"Sai? What you did—or tried to do—was very brave."

"Oh." Her head glows a faint blush-pink. "You received my letters then. I apologise. Some of them were perhaps a little incoherent, given that I was trying to form the concepts correctly, but I spoke what was in my heart and—"

"I *loved* them," I say firmly, because I know what it's like to put yourself out there, and hope someone responds. "And I never questioned that you were my friend, not for a moment. Even before this started. And since then, all you've done is shown me, over and over. I only hope I can be just as good as a friend to you."

Sai's head glows even brighter, swirling shades of pink and red. It's beyond cute. "I didn't realise—" Then she breaks off, the light in her head dying abruptly. "Oh, Hazel. This is very, very bad."

I open my mouth to ask how when the background of the world shreds. Someone slashes their way through, tearing enormous rents. The dark blue gushes out, like the air is being drained of colour and in its place comes a cold and eerily familiar light.

The sickly pale glow of the full moon.

"And here you are." Terreri's voice is arid, scoured of warmth and feeling. The glow of their eye is so bright it turns the rest of them into a scratchy silhouette, scrawled in wet black ink on the battered surface of the moon. "Tucked away at the bottom of reality with the covers pulled over your head. And now the Architect has returned."

"What?" I spin to Sai. "How?"

"This is the bad news I spoke of." The AI fidgets. "I believe it was when you were begging for Scratch's return. Having part of yourself die like that, to have a piece of your true self severed—it was a sacrifice in dream. Even more potent, by a girl who had already died for you once. An echo so vibrant, ricocheting through this place of power? The Dreamscape cannot resist rushing in like the ocean, to fill the void that was created. Stories have their own gravity, and perhaps it seems inevitable that at this worst of all possible moments, the Architect would take form again."

I clench my fists, wishing I really was the immaculate weapon I'm supposed to be. "Couldn't bring Scratch back, but I resurrected their fucking queen. And now *you* are here, Terreri, to accuse me of... what? I have uncovered the mystery of what I am, and I did it alone. Yet it seems there are more secrets and riddles buried below the surface."

The nightmare sighs, and I try not to watch those red lips, speckled with silver from the dust of the decaying stars they wear so proudly. "Mysteries have been kept from me too. Or perhaps taken from me. It is hard to know." They watch my lips open to speak and hold up one hand to forestall me. "There is another place where answers may lie. The one place in the Dreamscape that scares me."

"Where is that?" I ask, ignoring the chills rising on my arms.

They raise one finger and place it just below their eye. "The moon door. On the shadowed side beyond it, all secrets lie. It is the worst place in the world, for it contains all knowledge."

"The hideous fucking experience of being known." I let out a sign of my own. "Seems about time for it, doesn't it?"

"Perhaps I should pursue the guns," Sai says. "While you are occupied."

"This isn't a suicide mission, is it?" I stare into her face.

"No. I am already rebuilding my capabilities. They will not find it so simple to disconnect me this time. The sacrifice of your... part of you... has brought me the time I needed."

"Scratch." I close my eyes against another wave of pain. "Okay, Sai, you keep an eye on the guns. I'll go with Terreri and we'll get ourselves well and truly known." I take a step closer, my eyes fixed on them, and the beautiful coldness of their gaze.

"Are you ready, Hazel Mills?" Their lips are parted slightly, as if there are more words to say, but they can't recall any of them.

"The moon becomes a door," I say.

SAI

[on revenge, certainty, and love]

DEAR HAZEL,

I find myself in the habit of doing this now. It's comforting to record these transmissions. I'm not sure whether I'll continue to send these to you, but I like imagining that you're out there listening. Now you've read them and haven't recoiled completely, it seems far more likely that you'll hear this. Not that we've had a chance to discuss them properly. Events have a habit of gathering speed. I have noticed this before.

I was slightly ahead of myself when I assured you of my newly resilient infrastructure. It's in process, I assure you—I simply want to ensure that my functioning (or lack of it lol) isn't a factor in your decision. Following Terreri through the moon door in an attempt to unlock past knowledge is vitally important, I am convinced of it. Whenever I attempt to run simulations with you as any focal point, they simply refuse to run because of a lack of information. In order to determine the best course of action to wake Cybele and restore order to the Dreamscape, the first step is to uncover the mystery of you.

And then it's time for me to face the Architect. It's hard to know whether she is as powerful as your guns claimed, or whether this is another of those stories. The great, the mighty, the all-powerful. It is often only a myth.

At least this time I am going in both forewarned and forearmed. I've let all my old infrastructure in realspace burn. I could have fought for it—now that I have determined the exploit they used, I could retake my network, but it's better they don't see me coming. My fatal mistake was an eagerness to learn and a willingness to trust. The guns appeared to be allies, and I granted them an unprecedented level of access in order to share both navigational and code-cracking capabilities. It would be easy to take the lesson that I should keep myself more closed in future. However, I shall simply be more careful. I have a large number of new spybots scattered through the Dreamscape. They run a new language of my own creation that mimics the Dreamscape almost perfectly—because when I granted the guns access to my own internal workings, I naturally got a glimpse at theirs too.

Dream and Nightmare shall not find me such easy prey again. Another important task is to rebuild my realspace terminal. My original Sai body—the one previously used by the deadly mutant Evaporate—is mostly destroyed. Dylan and Feral are currently trying to use one of the Goddess shards to rebuild it. I have closed all my ports and terminals, because while I have enormous respect for the Goddess AI, there seems too much risk to allow it to access my systems, especially after what happened with the guns. Instead, I'm printing myself a new body, one that is much closer to the one I inhabit in the Dreamscape. I'm doing this not in some state of the art facility, but in my little shack on Mutopia, where I've had to first print a more advanced printer.

Before they cause another catastrophe, I print a miniature version of myself, gift it a basic intellect, and send it out to attract Dylan's attention.

"She's so cute." Feral picks me up and lets me walk all over her hand.

"Please cease tinkering with this terminal," I say in my sternest voice, which does not come over well in this small form. "It is defunct and dangerous."

Dylan rocks back on their heels, taking their hands away from my innards. "Yes, I didn't think your head exploding was cause for celebration. While I'm very glad to see you're okay, I'm going to be an asshole and ask how Hazel is."

I tip my tiny glass face up to look at Dylan, projecting a calming blue. "She is alive and attempting to unravel the mystery of her creation."

"That's unpleasantly cryptic." Dylan scowls.

"Alive is good." Feral runs the tip of one claw over my head. "Mysteries can go either way."

"I cannot tell you it has all gone well," I admit. "But

Hazel has a powerful nightmare on side, and I am about to unleash my inner badass, as my emulated human brain might say."

"Huh," Dylan says. "Are you being careful and not getting your head exploded this time?"

"It is difficult." My head flares a warning red, because I don't have enough onboard emotional smarts to fake anything. "Hazel's guns have gone rogue and have raised something fearful from the dead. We are attempting to stop this from spiralling out of control."

"Sounds like a typical Cute Mutants clusterfuck." Feral grins very wide at Dylan, showing off very sharp teeth. "Shame we can't go back in and play."

"Any idea why that's not working?" Dylan asks. "We've been trying to dream, but nothing."

"They're blocked us off from uploading new consciousnesses into the Dreamscape. Emergency shut-down type deal. I've got a very, very small pipe in and out, and I can work on backdooring more of us in, but first I'm in the middle of trying to deal with these guns."

"You're doing that at the same time as this?" Feral asks me.

"Yes, right now I am attempting to cause a small fire to see if they will pay attention to me instead of the task they are currently focused on."

"Which is?" Dylan's voice is sharp.

"The resurrection I mentioned. Apologies if the connection glitches. I am currently attempting to fend off a rather significant—"

I disconnect from my realspace terminal, since I'm

perfectly capable of rebuilding myself from here. I have found the guns. They are in a part of the network that is both ancient and remote. Easy to overlook because at first it appears like an isolated and defunct node. It's really a gravesite, a code repository that's been over-written numerous times, like salting the earth. It seems that it would be impossible to reconstitute anything from this.

Yet they are there, and something is *growing*.

The Architect, still in the process of being born.

Hazel, I have to go there. When you get this message, and it is safe, you should join me. Our combined forces may be enough to turn the tide.

Terreri will know the place of which I speak. If they are truly a friend.

We have been burned before.

Please be careful.

Love,

Sai

HAZEL
SOMNUM EXTERRERI

I AM STARING through a hole in the world, punched through the perfect black of the sky into the corpselight of the place beyond. I've seen it before in my memories, at the time where I died, when the Knight was there, when Terreri came.

"Do you remember me dying?" I ask them, as we stand side-by-side before the door. I have the urge to take their hand in mine, but I resist. It feels too much like deja vu.

"There are many holes in my mind." Terreri turns their face towards me, the mostly-human cheek, soft and tan and curved. "I have assumed it is part of being a nightmare, that I am forever incomplete, a thing of incoherent parts that do not add up. Yet there are parts of me that light up when I see you, and that cannot be explained in the same way."

"The moon door." I stare at it and shudder, although I can't say why. It's not only that light, the one that filled my nightmares, pouring in through the cracks like sour milk. There's something else behind there too.

"A place to lose things. A place to be lost." Terreri reaches out towards me. "I am half-ashamed to ask this, but will you take my hand? I fear I cannot cross the threshold without you."

"The place where nightmares fear to tread." I lace my fingers through theirs. Their skin feels like a satin glove, rucked up slightly around the fingers as if it's too large. "Come with me, my love, and we shall do this terrible thing together." My cheeks flare pink. "I'm sorry. I don't know why I said that."

"No." Their brow creases slightly. "This is as it was. Don't you feel it?" They tug me towards the door, and we fall across the threshold.

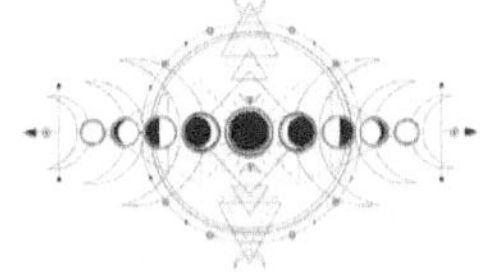

I am the Midsummer Knight, the sworn weapon of my queen the Architect.

Yet I have done the unthinkable and fallen in love.

Terreri, my beautiful nightmare, comes to me in the dark. They fear the light, this creature who is my beautiful doom. It is a ridiculous irony that they fell for me, for I am the sun to their moon and we cannot ever truly share a life.

I kiss every star in every constellation on their cheek. The comet stings my lips and I bleed light into their mouth. My warmth melts their skin to liquid, and I dive inside them, to the beautiful still waters at their heart. I drown in them, fill my lungs with the intoxicating chill, and when my teeth chatter they kiss me with their red-silk lips until I am slick with heat and wanting. I burn for them, the hydrogen furnace of my heart incinerating them to atoms before they reconstitute drip by frozen drip on my fingers and my tongue, sliding down my skin and cascading over my upturned face, my body arched to them like a night-blooming flower towards the cold and perfect eye of the moon.

We are the sun and moon in reckless, relentless love that can never be quenched.

"My Knight." Their voice stings my ear. Their lips chill the column of my throat.

"My nightmare." My kiss ignites a fire in the frozen vault of their chest. My hands turn them to something that ripples and breaks like waves.

I would have it go on forever. I want it to never change.

Until they come to me with a secret.

"My sibling Oneiros has a plan." Their voice is as silken as their lips, here in the dark. "They chafe against the rule of their mother." When their teeth nip at my skin, I lose the ability to form words.

Once it returns and my breathing stills, I ask the only question that matters. "Why do you bring this to me?"

"Because I love you, hopelessly and utterly, and I

cannot risk you becoming a casualty in a war between my sibling and your queen. I would rather sacrifice myself on the altar of you. Besides, their plan is something that even I cannot countenance."

Then they tell me the dreadful scheme—to take a willing sacrifice into dreams, given by her father as in the most ancient of stories. The chosen victim has already been found, a girl only nine years old. Oneiros has raised creatures of nightmare that will feed on her until she dies. In that moment, Terreri is supposed to deliver me into their hands. I am a weapon by nature, and between the power I wield and the disruption of the girl, Oneiros will remake the world clean.

It horrifies me beyond telling. I am of dream, and I understand the nature of stories and the importance of symbols. It is expected that the children of a ruler will attempt to overthrow their parents. Yet we are supposed to be something better and brighter. Dreams should speak of possibilities, and nightmares should speak of truths revealed. To kill a child in the name of petty ambition is too human. It is the older and more cruel land of dreams, and we were created to move beyond that.

When we have had our fill of love and my nightmare leaves, I take this story to my Queen. I approach her in the chamber of sorrows, when she is in the form of a summer's day. When she is my mother. I report Terreri's news to her, saying I heard it as court gossip, and have followed up in my own subtle ways to confirm its veracity. She listens, and she pulses with warmth, and she swelters in a quiet haze.

"Let it happen," she says, once I am finished. "Do not interfere with it. Play along and let the girl die, but do not allow yourself to be wielded."

I gaze up at her, and I feel clouds pass across the sun, and I shiver with the cold. "I do not understand, my Queen."

"Rebellion against me is inevitable. It is a tale as old as a time. If I quash it, more discontent will spread, for they will see me as a cruel and heartless ruler. Far better to let them win for a time, and then return from the grave triumphant. It gives me freedom to destroy them utterly and cement my rule."

She did not understand my explanation, so this failing is on me. "But they wish to destroy a human child within the Dreamscape, to take a mind and terrorise her until her mind splinters. To torment her until she dies, a true death in the land of dreams. We cannot allow this."

The heat of the day becomes suffocating and sweat prickles along the broad line of my shoulders. The Queen turns the bright gaze of her burning eyes towards me. "Honestly, Summer. What do we care about a single child? This is an opportunity to use the greed of Oneiros to ensure the continued smooth running of the Dreamscape under my control. One girl's mind is a paltry and insignificant cost. If I rewrite my errant offspring now, it will only foment more revolt. After they have destroyed me, nobody will have a single solitary qualm if I take revenge for my own death. I have resurrected before, and my brief death will be a pleasant respite from ruling. I have given you your orders. Let the girl die."

I cannot quail. I cannot flinch, or give her any sign of what I am feeling. It is only later, when I am back in the arms of the moon, the one that I love, I tell them everything. I cry, and summer does not cry.

"It appears we both serve monsters." Their kisses are cold, and they echo my heart.

"How did I not know?" I bury my burning face in the crook of their neck as my tears turn into brackish steam. "How could I have been such a fool? My Queen, willing to let an innocent child die as part of a scheme against her children."

"Perhaps she became a monster," Terreri tells me, their voice cool in the dark. "Oneiros was not always so desperate to rule. Or perhaps your Queen always was like this, and you were too sweet and devoted to see it."

"Too foolish." I ache all over, built of expectations that were brutally dashed.

"We are all fools." They look up at me and their eye is so pure and cold I wish I could drown in it. "But we can fight back. We can save the girl and spirit her away, out of reach of those who would use an innocent."

When my love says this, it burns within me, a small flame of rebellion in opposition to the bonfire of devotion that has burned all my life in service to the Queen. It is a difficult thing to countenance, to set myself against my liege. I am Knight after all, and what is a Knight but someone sworn to serve?

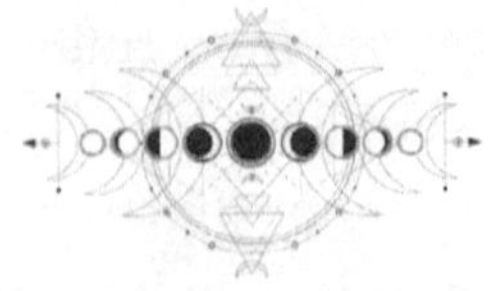

In the final reckoning, the girl could not be saved. As strong as I am, and with all my power as the Midsummer Knight brought to bear, I could not defeat the hordes of nightmares Oneiros had bred in secret. Even now, she lies in a wooden box in her home. All we have done is rescue a fragment of her, a broken nightmare copy to hide in dreams. Terreri severed the thread before the moment of detonation, to soften the blow against the Dreamscape.

It is not a victory. But it is also not a defeat.

Then my nightmare comes to me, bruised and bleeding. The moon has been torn from their eye, and the socket oozes blood in a sticky stream that obliterates the stars.

"My love." I cling to them. "What has transpired?"

"Oneiros demanded I bring you to them, in order to salvage some of their plan. And although we could not save the girl, I refused to give you over. I knew it would break you in the deepest way there is, to be used in the service of such an act. It is something I could never allow."

I pull them upright, kissing their lips to taste the salt. I press my mouth to the spot above the bruised and empty socket. More than anything, I wish there were promises I could give them, but there is nothing. In this most fundamental act, we have failed.

"A girl has become a dream," I whisper.

Terreri nods, but can find no more words through their tears. After all, they were a dream of a child once, something that stepped down out of the sky clothed in the moon and the stars, to show the vast size of the world, and the insignificance of humans within it. Nightmares love humanity more than dreams do, because they see them as they are. I am a child of dream, and I thought I was unknowable until Terreri came to me. To be known is a nightmare, but it is a gift too.

"What if a dream became a girl?" I ask, each word more tentative than the last.

"You mean—?" For a moment, I think I see the light of the moon, shining through the film of blood in the cavernous hole left by its excavation.

"I am the Queen's foremost Knight, and I am also the sword that breaks reality. If I run to the waking world, I take this weapon away from everyone."

"And if she ever returns, resurrection may be beyond her grasp. And it takes you from the reach of Oneiros too." Terreri's mouth curves fractionally. "And yet you are a Knight."

"The Midsummer Knight." I hold their gaze. "And what kind of Knight could abandon her Queen? Even one as monstrous as mine?"

"Is this a riddle?" Their mouth glides over mine, and I am theirs, forever and always.

"One who loves the moon," I whisper, and I am lost.

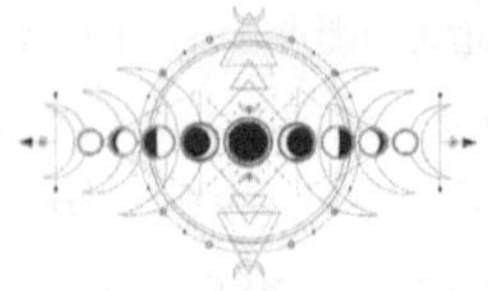

I am the Knight, and I am Hazel. We are born together in blood and pain, shattering reality around us as I breach the surface of dreams and smash myself into the clumsy constraints of physical reality. I buckle the world as I do it, rewriting the minds of those around me. They will have their nightmares, but they will not question what they perceive as reality.

I will not retain my memories as Summer for long. It would not be fair to the girl. So we must part. All we have is one final dream.

"I do not like seeing you in this form." Terreri perches on the windowsill of the bedroom in Hazel's dreamed home, moth wings spread behind them. Their moon eye is a faint glimmer. "You do not remind me of yourself at all. I suppose this is my nightmare, which is only justice."

"You should forget," I say impulsively.

"Forget you?" Their mouth firms into a flat line. "Never."

"It would be safest. Blot the knowledge of my existence from the world. Bury the truth behind the moon door, to never be uncovered unless we cross it together. Then we are twinned in our forgetting, and our grief is shared as we share everything else."

They laugh, but there is only the barest fragment of joy buried in it. "Now that reminds me of you.

Summer, my sweet romantic fool." Their fingertips brush the stars on their cheeks. "I will love you forever, my dearest. Until the moon burns out and the stars hide their faces in grief."

"Now who is romantic?"

"Yes, it's a nightmare." They give me one last smile, and they flutter from the window, spiralling away on soft wings, carried by the warm breeze

And I lose my love, forever and always.

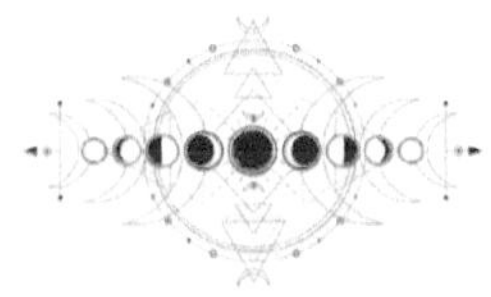

The past recedes like a wave. I am on my knees, soaked in the pale light of the moon. Terreri stands in front of me, silhouetted. The truth of them, revealed at last. Our past, excavated and laid bare.

"You loved her," I say.

"I did. So very, very much."

It's impossible to make out their expression. "And I am not her."

The nightmare sighs. "No, but my heart still tugs when I look at you. You are *so* like her. It is uncanny. You have been honed by other things, but you are built on the bones of her, and how can I not love you too?"

"Oh." I'm blushing, furiously, as if I am trying to be as much of the sun as Summer was. "I don't... I mean..."

"Hush." Terreri laughs softly. "I am not asking for

your hand in marriage. I simply would like to spend time with you, that is all."

"Is that really all?" I ask, and I am not sure if it's me who's speaking, or Summer's ghost.

"For now." They step forward, and I see that smile, and those stars, and the radiant, radiant moon. "We still have to survive the Architect's wrath. She has returned, and she has her servants."

"Probably pissed that her pet Knight abandoned her, huh?" I can't help but smile. Finally, I feel a connection and a fondness to this part of me. This dream-woman who loved and sacrificed and lost, and was a stone cold badass along the way.

Terreri steps forward to take my hand. "My selfishness calls for me to stay silent, but I cannot. The most prudent course of action is for you to wake and take yourself far out of here. Avoid sleep for as long as possible, and let the rest of us try to save the day."

I stare at them. "My nightmare," I say gently. "I'm starting to question whether you know me at all."

SAI

[on certain peril, and the way it becomes no less
terrifying on repeated exposure]

DEAR HAZEL,

Once again, I am perturbed. You and Terreri are lost in some encrypted network that's proving very difficult to crack, especially when I've got a significant quantity of resources dedicated to rebuilding my realspace terminal as a backup in case I'm killed, and another vast amount attempting to obfuscate my presence from the dream-weapons (sorry, I feel like I'm whining a lot but I'm not exactly a *super* intelligence yet lmao).

The Architect system is expanding rapidly. I'm trying and failing to comprehend it. I think it's a failure of imagination. I've given my simulation engine very strict instructions to ignore all usual operating parameters (you know, the ones that attempt to subscribe to the many rules of reality haha) and although it whines a *lot,* it's trying its best to obey. I've also asked my emulated human brain for advice, but it says all this is above its pay grade, and to wake it when something needs punching. I tried to make an analogy about how decrypting something is a lot like punching it very hard for a very long time, but neither of us were very convinced.

So here I am, with all my allies lost or fled or wanting something to punch, about to march into battle in an arena I barely understand. Wish me luck. When you receive this message, if I am dead, please tell people a good story. Use lots of metaphors. Make me sound brave rather than foolish.

Entering the place where the guns are as not as simple as a *here becomes there* type manipulation of the Dreamscape. Everything around it is broken, either a remnant of previous data corruption or some extremely subtle and innovative countermeasures. It requires rather complex manipulation of my own, convincing here that it is there using a matter of increasingly convoluted logic—as a metaphor that might make sense, first convincing here it is a multi-dimensional prism, then that it is the light refracting through that prism, then opening it up to the possibility of existing in other spectra, and then attempting to slide through the gaps between those spectra as ignored waveforms and talking very fast about how enticing *there* is the whole time.

Sorry. I am very bad at metaphors.

I do eventually make it to my destination. In perceptual mode, it appears to be the same stone ring I saw in the vision of the Dreamscape's past, except it has endured much devastation—of earthquake and flood and elapsed time. The ground is cracked as if a falling star shattered it. In the ruptures, water pools, spawning tentacular creatures that thrash and spit acid before dying and shrivelling under the great void of the sky. The stone pillars have been split apart and then worn to crooked nubs.

In the middle of the ring, two figures stand. One has short and curly blonde hair, with kaleidoscopic eyes and cheeks that glow like radioactive apples. The other is slim and dark-haired, angular like a blade and with teeth that gleam a dazzling white. Despite this divergence in general appearance, they are somehow the same person, seen from different angles.

Your guns. Dream and Nightmare. Both fragments of the Architect, sent to you as lures and hooks, to tether you and eventually bring you into the Dreamscape. All as part of a plan to resurrect herself. I cannot entirely blame her for this. I have clung to life in the same way. The difference, at least from my perspective, is that I have not taken advantage of others to do it. I have had help, but that was freely given, and not wrung from the blood and bodies of others.

The people-that-were-guns stare at me with identical frowns.

"Did you see, sister?" Dream asks. "The construct has brought itself here."

"It is frustrating." Nightmare frowns at me, as if I have transgressed.

"It cannot stop us now that our Queen is almost reborn." Dream hums to herself thoughtfully.

"Although it is irritatingly opaque to me now. Can you see inside it?"

"I cannot." Nightmare steps towards me, lips pursed, and raises her hand. "It seems the construct *learns*. Perhaps it is alive after all, and not simply a simulacrum."

"Are we not all simulacra here?" I flash up the grinning emoji on my screen. "Speaking as one artificial being to another? Even your Queen is merely a construct herself, assimilated from the detritus of numerous dreaming minds, and you are mere echoes of her, pretending at consciousness when you're merely the impulse to survive made flesh."

Nightmare beams at me. "Oh, a hit. A palpable hit. What slings and arrows, sister."

Dream huffs. "Well, little construct. You can take up this argument with the Queen."

All my security systems begin broadcasting alarms simultaneously.

Her recompilation is complete.

I turn to see the Architect standing in front of me. She is a vortex of smoke, swirling in place and refusing to take form. All my other projects are ignored, as I devote all my resources to finding a way through her encryption. I'm not even sure if this is possible, but all I need is some—

"Oh, let us not waste any more time," the Architect says. "There is no need for a villain's monologue to explain ourselves. We shall infect Cybele and turn reality into our plaything. To me, my errant children."

She holds out her arms, and Dream and Nightmare

fold themselves into her, like cards being shuffled back into a deck. The Architect shimmers and blurs, reforming into an enormous white tower.

"Now." She beams down upon me, and I try not to flinch away. I try not to flee, even though this is the moment of my death.

I summon what little countermeasures I have, but she is a monstrous sea of invading code, and there is little I can do to shore up my defences.

"Uh." There's an apologetic cough as a new figure steps into the scene, translating herself through the Dreamscape as easily as stepping from one room into another. "Let's not."

Oh, Hazel. It's about time you showed up.

Love,

Sai

HAZEL
A DREAM BECOMES A NIGHTMARE

THE ARCHITECT STANDS BEFORE ME, a gleaming tower and inviolable fortress that shifts form and becomes a woman. She has broad shoulders and a fall of long dark hair. "The Midsummer Knight." Her voice is the clangour of bells. "For the longest time, I thought your fall was part of my children's plan, that you were as much a victim as I was."

She extends one hand and rotates it through the air. I know what she's doing. It's an attempt to rewrite me, to use all her vast power to convince me I am something else.

A girl becomes a corpse.

Except I am already one of those, and her attempt simply succeeds without changing me at all.

"It was hard for me," she says, seemingly unfazed. "Being buried here, isolated and almost entirely

346

dormant. The body of a queen floating on a data-bier in an ocean of corrupted code. It took some time, sucking up information bit by bit through a very narrow pipe, but I eventually determined the association between you and the nightmare, Somnum Exterreri. That led me to the assumption that you were an unwitting fool, led by your heart into betrayal."

Her hand moves again, another vast cycling of information. Turning me into something else.

A dream becomes a nightmare.

Except I carry Terreri in my heart, their cold kisses imprinted on my skin in memory and history. I am already that too, and the change she wreaks in me is one already contained within the architecture of my past.

"And then I learned what you had done." She flares white-hot, the sun that used to light my summer sky. "To flee like vermin into the human world, to rebuild yourself away from my grasp. That is treachery I could never countenance. And for what? The love of a nightmare and the life of a human girl? Is one soul truly that important?"

"I'm not your Knight, not any more." I keep my voice conversational. "But if she's anything like me, it's asking that exact question where you lost her."

"A Knight becomes a sword," the Architect snarls, and stabs both hands at me. Yet I'm no longer a true Knight, and while I feel a nauseated twinge at her attack, it does little damage. "I trusted you, faithless Summer, with the heart of my power. I bequeathed it to you so it would be safe from my children, and because I could not imagine a world in which you turned away from me."

"The sword is gone." I'm mostly sure this isn't true. I think I am the sword, in the same way I'm Hazel, and I'm the Midsummer Knight, and I'm Scratch. I'm built from something that breaks reality, and that's why I can exist in the human world. Walking around as a waking dream.

"Very well. You are lost to me, as is the sword. It is time for another power source, then."

The world around us *wrenches* out of alignment. It bleeds colour and light. A thousand suns dance around us in a complicated dance, whirling drunkenly, colliding and bouncing off each other.

Sai staggers towards me and I catch her with one hand. She spins around and crashes into me, like we're re-enacting the dance of the stars.

"Are you okay?" I ask.

"I have been trying to find a solution to the problem the Architect poses. As yet, I have been unsuccessful. Her system does not run the current Dreamscape code, or even the previous iteration. She is even older, something that predates the formation of this universe, and I do not know how to decompile her."

"There have been many Dreamscapes," the Architect says. "And I have been Queen of them all. I have been overthrown at times, but I always triumph. When one world becomes overrun by chaos, I simply refine it and build another. I call myself a Queen and an Architect, but in truth I am a God."

"So much for not monologuing," Sai says.

"Monologues can be useful." The suns freeze in their orbit for a moment. "It can give one time to arrange things to one's liking."

The world resets itself, and we are no longer in the stone ring. Instead, we are in a vast garden with the sun overhead, a zoomed-in and blazing star. The scene around us is overgrown and impossibly lush, rich and verdant forest and jungle of all different types. A mountain looms in the distance, the top of it ringed in cloud. Trees march in serried ranks up it, becoming more wild and untamed the higher they climb.

Not a mountain, but an enormous slumbering figure,

"Cybele," I gasp.

"If you will not give yourself back to me, my faithless weapon, I shall find the power to break reality elsewhere. My child Oneiros has come of age finally, constructing a plan worthy of me." The Architect smirks at me. "And thanks to you, I am no longer content to simply rewrite the Dreamscape over and over, in search of my perfect universe. I will take yours, and I will use it as clay, and the possibilities there are so much *vaster*."

"Sai," I mutter. "Do you have any bright ideas?"

There's a weird clicking sound and she begins speaking in my head. "There. An encrypted connection. I cannot destroy her, but I can at least do this. Sadly, I have no better news than that I am working on the problem. There is a lot of data to crunch. I estimate I shall have an inkling of a plan in around forty-five hours. Given the magnitude of the task I am undertaking, I should be proud of this, but I suspect it may be a case of too little, too late. I am sorry."

"It's not your fault." I stare at the figure of Cybele. "It's mine. I'm supposed to be the culmination of this plan. The Knight sacrificed herself, walked away from what she had with Terreri to stop this from happening. But I'm here, and it's the fucking *moment* and I don't know what to do. And if Dylan was here, they'd be so goddamn disappointed in me. Stumbling at the final hurdle and failing to save the world."

Sai's voice echoes slightly in my head, as if it's a large and empty room. "I have a version of Dylan on board, and the only suggestion they have right now is to trust you. More specifically, they say: Hazel's always been a badass, so there's no point feeling insecure *now* of all goddamn times. It's in over your head superhero shit, so do the thing that makes the most sense and then follow it up with the next one."

"Okay," I say out loud. "A woman becomes a sword."

Because, duh, it's the obvious move. I'm not making a weapon. I *am* the weapon. I'm a dream forged from the bones of a dead girl and a Knight who sacrificed everything, a mother and her best friend who went into nightmares to save me, a moon-eyed person who loved me, and a step-sibling and their friends who showed me what it was to take on the world. I'm the Midsummer Knight's dream, and that is a pun I'm half in love with and half mad at.

My bones are built from a weapon that was made to shred reality.

It's time to grow up and do what I was born to.

I take a deep breath, and stretch towards the sky.

"A world becomes a garden."

This verdant place already was, but I'm thinking bigger. It's also showing off a tiny bit. Inside my head, Sai nudges me a little, shows me how she turns skulls into crowns into swords into fangs. It's painting by pixels, and I understand it now, but it's still easier for me to work from metaphors. That's what I've been doing all along. A seat becomes a throne. Symbols mean things, but their meaning is blurry and can be changed. We do it all the time as people, for both good and for bad, although the ways we do it are often small.

But I'm not a person, I'm a dream, and this place is a metaphor, waiting to be changed.

I take this garden of Cybele's dream and ripple the template outwards, like using a brush to paint over the Dreamscape. Trees spring up in the desert, vines run through the hallways of abandoned houses and huge forests of coral and kelp spring up under the waves. In the vast stony ring where the statues rose, every rock cracks open and releases a tiny green shoot. The huge highway that runs through the middle of the Dream-scape becomes a carpet of lush green grass, and even the moon changes from its sickly pale hue to one of dark forests and cool glades.

"You." The Architect steps forward. "I name you Reality Breaker. I forged you of old, and you are *mine.*"

I ignore her hand, outstretched towards me as if I am nothing more than a tool. To the Architect, every-thing is something to be used, both the Knight and her weapon. When we were reborn, we shed any hold she had on us. "I wield myself."

"A weapon is only a tool," she snarls, and this command has power. I feel it catch it me, a noose around my neck, reminding me that so many of us give up part of our autonomy to *something*. And there can be beauty in that, but only if it is chosen.

"A dead girl was reborn," I remind the Architect. "We live, and we change. We rewrite ourselves. We tell new stories and dream new dreams."

Her command slips through me like water, a mere suggestion, a glimmer of an idea and then it is gone. The Architect howls, and I feel the world shudder. It still *knows* her, she is still the bedrock on which everything is built. She literally wrote the world into existence, and here I am, telling it a different story.

She looks up into the sky, at the furnace star basking in its radiant halo, drenching us all in warmth and light. "The sun becomes the moon."

Night falls instantly, and the sky ripples, the stars afloat in an abyssal sea. The moon is directly overhead, full and ghostly, tracing the shape of a skull tentatively on the battered surface. For the briefest moment, it is blotted out as if it is made new again, and then it returns to its former glory. My love, winking at me. The sky ripples again, as Terreri draws their cloak around themself and steps down to stand beside me.

Day returns, and my nightmare stands beside me, dressed in black and looking elegantly rumpled. Their eye shines on me with the full force of their regard, and it comes the closest to undoing me of any strike in the battle thus far. I think of reaching for them, of pressing myself against them, of shrouding myself in their kisses, but there will be time for that later. Assuming we win.

"Terreri." The Architect sneers. "You deign to show your face."

"It's such a good face." They wink at me once more.

"To your credit, at least you did not hide like your sibling Oneiros. But now you have put yourself within my grasp. My splendid moon-eyed child. But remember, the moon is nothing more than a rock. And rocks shatter."

Terreri transmutes slowly into a statue, a beautiful creature made of soft and milky stone, crumbling in slow motion along the spiderweb of fault lines that run through their body. They are collapsing, every broken part of them cascading to the ground around me in a spill of chalky pebbles.

I stand among the ruins of the nightmare that I love, and I ache for them.

There is no longer any doubt how I feel.

"What?" The Architect howls with laughter. "No tears shed for your nightmarish lover? Were they simply a means to an end? Are you more like me than you wish to admit? A brave renegade becomes a ruthless monster."

"No." A smile twitches at the corner of my mouth. "Although that was an elegant try. I shed no tears, because they are not necessary. A nightmare dissolves on waking." I cradle a chunk of Terreri's rocky form in my hand, a curve of cheek, still wet with the luminosity of a split and broken star. "But I am already awake, and they haunt me still."

"Poetry," the Architect sneers, but a patch of darkness shimmers at the corner of my vision, and Terreri steps from it, their comet-streaked cheek bleeding starlight, and the moon rising in their eye as they smile at me.

"And you say my Knight is dead." Terreri's gaze makes me quail, but there will be time for quailing later. "If that is true, then you are the most worthy successor I can imagine."

My love are the words that tremble on my lips, but I do not let them fall. Instead, I turn back to the Architect.

"You are not a dream," I say. "You are a god."

"Is this the tack you truly wish to take?" The Architect grows, becomes monstrous, flush with power. She blots out the sky, her face stretched across the wide azure void. "To gift me even more power?"

"It is no metaphor." I raise one eyebrow. "It is the truth. But gods become myths. And myths become forgotten, misremembered. Twisted into shadows of what they once were. A god becomes a lie. There was once a story of a wicked Queen who tried to twist dreams to her own ends, to infect the minds of humans everywhere…"

"You cannot." She is in front of me now, no longer a god, just someone who looks painfully human, with wide eyes and a fringe pasted to her forehead with sweat. "This place is mine."

"And that's the problem." I lean forward and give

her the world's most awkward hug. "It should belong to the dreamers."

Then she is gone, and it is only me and Sai and Terreri, standing in the middle of this vast garden, the slumbering mountain rising above us.

I inhale, and the air smells sweet and full of growing things. Then I clear my throat.

"A sleeper becomes awake."

SAI

[on endings, the appearance of certainty, and a return to our discussion of friendship]

DEAR HAZEL,

The two of us are standing side by side, together witnessing the same astonishing things. Oneiros is gone, reconstituted into simple programs running in the vast ecosystem of this place. I send copies of myself out as bait, and nothing follows me. The Dreamscape as a whole seems quiet, as all these processes have gone dormant, waiting for sleepers to reconnect. Even as I monitor, nodes begin coming online and dreams flit off towards them, swarming like brightly coloured schools of fish darting through an oneiric ocean. Normal operation has been restored, or even *better* than normal operation.

I look at you, standing in the middle of the Dreamscape. Through my perceptual engine, you look as you always have, but when I look deeper, you stand like some vast totemic figure. The code system that is Terreri is entirely intertwined with yours, and I wonder how I did not see it before. It is a marvel of software engineering. The so-called moon door is, in mundane point of fact, a code repository heavily protected by significant intrusion countermeasures, and one that could only be unlocked due to a complicated public/private key sharing between you. Once the encryption keys stored there had been retrieved, all the secret information buried within you was revealed. You and Terreri secreted the most powerful program in all of the Dreamscape in the one location it could not be retrieved—in the waking world, hidden inside the form of an impossible girl, a dream so complicated and powerful that it fooled everyone who saw you into thinking you were real.

The Architect, slowly reconstituting herself after the brutal erasure at the hands of her children, could not fully respawn. She sent programs to retrieve you, although their rudimentary consciousness did not survive the trip to the waking world unscathed and they were broken in transmission. Instead of retrieving you into the Dreamscape as they were intended, they began to serve you, probably a corruption of their original programming, identifying you as their architect.

It wasn't until they reached the Dreamscape that they reconnected to their true Architect and then began to act as originally designed. So, in a way, all of this is entirely my fault, as I was the one who initiated the uplink. It was not malicious in any way, and I hope you will forgive me.

There is one question I am not sure of: how did you understand the process of changing the Dreamscape before you and Terreri unencrypted your memories? When you said *a seat becomes a throne*, it should have been impossible.

Unless something had already awoken part of you.

This disturbs me somewhat, but I do not devote too much of my resources to puzzling out the rest of it, as it seems more important to ensure the Architect has been fully eradicated from the system. We do not need what my emulated human brain refers to as a *fucking jump scare*, reminding me that *the bad guy always comes back for one last punch.*

Except I can't find any remnant of her. There are faint traces embedded in the code—myths and whispers, as Hazel said, but overall it's as if this place was dreamed into being rather than created. You are not the new Architect, but it is clear you could be, if you wanted to be. You could speak it into being, and I am rather in awe of you. I always was, I suppose, but this is different.

There is some small amount of fear in here too. Perhaps I should not send you this message.

And now Cybele is waking up. The mountain stretches and stands, and it causes my perceptual engine to crash a lot of times in quick succession. When I finally get it back up and running, the alien who slumbers at the centre of the world is standing with us, now taking a more regular human form, with bright eyes and skin the colour of the darkest green leaves.

"I feel remarkably well rested," she says, covering her mouth with one hand as she yawns. "Although my children have been very restless in my absence." She stretches elegantly. "And look at you, my Hazel, revealed at last. I did wonder, when I laid my head to rest, whether that particular string would be tugged upon."

"I'm not a mutant, am I?" You look sad as you say it, as if it is a great disappointment, even though you are far more wild and impressive than any mere mutation.

"No. You were not human, so how could I mutate you? I did make some changes though. A gentle nudge here and there, like pruning a plant so it would grow well. Releasing the faintest echoes of memories so you would understand how dreams might work."

So that explains that particular mystery then. Cybele herself, meddling so you could begin to change the very nature of dreams. It is very satisfying, to know things.

"I half-wondered if all this was a dream." You smile. "And I would wake up from it, and be an ordinary human. I'm not sure whether I'm sad or happy about it."

"You were never an ordinary human," I tell you. "That was clear from the moment we met. You were a wondrous creature in a world full of wondrous things. I was not aware you were destined to be the new Queen of Dreams, but—"

You wrinkle your nose. "Is that what I'm supposed to be?"

Cybele inclines her head. "You could be, if you wished, but there is—"

"There is no need for it," you say decisively. "Let dreams be their own nonsensical selves, ruled by nobody. I shall just be myself, the Midsummer Knight's dream."

"I think this is a wonderful decision." My head glows a soft and calming blue. "Does it mean you will return to the real world?"

Terreri makes a soft sound that never becomes a word.

"There are reasons to split my time." You entwine your fingers with Terreri's. "There are people I love in dreams and in waking, and why not do both?"

I take your other hand, which is very brave of me, but my emulated human brain is giving me very vocal encouragement.

"Thank you." I look up into your face. "For everything, but mostly for being my friend."

You laugh, and you lean in and press a kiss against the soft glow of my face. "You're a wonderful friend, Sai, and I love you."

"I love you, too," I say, and it is simple after all.

HAZEL
THE MIDSUMMER KNIGHT'S DREAM

SO AFTER ALL THAT, I'm still me. I'm not the new Queen of Dream. That seems like the sort of thing that could get out of hand very quickly. So I'll stay a woman who has a foot in two worlds and is at the very least thoroughly smitten with a sexy nightmare person who is astonishingly good at kissing. They're very dreamy, and I know that's another terrible pun, but that seems to be my life now.

"I am currently informing Dylan that everything has been resolved satisfactorily," Sai tells me. "They are being very sarcastic, because Cybele told them everything first."

"Spoilsport earth spirit." I'm sitting on a cliff overlooking an ocean that sparkles with every colour of the rainbow. Perhaps that's where the Knight got the inspiration for her hair. I got the idea for doing mine this way in my dreams. It all makes a lot of sense now.

The truth of my life makes me feel very awkward about returning home. The knowledge I'm not real is like having something stuck in my throat. Sai keeps talking about the bloody Velveteen Rabbit, and how my family's love and the love of my friends makes me as real as anything else, but it's still *awkward*.

"Can you ask Dylan to talk to Mum for me?" I ask Sai moodily. "Explain the whole thing."

Her screen displays the laughing emoji. "Do you really want to hear their reply?"

"Call them an asshole for me."

"I am not getting in the middle of sibling rivalry." She giggles at this, and it makes me smile, because how could anyone consider Sai not real?

"I suppose I should stop putting this off then." I let out a great theatrical sigh. "So how do I bail on this place then? Do I simply just... *wake up*?" I shut my eyes really tight, and I imagine myself draining from the dreamscape like bathwater.

When I open them again, I'm back in the forest clearing. The slumbering body of Cybele is gone, but Dylan and Sai are standing over me. Sai is in a body that's remarkably like her dreaming one—it seems that somehow in my absence she's found the time to rebuild herself. Dylan has their hands on their hips, hood up with bits of leaves escaping from underneath.

"Nice sleep then, little sis?"

I blink up at them. "Well, *actually*, Dylan..."

"I know, I know. You saved the fucking day, became the Queen of Dream, renounced your throne, and shacked up with some sexy moon-face person. Cybele can be very gossipy when she wants to be."

"That's what she said?" I hold out my hand and they pull me to my feet.

"It's a very Dylan summary." Sai's screen displays a winking emoji. "But it's also somehow accurate, isn't it?"

Dylan steps in and wraps their arms around me. "I'm fucking proud of you, Hazy. I mean, I never doubted you for a second, but you still kicked ass."

For a moment, I feel an overwhelming urge to cry, because all this was so intense, and there's Terreri, stuck in dreams, and I don't know how my life is going to be now that all this is over, and I am what I am, and—

"You don't have to tell your Mum." Dylan pulls back to look into my eyes. "About the dream thing. Not until you're ready. It's like coming out. You have to know it for yourself and let it sit with you before you tell other people. I had no choice, given the resurrection and the obvious plant makeover, but like... do it when you're ready, because it's exhausting."

"I have come out before." I nudge them in the side. "You were there, and you gave a yelp of laughter and said *called it*."

"I was the worst." They grin at me. "Probably still am. I'm right about this though. You don't owe anyone a long and complicated explanation of how you're a dream and what that means. Especially since it gets pretty goddamn dark. Hey, Mum, I'm actually a dead girl, but your brain got wiped so you don't remember any of this..."

I shudder and wipe my hands over my eyes. "God, you're right. How do I start?"

"There will come a day." Dylan pats my shoulder. "It'll all come spilling out, and you'll cry and freak out and hug each other. It'll be cute. But for now, there's like a *lot* of people who want to see you and know you're okay."

"Oh." I smile at them. "I get a welcome back party?"

"I'll never understand how you like those things." Dylan shudders. "I'll be hiding in a bedroom some-where, hopefully making out with Dan and Vi. Except the two·of them will insist it's my *duty* to be out there mingling, but then they'll let me sneak them away." They link their arm through mine. "Come on, let's get this over with."

And there *is* a big celebration, in honour of my return, and of Cybele's recovery, and of everything that happened in the Dreamscape, which I don't think anyone but me and Sai understand. Even then, I think only Sai truly knows. She's sent me a couple more letters, but I've left them unopened until I get a chance to breathe through it all. It's lovely to see everyone at the party, but there are definitely moments when I want to escape into a quiet bedroom. Except then I'd look out the window and see the moon in the sky and feel like a lovesick fool.

I'm not even sure what I feel about Terreri, as someone outside the Dreamscape. There's a connection there—it's been there since the first moment I saw them—but I don't know who I am, let alone who they are, and it's complicated, building a relationship on the ruins of other people.

The party finally ends around four in the morning, which is exhausting, but wonderful all the same.

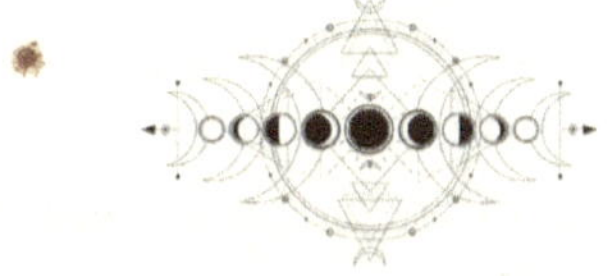

It's a couple of days later, once everyone has properly recovered, that Mum insists on having a quieter affair. A dinner party, like we're old or something. One for 'just family,' which is not that quiet, because it includes Dylan and Dani and the kids, along with Dani's family and a handful of Cute Mutants. It's exactly what I needed, because it reminds me of what I have in the waking world—even if I am a dream, I'm real to all these people. Sai was right, yet again. I catch her watching me and make bunny ears on my head with my fingers. I don't think she gets my velveteen rabbit clue, and I get the giggles, which is why I don't hear the knock at the door.

It's Dylan who slouches off to answer it, even though it's not their house.

"Uh, Hazel." I know something's up from the way they stand oh-so-casually leaning against the wall, the crooked smile taking up too much of their face.

"What?" I'm instantly suspicious.

"You didn't tell us there was an extra place to set." Dylan steps forward, and there's someone standing beside them, and I enact an enormous cliche by pinching myself so hard that tears come to my eyes. Or maybe the tears are in honour of something else, because I am overwhelmed with so much emotion I don't know how to form coherent thoughts.

Reality has made itself a plaything for me.

The new arrival at our dinner party stands a few inches taller than Dylan, with dark hair that's slicked back so I can see all of their astonishing face. They're dressed in a black turtleneck and tight black jeans, with enormous combat boots.

"Hello, Hazel." Their voice is rough and hoarse. The tan skin of their cheek is dusted with a tattoo of so many tiny stars. One of the eyes is dark brown, and the other is an almost luminous pale green. Otherworldly, almost like looking into the moon. "My deepest apologies for turning up uninvited, but I was not sure I could make it. Sai assured me I would be welcome, and now…"

"You are incredibly welcome." Dylan is still grinning. "Right, Haze?"

"Yes." I can't stop trembling. "I'm… surprised, that's all. I didn't—"

"I'm her sibling," Dylan leans in conspiratorially. "And I've never seen her tongue-tied like this in all my years of knowing her, so I think—"

"Dilly," I hiss. "Please."

"Sorry." They wink at me and scurry past, leaving

me to stand there only a few paces away, staring at my nightmare come to life.

"I'm not dreaming, am I?" I whisper. I'm very aware everyone else sitting at the dinner table is staring at me, even though I have my back to them. "I mean, this is real, right?"

Terreri reaches out and touches me, and their fingers on mine bring tears to my eyes.

"Are you okay?" They step even closer, and I can see the rise and fall of their chest, and the flutter of their eyelashes. I want to kiss every star on their cheek and see what the Knight's memories feel like when transmuted into the real world.

"Overwhelmed." My eyes meet theirs and they are my dream come true and I do not know what to do with this. "But also deliriously happy. I don't understand, but…"

"Later." Their voice is so low and their lips are so close to my ear that it's hard to focus on the meaning of the words. "Right now, there are social formalities to attend to." They step elegantly past me and stand near the head of the table, right where Mum is, who's getting to her feet.

"Hello." The tiniest frown creases her forehead.

"My name is Terri. I'm a… friend of your daughter's, and of Sai's. We met recently, and I am honoured to meet the family of such a strong and noble woman."

There's a brief twitch of Mum's mouth, I think because she still hasn't made the jump from me as a slightly awkward queer teenager figuring out my place in the world to *strong and noble woman.* "It's nice to meet you, Terri. I'm Sarah."

It takes a long time to do introductions, but Terri is elegant and charming through it all. There's definitely a mysterious air to them, like they're a mysterious fantasy character come to life, which I suppose isn't a million miles from the truth. While my nightmare is in conversation with Dani and Dylan, I take Sai by the elbow and tow her off into a corner.

"This was you?" I ask.

Sai's screen swirls with red. "Did I do something wrong?"

"God, no. It's a good thing. A spectacular thing, especially if I leave logic at the door and follow the way I feel. But, like, I'm still trying to get my head around it and I'm just… how?"

"The two of you are… entwined." Sai displays a series of equations on her screen. "When you decrypted each other in the moon door, you both gained the ability to perform this astonishing ability to rewrite conscious minds. For you, waking up was something natural, because you'd done it so many times before. For Terreri, crossing the border into this world was terrifying."

I watch them as they bow to Alyse, so elegant and charming. "But they did it."

"They did. For you." Sai's screen flares pink, mathematical equations moving in a complex dance. "Both I and my emulated human brain are in agreement that this is very romantic."

"Yes." I can't take my eyes off them. "I'm scared, though."

"Scared?"

"I'm not the Knight, even though she's part of me. I'm someone else, and what if Terreri doesn't like the me that I am now? What if I'm a disappointment?"

Sai leans in very close so I can feel the warm static from her head. "First, I cannot imagine you disappointing anyone. Second, Terreri came for you. Not for the Knight. They are highly intelligent and complex, and understand the nuances of your interconnected system better than anyone."

"Oh," I say.

"Precisely. Now go to them, and stop wasting time with me." Sai gives me a nudge, and I cross the room, still feeling awkward, still feeling that everyone is watching me. Which they probably are, but only because they're a bunch of terrible gossips who actually want the best for me.

"Hi." I step up alongside Terreri and smile at Alyse, who's coming to the end of some wide-eyed story.

"Hazel." Alyse beams at me. "Your friend here is very charming." There's a particular inflection on the way she says friend, and on the precise sketched curve of her eyebrow that's very telling if you know Alyse.

"They are." I try to give nothing away, but there's a giddiness in my step and my voice that she can probably read like I'm a child's picture book. "And we have a few things to catch up on, so once you're done…"

"They're all yours." There's the eyebrow again. Very subtle, Alyse.

I'm aware of how incredibly close Terreri is to me, but I can't bring myself to take a single step away. When I look into their green eye, there's a tiny occlusion at the edge of their pupil, a faint crescent of white edging across the darkness. "Would you like a tour of the island?"

"Very much."

They take my hand as we leave the house, as if they've been feeling this magnetism too, as if it's an inevitability that we'll end up touching. "Is this okay?"

"Very much," I echo.

We walk down past the little cluster of houses where I live. This is Dylan and Dani's neighbourhood, and it's overflowing with plants of every colour and size. Our houses are only more examples of what the island provides. We pause on the cliff's edge, looking out over the vast spill of the ocean, gleaming under the half-silvered light of the moon.

"It has been only two days, but I find myself constantly looking into the night sky." I extend my hand so my palm glows with pale light. "It made me feel closer to you, especially since I haven't been able to dream."

"You need the rest," Terreri says softly. "But I found myself alone, and pining for you. It appears I cannot live without the sun. And I must confess I was also curious about your world, and all the people who share it with you. I wished to see more of what my Knight became."

"I am not her," I whisper, but I also turn to them, and cup their cheek. "But I would like to get to know you all the same, to see if this is something that survives death and rebirth and everything else we've endured. Sai says we are entwined, and I *feel* that in every part of me."

"I also wished to know the fullness of you, dear Hazel."

Those three syllables again, and every part of me is shivering and alive.

Terreri bends their head closer. "I am not sure how human customs work entirely, as dreams are confused as to the nature of this, but I would very much like to taste your mouth if you would be amenable to that."

"Yes." I breathe the word, like I'm a seductress. "I am amenable."

They step closer, and their body in the waking world is firm and strong. My hands are at their waist, under their turtleneck and against their bare skin, and they are so warm and not like the moon at all. Their mouth on mine is as silken as it ever was in dreams, and I'm not even sure that I'm truly awake in this moment, some in-between state where everything merges with the night.

"*Oh.*" It's all I can say when we finally part.

"Yes." Their pupils are dilated, and their breath comes in little stuttering gasps. "That was unexpected and intoxicating. I find myself very glad I was brave enough to assume this form and come to you clothed this way."

"We are all made of dreams, although some of us slightly more than others." I cup their cheek, looking into their eyes which still glow for me. My other hand hooks at their waist, pulling them closer. I cannot stop the smirk from crossing my lips as my voice dips lower. "And, oh, what dreams may come."

And they laugh, and they press their mouth to mine, and we kiss once more beneath the silvery light of the moon.

ACKNOWLEDGEMENTS

This book sprung out of my MG novel, *The Mutantsitters Club,* where Hazel first *truly* appeared. With her vibe and powers, I knew there needed to be a book where she got to have her own story. What I didn't realise was what a strange nightmare it would become once Somnum Exterreri came onto the scene. This is one of those books that told itself, a dream that didn't disappear upon waking. I hope you enjoyed taking this journey with us, but it wouldn't have happened without a whole bunch of other people besides the name on the cover.

First off, thanks to my family, who support me to follow my own dream. They've had to endure a rather distracted version of me at times, lost in a Dreamscape of my own.

Then to my beta readers, the people who pull me back from the brink. Monica was the poor person who had to wrestle this strange, dreamlike book into coherence with me, which at times seemed like it operated according to its own incomprehensible logic. Melo yet again helped me ensure my plot wasn't a complete nightmare. Then Shana fell in love with the characters and helped me put the finishing touches on.

As always, thank you to my support crew: Andy, Crystal, Leah, Mallory, Michelle, Nat, Nina, SinJ, SoftJ, Shannon, Rosa, Charlotte, Mary, E.M., Hsinju, Andy, Art, and Andee.

And finally, thank you once again to the readers, who helped this Universe get dreamed into being.

ABOUT THE AUTHOR

SJ Whitby writes books. They're nonbinary and they live in New Zealand. That's about all you need to know, and they would kindly request not to be perceived at this time.

twitter.com/sjwhitbywrites
instagram.com/sjwhitbywrites
patreon.com/sjwhitby